BONES OF SILVER

BONES OF IRON

The Stars Hereafter Chronicles, Book II: *Bones of Silver, Bones of Iron*

ISBN-13: 978-1-9990749-2-0

Cover design, illustration, book design and image editing by Robert Grey.

Engravings by Channarong Pherngjanda.
River Iteru original image by Quirkjunkjournals.
Divine Island gateway original image by Iftikhar Alam.
Songuset original image by Oleg Gapeenko.
Tel Ba'al backround original image by Ojosujono96.
Vintage hawk engraving courtesy of Gordon Johnson.
Khémian desert dunes original image by Son of Moon.
Ship aflame original image by M. Harits Afaris.
Fairy chimneys original image by Myron Standret.

BONES OF SILVER BONES OF IRON

THE STARS HEREAFTER CHRONICLES | BOOK TWO

RUPERT SMITHSON

HUMMINGBIRD HILL

The Stars Hereafter Chronicles, First Trilogy

The Stars Hereafter Chronicles, Second Trilogy

The Stars Hereafter Chronicles, Third Trilogy

CONTENTS

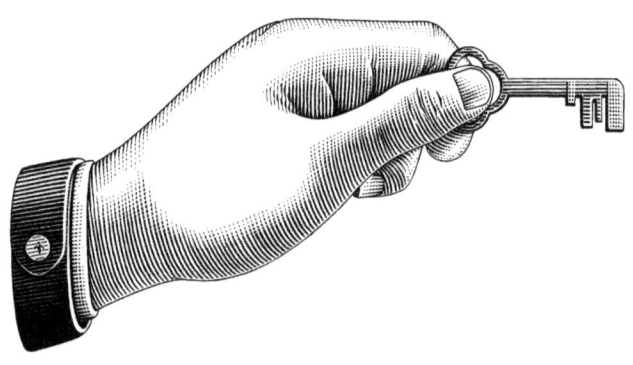

"In Khémian thinking there are twelve of They of Bones of Silver.

But there is only one of He of Bones of Iron.

Yet the twelve must be united in order to match the one's iron strength."

＋

Masudah *of* Zau

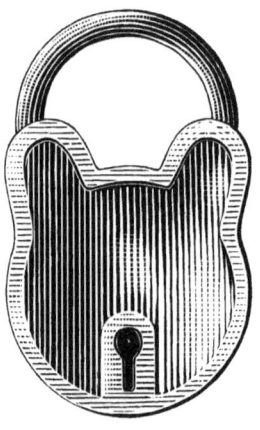

I

Destination Black Land

"They call it a wake," Commander Kinga said. "I call it denial."

In the moonlit near distance, the cold night that reeked of smoke made her people seek each other's company to disperse the dark thoughts that come when disaster has struck and one is alone.

Sir Rowan Berry glanced at her face, a cast of grim restraint framed in untidy pale hair, her eyes a shade of violet in the moon's silvery light, her gaunt body clad in antiquated lacklustre armour. The haunted Arbaro woman surely remained upright only because the survivors' hollow eyes watched her every move.

The two looked out over a smoking wasteland beneath a wolf moon, a vast forest of burnt spikes, once evergreen, now mere emaciated vertical silhouettes under indifferent stars. Blackest of the darkness below gaped the void once the rocky roof of Gormlin Cave, the Arbaro underworld domain, now a pit of scorched rubble. On the hillside under the remaining living trees spread an encampment marked in the gloom by dim firestones. Survivors of the lizard king's attack from the skies had maintained silent vigils for the past week, and conducted the backlog of funerary rites and nocturnal devotions.

"We mustn't give way to despair," Rowan said. "To break our hearts is what our enemy wants, hence our souls to reap. They know not what they do. They're dreaming, sleepwalking, possessed. Yet we can't wake them… they're a form ignorance itself has taken. But I believe they're doomed to fail."

Kinga shook her head and inhaled, nearly gasped. "Before this tragedy, my greatest fear was that I would leave my children motherless." Her long bright hair shivered in the moonlight. "One moment the endless forest under the blue sky… so peaceful… the next a wide column of white light flashed from space into the ground…" Her hand shook and came to rest on her mouth. Her pale eyes stared. "Our much loved home is an open grave now. The people look to me for strength, but look at my hands… I am quaking. I have none." Desolation looked out from those pleading eyes, and she gripped his arm.

Words failed him. The sorrow here flooded his inner being, so deep he might drown in it. But he placed a hand on the vambrace that shielded Kinga's sabre arm. To touch a woman reminded him of Samarit Longbow far away. As always, memory of her buoyed him up, enough to think before he spoke. His journey through the underworld across the continent and eastwards on his mission to Black Land, otherwise known as Khémia, had taken him from the ruins of Wishbone Warren to Gormlin Forest here in the foothills of a high range, the Fell Mountains.

"We had been happy," said Kinga, no doubt observant of his hesitance, "to forgo the worldly quest for more and bigger and better. The crystals given to us by the League for light, healing and gardens underground were quite enough. How incredibly naive."

Sophistication had neither protected other League of Domains caverns below ground. All had collapsed and been made into crypts like Gormlin, laid waste or else their positions exposed and made vulnerable.

But Rowan sighed, and said, "I'll speak to your people… then I must go."

Kinga led him back to the camp, as the current vigil had just ended, yet the people remained loath to disperse. The long night would grow longer, and with it no escape from empty isolation.

Thus Rowan spoke to the solemn company: "I grieve for your great losses. We must sorrow for a time, but never bitter and never without hope. Bury your dead, Arbaros, but move away from the grave as soon as you can. Winter is coming…"

Their faces stared, haggard and stony –

His voice flagged like a sail void of wind – he could not tell them that hope, like a crutch, would have to be abandoned for something better. He could not speak of faith, for he had none, and leaned on that crutch himself.

The people turned away, back to their grim duty.

And he dropped his chin, and closed his eyes. Perhaps he should have lied and told them everything would be all right. Perhaps that would only have added to their burden. Heavy of heart, he turned away from the Arbaros, doubled back along a stream bed, and headed for the next portal on his map.

✦

Each time he ventured topside he confronted devastation and mourning among the newly bereaved and homeless. To the survivors he expressed sympathy, but no more than that, and made haste to remove himself from the field effect of grief. At times one of the dispossessed wanted to join in his quest. The pain in their hollow eyes told him he must travel alone or be dragged down into despair, always a danger to an empath like him.

✦

One day, forced to climb to the Surface in order to skirt an extremely dense field of black basalt that tolerated no tunnels, he spied a cryptid in a wilderness canyon below, a product of an experiment, either by the Primordial Architects or by the reptilians, also known to tinker with genetics without compunction. Carefully concealed behind a boulder, he observed the creature drink from a clear stream. Rowan estimated its stature at seven feet, half a foot taller than himself. But this otherwise naked muscular beast's coat of stringy hair covered its dark humanoid body like shaggy trousers. Its head adorned with short black curved horns poked through a mop of hair somewhat like Rowan's cherry-red felid mane, only more reddish-brown, which matted fringe did hide the thing's eyes. Stealthy and silent as only a felid can be, Rowan remained undetected by the wild black goat-man.

In time it grew rigid as a stump, then like lightning struck an object that drifted just beneath the surface of the icy stream. Its claws had grasped another cryptid: a trout covered with white dripping hair like a drowned rabbit missing its ears and legs. The humanoid apparently relished the raw meal, once peeled of its bloodied fur. After a satisfied belch, the goat-man scratched his hairy belly and disappeared into the forest on the opposite bank.

◆

The mythic beast remained lodged in Rowan's thoughts on his descent of the south side of the mountain pass into an immense sunlit conifer forest. Thus inattentive to the external, at the snap of a twig nearby his hair nearly stood on end, confronted with a small herd of deer dappled in noonday sunshine under the canopy of green. No ordinary cervids, however, they walked on two hoofed ungulate legs, and had arms with hands. Their torsos and shaggy heads conformed to the humanoid pattern as much as did anders, canids or felids – but deer-skinned, with long cervid ears, and antlers on their heads –

"*Who goes there, strange one?*" asked the alpha, brusque as he paced back and forth. A noble rack of antlers adorned his handsome head. He stood guard over the smaller males, as well as the does and fawns behind them. The stag-man's brown eyes blazed.

The herd tightened their circle like a noose, and wielded sharpened sticks.

Despite their defensiveness, Rowan took in their lithe coppery-bronze beauty in the dappled green and bright golden forest light. The large dewy eyes, tawny coats and the white spots of the fawns; and the soft-eyed does: gorgeous femininity coated in honey-coloured hide.

Their grip on their wooden spears relaxed.

"*You are not wanted here,*" the leader said.

"I come in peace. I'm only passing through your territory to a destination far to the south."

"*You smell like a big cat.*"

"Please note my lack of fangs or claws, only felid markings on my face. I walk on two legs, like you. See my clawless hands. We have an ancient ancestor in common. We're cousins."

"*Be on your way then. Go. Go now!*"

Rowan took steps to advance past the stag-man, but halted. "Tell me, have you seen any Snake People or other reptiles, as much as twice my height with blue-feathered combs, lizards with no tails, who walk on two legs?"

The stag-man's dark eyes grew even larger and more lustrous. "*We run from them. They have chased us out of our feeding grounds. We are hungry. They too want to eat us. But we are quick and their minds are dull. They will not eat us, not if we keep running.*" With that he dashed through the tall trees beside the trail to join the herd on the path, which fled in the direction from which Rowan had come, to higher ground; their muscled tawny haunches' short tails flashed white, and all quickly disappeared into the forest.

◆

Rowan's hand often moved up of its own will to clasp the obsidian pendant that hung from the gold chain around his neck, a gift of occult protection from his sister Blue. At those times he rotated the plain gold band on his ring finger, the special ring that Captain Masudah of Zau had ordered a smith in Perkona Ola to fashion as a talisman for the magic of invisibility. He noticed the habit now, and dropped his hand, and relaxed. He did not want to use magic if he could help it, due to the grave dangers associated with such powers. He had only to think of his elder sister Blue's abuse of shape-shifting and hypnosis. Her subsequent apparently permanent disappearance at Wishbone Warren in ruin like Gormlin Cave proved that it should be used only as a last resort.

With gratitude for no further encounters with trouble, he soon came to the next natural portal near a cave mouth that would otherwise have taken him into the tunnels known to be dangerous, patrolled by the Snake People now. He calmed his mind to a still mirror, and set the portable scanner on its small tripod, a lucky find in a mound of rubble on the way. In short order a transparent circle of wavy distortion appeared in the visual field, and rippled the rocky background like a stone thrown into a clear pool. Rowan bowed to the invisible powers of the universe, stood erect, donned a headband that held a crystal lamp, another lucky find, entered the opening to the interdimensional field and picked up the scanner on the way –

*

At the end point the rippling ceased and the environment revealed itself: a subterranean underbelly of stalactiforms, calcium salts that had formed long icicles of stone over many millennia. None had broken, proof of the stability of the bedrock, never shattered by earthquakes in all that time. As he moved forward, guided by the scanner in locus mode adjusted to automatically adapt to variations in natural granitic radiation and the planet's electromagnetic and gravitational fields, a built-in detector tested air quality, a welcome supplement to his keen sense of smell. A cave system might include old mines with rotting wooden beams and rusting iron rails that absorb oxygen. Even stirred up mud potentially released toxic carbon dioxide. But in general, travel underground presented more tedium than danger, despite the risk of hypothermia, falling rocks, floods and exhaustion.

Rowan switched off the headlamp. He had reached a limestone cavern inhabited by thousands of glow-worms that lined the ceiling like a starscape. Their bodies glowed luminescent, but they had spun long strands of light as well, which hung several feet from the ceiling to attract mayflies, mosquitos and moths, an encouraging sign that he must be near the Surface of the large island he sought, the southernmost that belonged to the Continent of Evrys. The scanner confirmed it. He knew he must soon descend below the seabed to eventually reach fabled Black Land on the northern coast of the Continent of Afara, where the rich river delta spread, home to his Khémian ally, warrior-priest Captain Masudah of Zau, that is, if he had survived the destruction of Perkona Ola in the north, a major cavern city also collapsed by the white fire from the sky, Rowan's late residence.

He checked the scanner, and reviewed the readings of the road ahead. The undersea tunnel had been created in the distant past as the second and longest stage for rail travel to connect the two continents, nearly one hundred miles in length from the island to the continental shore in the south. Long abandoned, he reckoned he needed oxygen most of the way, as the rusting rails would still be absorbing the life-giving gas, a big challenge, as he carried no tanks nor could they be refilled at any point in any case. Masudah had made the same trip several times and had explained the magical method he and his Khémian comrades employed to still their breath at intervals long enough to survive. He had been told that to understand Khémian magical science, he first must be born Khémian, yet an outsider if gifted and committed could progress in such a way that a bridge to his own native culture's lost tradition might form instead. Because his culture of origin had been destroyed by the reptilians before he had outgrown toddlerhood, here and now he needed another method, a more material means than magic, the indispensable nanoids that still coursed through his veins at nearly full charge, a time-sensitive technique, therefore risky, but the bots could be programmed via a small device disguised as a copper bracelet with engraved runic symbols, a piece of gear assigned to League commandos to conserve oxygen yet not diminish vitality if stress levels remained low. In the current situation, he calculated the limit at roughly twenty-four hours, given the level grade of the rail line, relatively easy on foot. But he would still need to traverse the tunnel at a more rapid rate than his usual pace to decrease the thirty-three non-stop hours of travel time estimated. He decided to rest beneath the glow-worm starscape before resumption of the most dangerous leg of his quest thus far.

II

Threshold

LIKE AN EXHAUSTED wild lion ancestor having failed to grasp its prey after a long chase, Rowan panted and leaned against the damp walls of the undersea tunnel. The scanner had become difficult to read, let alone vision at all in the dim light of the crystal headlamp. The correct direction eluded deduction. He must know, and soon. He might be walking back towards the north, but for how long? Possibly the heat and humidity caused the disorientation. The magma beneath his feet coursed closer than expected here, which made the ambient temperature well beyond normothermia despite the cool depth of the Middle Sea high overhead. The late Squire Krumb's pharmaceuticals, the little yellow pills that cooled the blood, would have been most welcome now. Reluctant to close his eyes for fear of passing out, he stared at the compass among the other gauges in the scanner interface. The symbols that indicated the cardinal directions had become a complete mystery, but in time he somehow remembered that the one with the arrowhead meant north. Then he knew his course lay in the direction his feet had taken already, very fortunately. He need only plod on and take care to check the compass often. But the trek had become much like a dream. In dreams the most firm decision can mean nothing, when soon the scene has changed and the past evaporates. Inwardly he appealed to a higher power to continue to guide his steps regardless of state of mind, whether he could read the chronometer and other gauges or not.

On this long stretch of the journey, only the drip of water or the echo of his footfalls, often mistaken for a stalker, met his ears. But now another faint sound – from the exit at the far end? – no, something heavy dragged along the track bed, slid, halted – slid again – and sniffed – yes, the dim light of the headlamp briefly reflected two points of red some thirty feet ahead, about two feet apart.

Another form of intelligence not his own intervened. Another being took advantage of the exhaustion and psychically examined an intruder.

But felids were renowned for their independence, focus and iron will. His slow hand moved to his plasma pistol holster, raised the weapon grasped firmly now in both hands, and checked the row of indicators on its barrel – full power. He peered with care along the length of it to guide his aim, and let the pulse strike exactly between the two red reflections. He moved closer, pistol at the ready, and with caution approached the thing that he hoped lay dead on the tracks, a pool of blood beneath its head, the business end of a giant snake, its girth sufficient to devour a man whole. Too exhausted to acknowledge fear, he admired its iridescent patterned scales, beautiful even in the dim light. The Snake People had clearly been derived from the giant lizard men all too familiar since Rowan's early childhood. They only lacked limbs and the fantastic feathered combs of their cousins. This dead reptile, however, had been partially armoured in a composite mycelial-metal alloy like the bipedal Reps. Fortunately, its headgear had slipped to expose its upper face, what Rowan had heard scraping along the rusty iron rails. The creature's central cranial suture had been exposed, thus Rowan's shot had found its mark.

His sensitive ears piqued and swivelled in his chosen direction, and picked up more evidence in the distance. Much more. A veritable ganglion of snakes blocked his path. From out of nowhere clarity of mind flared and energy filled his form, a kind of second wind. The intuition arose that the beast's shed blood might be responsible, a crude form of vital power he had possibly assimilated psychically. At the same time he understood the encounter had already consumed other more valuable resources. If the exit to the tunnel were not very near, this flare of energy might be as brief as a meteor. He moved sideways to get past the long snake, with no choice but to confront whatever number of similar monsters lay ahead. Confirmation that the end drew near came as the light grew slightly stronger and the grade of the track increased as it rose to higher ground. Yet the hisses and cloud of red reflections promised a challenge to which he must respond or die. Only one hand on the pistol now, the other instinctively touched the obsidian pendant, and he drew his hand to his lips and spoke the magic spell of invisibility into the ring of gold –

The hissing ceased. The many red eyes scanned blind.

Rowan knew no temptation to kill, his intention only to move towards the burgeoning light, the end of the tunnel, but very careful not to touch the iridescent serpents that curled about each other, the young of the dead mother.

Their heads rose and fell, eyes stared, forked tongues darted into the darkness to discover what had become of their parent's vanished prey.

He knew better than to exhibit any emotion. Creatures like these no doubt smelled it just as well as pheromones, as did their humanoid lizard cousins, who relished negativity, especially panic and dread. Very carefully he stepped past their darting heads, and stepped away. The bluish light rapidly grew brighter and the air freshened –

Behind him now, the long tunnel had given way to a landscape of sand hills under an incandescent noonday sun – but the air rich in oxygen compared to the tunnel filled his lungs with life. Rowan breathed deeply of it, and turned back to face the dark opening, then moved quickly away even from the remnants of the still somewhat exposed railway iron outside, and all the while sensed the environment in every direction via the remote-viewing technique he had been taught in an unacknowledged program at the commando school. The white sun beat upon the Surface world without mercy, but cooler than the tunnel, a blessed relief. But he must not rest, not yet. However, perhaps due to the quick onset of extreme fatigue, he forgot to break the magic spell of invisibility. If anyone else had been present, they would have seen his tracks appear in the sand, then the deeper impression of his unseen body as it fell in a heap.

◆

The moonlight on his upturned face made him flinch. Or maybe the scorpion that crawled over him did – he rolled away quickly and stood, but only then realized invisibility remained. He wondered at what cost, as supernatural powers took as much as they gave. Inwardly he examined his being, but could not recall his mission. He only knew he trekked a long journey. *I only ever wanted…* He decided to let the meaning reveal itself. Right now he must reconnoitre the surroundings: sand in long stretches under the bright moonlight, in the distance broken by dark patches out of which arose large broken boulders. Behind the boulders on higher ground stood a cylindrical tower, perhaps a beacon for sailors, a lighthouse for ships, but its lantern unlit. A short distance away leaned ruins of an older abandoned structure, perhaps a small fort. The remains of a watchtower loomed over its walls.

This is the Continent of Afara. Far beyond the northern horizon across the sea lie the islands of the Continent of Evrys. The Snake People… he shuddered, but gave thanks to the universe that he had passed them unscathed. But he must be careful. *How long have I slept?* Already the cost had added up – too witless to remember that he could simply check the chronometer, no accurate answer emerged, but based on the estimated time to cross between continents through the undersea tunnel, with a margin for delay due to exhaustion, it may have been as long as twelve to sixteen hours.

To reverse the spell required the correct words Masudah had taught him. But he could *not* remember them no matter how hard he squeezed his eyes shut. So he tried to visualize the warm brown eyes of the Khémian's tanned face, the cropped dark hair, the square jaw, the long straight nose beneath which an expressive black moustache rested like two strokes of charcoal. When he smiled they resembled black wings startled to flight by his very white teeth. And the metal buttons, red piping and pillbox hat with the sigil of the gold pyramid within a circular red field, all elements of the soldier's uniform Captain Masudah of Zau had worn when Rowan first met him in the Kéo Mountains – above Muddred Vale, the reptilians' military-industrial complex – far from Vugh Deep in which Perkona Ola once nested like crystals in a geode, well beyond the northern flank of the Kéos, some of the tallest peaks on the planet.

The visualization exercise freed the spell to appear on its own in Rowan's mind: with no further delay he spoke the magic words into the ring of gold. His legs grew translucent, then into solid form as the five-toed boots custom-made for elite commandos filled the footprints in the sand perfectly. Rowan expelled a big sigh and relaxed. But as Masudah often said, eternal vigilance is the price of freedom. Untrained mortals may live an unexamined life, not an option for commandos, especially those designated intuitive empaths. The intrusion of others' minds, worst of all in the form of friendly fire in thoughts and feelings from allies, might completely skew perception if care were not taken to shield his psyche. The alternative: to dull the mind, dim sensitivity and risk soul blindness as well as physical danger, the path of the fool.

But topside now, he slaked his thirst with the last of his canteen's contents. Thus he embarked on the next leg of his journey, into the unknown where he hoped to gain the knowledge he sought. According to the scanner, three weeks to a month of trekking along the arid coastline remained until he would reach the ancient city of Zau in the rich black lands of the great river delta of lower Khémia in the north of Afara.

+

The long dry days blended into weeks, just like the sand-blown sky and dusty ground mingled without seam if he looked inland whence sandstorms at times blew far out to sea. Rowan spent most of those waking hours in an inner landscape, nothing unusual according to psychologists, especially when suffering is present, even if only in the form of boredom. If each day is much like the next, time loses its meaning and thinking becomes mechanical and repetitive, thus devolves the soul. Intentional thinking is very productive as a countermeasure. *Stone walls do not a prison make, nor iron bars a cage.* The line of poetry brought to mind Masudah, who often quoted the sages, and had once mentioned that he had spent some years as a hermit upon commitment to the priesthood:

+

"One would think, Sir Rowan," he had said, "that living completely isolated and alone in a cave far off in the desert wasteland, only meeting the body's needs minimally each day and deep in meditation the rest of the time, would wear the mind to a blunt stump and kill the spirit. Indeed, this is the hermit's experience… at first… for him or her the challenge begins at this point. You would not have recognized the young Masudah. He was a naked ascetic, eyes like molten glass, long of wild matted hair and long of tangled beard that hung to his middle, with his ribs clearly visible beneath the taut sunburnt flesh. So much time with no one but one's own ego for company is very difficult until the goal is reached, as any hidden fears cannot remain hidden. They take the form of demons that attack or even possess the lonely recluse, or so it seems to him or her, and very convincingly. But they only serve the good. When no longer in hiding, it is possible to withdraw power from them and reclaim it. They are squatters. You, the landlord, may be called away, but when you return, you must let them know who is boss. The battle can be, how you say… protracted."

"Masudah," Rowan had asked, "why choose such a difficult path?"

"For freedom, Sir Rowan, freedom from delusion that hides like a sorcerer who casts spells from the shadows. Desires flare up, not even one's own, but inherited from ancestors. You see, the hermit discovers he is but a node in a web. Desires rise from the unconscious depths and insist on fulfilment. For instance, strange to say, unknown to me, my great-grandfather did not in his heart really want to follow his parents' wish that he become the great scribe that was later his fame in his own time. No, he wished to be an artist. His gift as a boy was as a sculptor, but the dogmatic forms in the temples and tombs required to maintain the society's beliefs, they held no appeal. They cramped his inner vision, thus offered no opportunity to express his love of wild nature, not as a profession. His parents had other ambitions for him. Artists in Khémia are inferior to scribes. No one in my family had spoken of this, yet it was clear to me the powerful desire that gripped my mind to alter the rocks around me came from elsewhere. But I even took to beating on them to make them conform, and bloodied my hands! Then I had a vision, as one is prone to do when meditating for extended periods. My ancestor came to me and spoke: 'Masudah, son of my son of my son, you must be true to yourself. Why else confine yourself to this desolate place all alone? Resist evil Apep, the god of lies, the reaper of souls! Know yourself as you truly are, not how others tell you. The great god Apep knows only the false. Be like a midwife in this womb of a cave and birth a new Masudah into the world, one in harmony with your true destiny.' There is much more to the story, but thus encouraged, I met a goddess, and found the beginning of my path, left the cave, returned to be taught of He of Bones of Iron, and now play my part with joy in the great drama of the world as it unfolds."

✦

Rowan trudged the wilderness, encouraged by the fond memory of his great friend Masudah. He viewed the Khémian as among the purest of beings, despite his seemingly contradictory roles as both priest and warrior.

But here and now an ordinary mortal would not have survived the lack of fresh water, never mind the boredom of endless miles of endless miles, acres and acres of empty acres. Even the sea at his left murmured sleepy and opaque; its tired waves broke on the shore in monotonous regularity. In the morning the relentless sun shot up into the vast hazy dome to blind unshaded eyes, but nanoid-enhanced vision adjusted with automatic precision. When the westering sun sank too slow each day behind him, the magenta fireball suspended in burnt orange flame baked Rowan's backside as if a blazing furnace had sprouted legs and followed in close proximity with its red-hot door wide open – until it fell behind and dropped below the rim of the planet. Then appeared the mercy of stars like cool diamonds that twinkled above, reflected in the tidal pools along the rocky shore. For a time the new moon reflected nothing of the sun well below the horizon. Only starlight illumined the scene. It became difficult to tell where the ground lay, as if all were within a flat black sphere of infinite circumference, riddled with pinholes and voids in the beach. To look at the stars reflected in the tidal pools this way made his mind play tricks; the ground felt as unstable as the antigravity disc that Samarit had taken him for a ride in soon after she had rescued him from the orphanage of his youth. He soon mastered flying that strange bio-machine – they had even visited her private retreat, the bamboo birdsong lotus pond, one of his most cherished early memories of her.

A smile played on his lips as he recalled beloved Samarit. It steadied the moonless landscape at night and made the journey by day a less tedious plod. But he could not help but marvel at how he had outgrown the callow youth of two-and-sixty he had been when he met her. At that time he knew nearly nothing of the world. Even what he did know was worthless. She had given him everything by stealing him away, even if it had only been an assignment to rescue an orphan as a stage in her training as a cadet. A League commando himself now, he had been adopted by the Longbow clan, unofficially, the main stakeholders in the former warrior guild.

Here and now the sun baked the desert he traversed, and his elder sister Blue spoke in his overheated mind, a strange possibility even though she had died: "Without me, little brother, none of that good fortune would have happened."

"Maybe," he replied aloud, "but you took as much as you gave, in fact more. Your actions early in life led to the death of Mama and Papa… and my long stay in the orphanage prison."

"Yes… sorry about that, little brother. I told myself I did it to save our lives, but to make up for it I gave you shelter, wealth, an education, even a title, which came with a servant."

"The good Squire Krumb… who died to save me. But, Blue, you sacrificed all that to a demon. You misled us, including Sam, not to mention key military officials, into volunteering for a stupid hopeless mission right into You-Know-Who's waiting claws."

"Yes… Kirzaka the Deathless, Talon of Maçina, in the heart of Mudredd Vale.… it sounds like an ad for a bad movie. I did that, I admit it… poor Samarit, put into stasis and left to a long slow death by decay…"

"Blue, I'm sorry you're sorry… I should have died too, but he made me his messenger… forced to stumble the frozen mountain trail back to Perkona Ola a barefoot raving maniac."

"Don't forget, Rowan, I also made certain Captain Masudah and his band of warriors picked up the pieces before it was too late."

"You're incredible." Rowan shook his head. "You pulled the strings so that Sam, only a teenage cadet, would pluck me from the orphanage in the first place. I can't fathom how your mind works, Blue, but I'm a long way from hating you like I did when I discovered the truth. I really do admire your genius, your amazing resistance to the reptilian influence in your life. You are, on the one hand, the most self-serving and destructive creature, yet on the other…"

"What? What, little brother?"

"It's hard to speak. I only hope your abuse of magical powers hasn't consigned you to oblivion forever, even though you're dead. I can't help myself… I hope beyond hope you can be redeemed, Blue, that you can be a proper woman some day… even if you're dead and… it's too late…"

◆

Ruminations retreated as signs of civilization appeared: at first beached fishing boats and thatched mud huts here and there. Black Land: as sleepy as the slumbrous sea, no one about in the noonday sun. Rowan did not feel inspired to knock on any doors. But he could not go wrong if he followed the west bank of the river southwards. The first Khémian he saw turned out to be an ibis wading in this very branch of the river Iteru, one of the longest in the world, which he believed would lead him to Zau on the east bank, near the middle of the western half of the delta. He admired the bird's long downward-curved black bill, black head and neck of a white body as it probed the mud on long black legs, a good omen. Masudah had once mentioned, in a discussion of the flora and fauna of his homeland, that the ibis served as patron to the scribes, who served as administrators, and sacred because of association with Thoth the god of wisdom, magical arts, science and writing, often depicted as a man with the head of an ibis.

River Iteru, Black Land, Lower Khémia.

Rowan moved inland along the west bank of the tributary. The green land remained very flat as far as the eye could see. This river delta, one of the greatest in the world, spanned approximately one hundred and fifty miles in breadth. One hundred miles inland from the sea at the apex of the delta marked the location of the great rebuilding project Samarit said had been interrupted due to events in the wider world, thanks to the reptilians' escalation of violence. At that locus the Khémians were said to be repairing the foundation of an ancient structure, to replicate the greatest of a series of pyramids near the point where the great river branched into two main distributaries as the well-nourished land, when viewed from space, fanned out far and wide like a lotus blossom in profile.

Signs of life increased as he went: wooden and papyrus boats with curved bows and sterns manned by fishermen at work with their nets suspended between two such reed craft. Later he noted boats with square or triangular linen sails. The wind blew mostly from the north, and these simple canvases aided in moving against it, as rowing would be a struggle, since the current did not flow strong this time of year. Ingenious simple methods of drawing water up and into the field exploited the river as well. Brown-skinned farmers in white garb worked in the distance beyond rows of palm trees. Donkeys with burdens trotted there too, and at times oxen that pulled carts. More rare graceful women with large baskets atop their dark heads sauntered, some trailed by boisterous young ones. So far, this ancient land radiated calm and peace, rich in soil and inhabited by peasants whose way of life had remained unchanged for thousands of years. No one paid him much attention. But then no village, let alone city, had been encountered yet. Rowan perceived that Mother Nature dreamt sun-drenched Khémia into existence, very ordinary in a way, but a miracle of freedom on the Surface of Eorthe, topside.

III

Beyond *the* Grave *of the* God

"Masudah is a very common name in these parts, stranger," the man replied in Common Tongue. He smiled and leaned on his pitchfork. Dressed in a fine linen loincloth, he nevertheless had just spread straw on donkey droppings in the street outside his pottery shop. Like Masudah, his skin had been browned by a lifetime under the southern sky, but his black hair had not been cropped in the style of the Khémians Rowan had met before, all of them soldiers. Like a thick helmet to protect his head from the blazing sun, the fringe had been trimmed very straight above the eyes, and the sides hung to the shoulders in an encircling even curtain. His shadow nearly directly beneath him, he had been the only Khémian in sight outdoors at noon two days later. "Forgive the unsolicited advice," the man continued, observant of Rowan's wet hair, "but it would have been wise to make an offering to the crocodile god before you crossed the river. His manifestations this far north are more common than believed. There are many deaths each year. It is fortunate the Lord of the Waters is resting at this season, and it may be that he gives you special permission. You see, he rules the military as well. He recognizes a soldier when his tongue, the river, tastes one."

Rowan knew the man's words were prevarication, a means of buying time to assess an outsider's purpose in visiting a part of the country sacred to its natives but only visited by foreigners interested in ancient history, and that exceedingly rarely. It was not, however, especially difficult to reach this sleepy destination by barge or boat on the easily navigable lower delta, but some days distant from the pyramid reconstruction site and some three hundred and fifty miles from the capital by river, the city of Abdju.

The man's dark eyes examined the stranger closely.

Rowan looked neither like a foreign academic nor a tourist. Experience in recent times had burnished the felid with the weathered patina of a warrior, his only weapons now a curved hunter's blade in a sheath on his belt and a small hidden phaser pistol. But it may be easy to assume danger lurked in his rucksack. Indeed, the portable scanner within potentially might be weaponized.

"My name is Men," the man said. "I would say Men of Zau were we elsewhere."

"And I'm Rowan Berry... of Vugh Deep across the Middle Sea."

"Ah, yes. Please, it is our custom to offer hospitality to strangers, who may be emissaries of the gods in disguise." He gestured towards the door. Inside the very tidy shop an array of beautifully crafted clay objects inhabited shelves:

pitchers, basins, carafes, pots and so on. Men led the way to a back room that opened onto a small garden shaded by plastered brick walls, where he offered refreshment in the form of wine diluted with water cooled by evaporation in a hanging permeable ceramic urn.

A woman, Men's wife Ahset, set a tray of cakes on a fine wooden table of simple but elegant design decorated with symbols in ivory inlaid in its edges. Dressed much like her husband, in white linen of the best quality, very fine, but also only enough to cover the hips to the knees, her upper body bare; her hair had been as neatly cut in exactly the same style as Men's. Both used kohl, a cosmetic eyeliner. The pair looked like twins in identical costumes.

Rowan had noted her dark eyes widen when she first glimpsed him. Felids would not be strangers in this land, only more common in the cosmopolitan capital. Perhaps it was Ahset's first encounter with the species, although he knew that Khémians worshipped all manner of gods with animal features, including the feline. In fact cats were said to be sacred in Khémia. The idea imparted some confidence, yet Rowan knew he must explore this aspect of the culture before deciding what it implied about him, a stranger in a strange land.

Ahset left the room with apologies that she must attend to her duties as neighbourhood community leader now that clouds had cooled the afternoon a little.

Rowan thought to ask, when the opportunity arose, whether air travel might be possible here. It had not occurred to him, not only because topside danger prevailed in all other lands, but because it seemed he had stepped back thousands of years upon exit from the undersea tunnel, as if it had been not only the lair of snakes but also a time machine.

"I believe the Masudah you seek does not reside here now," said Men. "I do not know him, but my elder brother, long since ascended to the stars, spoke of his friend Masudah who became a warrior-priest. You may find him at the plateau where the pyramid will be restored, but more likely in the capital far up the river. That is where the most important religious people do their work. He will be one of those. I have never been there, but it is a holy place. I intend to make a pilgrimage to the sacred city once in my life, when I am mature enough to understand what it has to teach, and when our children are ready to run the family business. But our city Zau too guards sacred ground. We tend the grave of a great king who became a god, one who rejected ascension to the stars, that is, to become a star himself, but instead remains in the underworld to judge the newly dead. Our religion does not expect perfection of frail human beings, however, only honesty. Thus the tomb is also a temple, a place for confession of the mistakes so easy to make in this dimly twilit life."

Rowan nodded acknowledgement. "If I were not on an urgent quest, I would explore all this. It's as if I can feel my mind expand as I travel, all the more so as I've entered your kingdom, so free of noise and hurry, but alive with a subtle power. You speak of twilight, yet the light blazes through every opening."

Men peered at Rowan closely, apparently deep in thought. Then he spoke: "Yes, it is sometimes quite hot here in the north of Khémia at this season when the sun casts short shadows and is most brilliant, but it is light of the mind we seek to banish the inner twilight. You will find a complex tapestry that is our culture as you move further south, rich with symbols that when understood reveal to the initiate all the truth an Eorthely mind can tolerate. This is hardly surprising, as all sentient creatures have limits, even gods. This truth *is* the light, the Light of lights… but there is no hurry. Our lives are short, but we return again and again over the millennia. None of us natives is born a stranger to the others. We are a vast extended family who have made our home along the sacred river since the Antediluvians, who were an ancient people since the Time Before Time, migrated from their lost homeland in the far west. Our children were once our ancestors and we will be born to them again. You know, even foreigners, if called to Khémia, have some past connection worthy of investigation. Perhaps this is the power you feel, as you are already familiar with it in some way, from a past life here."

"Rebirth," replied Rowan. "I've come across this idea in my studies. It's said to be a widespread belief, common to all cultures worldwide."

"You have doubts," said Men. "This is good. We must not swallow what others hand us if it does not taste good. Perhaps you will come to know of its truth one way or another. For now, it matters not. What is important is the quality of our experience here and now, not so?"

"Agreed. Speaking of which, I've enjoyed my brief rest. Thank you. But it's time to make tracks for the south. It's urgent that I find Captain Masudah. I'm sure you've heard the world is on fire because of the reptilians." Rowan looked down at his five-toed boots. "My home is gone, as are so many once underground in the caverns of the planet. For some reason Khémia is exempt, at least for now. I need to know why. Maybe it can help us in our struggle for freedom."

"I understand," replied Men. "The Apep, the lords of chaos… perhaps another time it will be my pleasure and honour to speak more of what we value, which also is freedom. You may yet be my guest in my home and at the temple of the god-king. There you may come to know the peace and beauty He bestows through the blue lotus rite."

Rowan, touched by this Blacklander's increasing openness, felt some regret at having to miss an opportunity to expand his knowledge of the world. But neither a tourist nor a researcher, he remained a man on a mission.

✦

Travel by land was not typical here. His host had informed him that local roads, little more than paths, meandered this way and that, and most often ended abruptly in some riverside field. Rowan took Men's advice and hired a boatman, whose craft, unlike the papyrus reed skiffs of fishers and hunters, had been built of acacia wood. Its square sail took advantage of the wind that blew in their desired direction of travel, south. They passed many similar boats and barges on their way north, which rode the current or were driven by oars. He asked the captain, "Why are no boats we've seen so far powered by motors? Surely that would be easier and more efficient."

The grizzled old turbaned sailor, whose dark face had been etched by long years under the white-gold sun that reflected in bright patterns on the water, grinned but with a penetrating gaze. "Perhaps too easy, sir," he answered in a voice that surely rumbled up from the riverbed. "We love our old ways, you see. And our old ways make life happy. That is all."

From the boat's deck the view of endless flat green fields extended from the river towards the desert out of sight far beyond each bank. In time the sandy wasteland came into view off to the west, then disappeared again as the river wandered further east into the delta. The pilot remarked that this meant they would soon reach Fustat, near where Rowan might find his friend, at the site of the great pyramid complex in the initial stages of construction – or rather reconstruction. Nothing of significance could be seen from the river, however. The plateau would have to be climbed after debarkation in order to discover its secret.

✦

Men and women lowered slabs of granite and basalt (some, Rowan discovered later, nearly seven hundred and fifty tons in weight) into place with precision over part of an inselberg, a geological feature that emerged from a site possibly a couple of hectares square. The slabs of stone automatically conformed to literally

19

cement themselves to the bedrock, which gave the foundation superior stability. The floor's surface appeared a perfectly flat plane. Not even a razor blade could be inserted between the barely distinguishable joints. Rows of people on each side guided the giant tiles while four operators made them float about four feet off the ground. Rowan's skeleton hummed with a not unpleasant vibration as he drew closer to observe. The operators wielded short hand-held cones of stone; the pointed ends apparently emitted the vibrations that kept the slabs aloft. To Rowan antigravity was a familiar concept, as back in his former home, the late Perkona Ola, all manner of machines had employed it, including flying discs. They too could be considered mineral technology, in that crystals powered them. But he thought the hand tools of the Khémians incredibly primitive in comparison, mere smoothed rocks with pointed tips.

"The cones are only the physical part of the technique," said one of the workers at rest whom Rowan had approached. "The operator is the engine. Or rather the body-mind is. A kind of hypersound is the secret." The young man's eyes appeared very soft, as if he were just waking from deep sleep. He looked like a more deeply bronzed and younger Men of Zau, only in a work kilt of cotton twill; he spoke slowly and showed no personal interest in the stranger who questioned him, and answered mechanically. The man nodded towards a row of low stone huts some distance away on the dusty plateau. "The overseer can answer your questions. A priest of the name Masudah could be any of a number. But Zau is a special place. Perhaps she knows of whom you seek."

Most of the huts stood unoccupied at the moment, but in one Rowan found a short but strongly built woman of late middle age, who sat on a reed mat in front of a flattened roll of papyrus. Inked symbols in black and red had been inscribed over its entire surface.

She sat with her spine erect but her eyes closed beneath thick black locks decorated with red, yellow and blue beads.

Hesitant to disturb such stillness, Rowan retreated from the doorway –

But she opened her lustrous kohl-rimmed eyes and looked directly at him. "And what does a warrior from so far away seek here?" she asked. "It could not be employment."

Rowan nodded a greeting. "Correct, madam, it's not work but a Khémian of the priestly class whom I seek. I'm Rowan Berry and come from across the Middle Sea, where I met my comrade warrior-priest Captain Masudah of Zau on his diplomatic missions to Vugh Deep. Some days ago in Zau I was told that he may be here near Fustat."

The plump woman continued her steady contemplation of the stranger. "Your home is gone," she said. "I offer condolences." Unlike Ahset, her lower torso had been clad in a long plain skirt with a high waistline that nevertheless left her breasts bare in the Khémian fashion, of fine translucent fabric suspended from straps over her shoulders. With the aid of a staff, she rose with grace to stand up on bare feet, placed her palms together, closed her eyes and bowed. When upright, she said, "We saw the chaos coming and prepare, but our work has been interrupted of late."

"Yes, the Apep are coming to cleanse the planet of their enemies, even here."

"I am Heqet of On, overseer for today. I am pleased to meet you, Rowan Berry of Vugh Deep." The woman tilted her head slightly and looked up at him, then past him through the open door through which heat radiated is if it were a door to a furnace, yet her office felt much cooler. "It is hard to believe," she added, "but this desert will one day be green, rain will fall daily, great forests will arise, all will blossom and thrive. In time the desert will return to the way you see it now, dusty, hot and very dry. Again and again it will follow this cycle. More than the Apep, our work must be prepared for this... time itself."

Rowan acknowledged with a nod. "Now, that's taking the long view."

"It is our way." Her gaze returned to her visitor. "I do not know of your colleague Captain Masudah. If he is a warrior, you will find him at Abdju. The priestly class was specifically formed to investigate the great god Apep and provide measures for our security, to the extent that is possible. You may know that Masudah of Zau, like all priests, will have been trained from a young age for this. Generations of our priests have planned what we continue to execute now as a countermeasure to chaos, based on successes in aeons past that served our ancestors well, once they had learned from their mistakes."

"I don't mean to interrupt your work," he said. "I'll be moving on now. But if you have a moment, how is it possible to move the blocks of stone as you do?"

"It is my duty to explain this to you." Heqet's eyes brightened. "There is hypersonic radiation produced in this unique locus, by the energy grid of the planet and the resonances of the water and the sun, the whole universe in fact, that creates a fractal vortex. This produces toroidal geometry that generates magnetism. We use stone of a specific kind to amplify and modulate it in architecture. The weight is not a problem. We do not even have to do what looks like float the stone. It is locked in position at the micro scales of measurement in a plane wherever we like. All we have to do is push it along whichever axis, vertical, horizontal or depth. The large-scale structure will be self-operating, but we can modify it with hymns and chants. All our technology, from architecture, surveying and measuring to quarrying, transport and engineering, is based on what we have derived from our study of the hidden monuments, and our religion, which encodes the knowledge. If it were not for this discovery, we of Khémia would still be shepherds and nomads, wizards and sorcerers."

"And annihilated by the reptilians, like so much of the rest of the world." Rowan's curiosity had been piqued. "So you back-engineered the artifacts. From what you're saying it sounds like what you're building here is some sort of adaptation to stabilize a continually changing environment over long periods, much longer than I'd imagined. Even the planning takes generations to complete. And it's ongoing, always under renovation."

Heqet chuckled. "Yes, but what else is there to do? This is life, constant change. Our work is our worship, the whole reason for Khémia being what it is. It is our joy, for which we are grateful." When she laughed her eyes sparkled. "We are uniquely placed in this land. And this particular site is not only at the centre of the world's land masses as they are configured in this age, but beneath our feet is a unique aquifer ideal for our purposes, which dances with Iteru, the great river. Clearly, it is our duty to harness the telluric energies for the world's benefit. Besides, we return again and again to it, life after life, to join as friends on a great mission of service. Little is lost but our personal memories. Even they return from time to time, but it is our culture that channels the body of information we need to continue our project. That is what is important."

"The finished work I've seen so far is very beautiful."

"We build with love, very important because the temples are, how you say… repositories of knowledge in their very design, in addition to being what you might call, how in your land you might say… generators of energy, machines built of the most durable materials should time attempt to destroy them, and it will. But that is not why we build with large blocks of the hardest of stone. All the main types quarried far away are heavy in quartz content and conduct the flow of power conjured out of so-called empty space. Other types act as insulators. We can channel it to precise specifications by cutting, forming and arranging the parts accordingly, like an engine of stone."

Outside in the distance a large circular saw whined as it trimmed a block of basalt. The shout of a man preceded a thump that vibrated the floor of Heqet's office.

Rowan replied, "It wasn't time but our enemies who converted the world to dust. May they fail to wreck your plans."

"The reptilians show little interest in us… yet," she replied. "They think we are fools who play with dirt, no threat to them. Their attention is elsewhere, as if they hate this world and cannot wait to escape. They seek power for that, but see us as a contemptible and poor resource, only of value should they need to scrape the bottom of the barrel, so to say. They do not possess the subtlety of mind to understand. They believe they have greater ambitions to attend to, and do not realize that our collective mind in tandem with the very land beneath our feet keeps them away. Even their thinking must conform to our will. We make them believe that we have nothing to offer, though we be anders who can be made to fear and tremble like any… but only if we permit it.

"Yet time is even more relentless and will succeed in wearing our edifices to dust and rubble… we hope not for many tens of millennia, however. Even then traces could remain like seeds from which the knowledge may be, how you say… reconstituted, barring a cosmic collision that might turn the planet inside out. Or another global deluge if the sun god Ra becomes hyperactive and melts the Land of the North Wind, where it is said in myth that a race of giants lives in caves of ice and the sun shines at midnight. Any intelligent being in the far future who merits the time to be curious will be able to sprout those seeds, so to say, and continue what we have begun. Yes, even despite the recurring cycles of ignorance natural to this world, or 'consensus realm' as the priests call it."

"I see," Rowan replied, "or rather I try to see. I hope I can learn even a little of what all this means. For now I can only think that somehow there's something here that can help my people far away survive, then rebuild but on a better foundation. Ignorance needs to be wiped from the face of Eorthe first."

Heqet's happy face took on a serious cast. "Caution, Rowan Berry. You speak of ignorance, but are you all-knowing? Perhaps your perception is not just an observation… perhaps it is a judgement."

"Don't you believe the reptilians should be condemned as evil?"

"I have been educated in the knowledge of energy. Emotions are neutral. Like any form of energy they can be creative or destructive. When they become attached to ideas of revenge and murder that erupt from the depths, they can easily, but only with your permission, absorb attention completely. Experience then becomes a contorted vortex, a whirlpool of pain as it drags the mind into suffocation and darkness. This is the great god Apep at work. Then there is no hope but to let the consequences manifest, which are always what we call evil. They have the power to poison and crush one's soul, and one will become lost in a lost world. I am only a lowly overseer, but trained to communicate with the architects and engineers. I know about energy. I know that it sleeps within us, as well as without. Our tradition is to use resonance between this apparent within and without to do our great work. Lacking this resonance, it is impossible."

23

"Thank you. I wish you good day," Rowan said. "And good millennia."

Heqet's smile returned. "Future generations, having once again fallen asleep in amnesia, will look upon what we do here in wonder. They will ask, 'Who were the ancients? Did they come from the stars? How did they make all this and with such precision? And why?' The monuments' very existence will be why enough. If we do not build our magical machines, there will be no future generations of intelligent species to ask such questions. This is what motivates us.

"But I talk too much and am not a teacher. Please, I invite you to explore the site if you wish. The magic is hidden in plain sight. Its secret we do not try to protect. It is only for those who have eyes to see, but even the little of what we have built so far is of great benefit to mind and body. Only the temples beneath the surface are forbidden to you, as they border an inverted world. Be careful of the places where we dig. Do not fall in and break a leg! Such an injury can take up to three days in the healers' dim underground temple to repair. How dull!" Heqet laughed again, her sturdy body jiggled while she leaned back a little, and her kohl-dark eyes for a moment squeezed shut in glee. She nodded respect, and said, "But you seem one who takes care of himself." She smiled into Rowan's eyes, and added, "I see you are in haste to carry on your search for your comrade. I wish you success."

Gateway *to the* Divine Island.

IV

Abdju

"Masudah is a very common name here, pilgrim," said the officer in charge of the gate, and echoed Men's words first heard back in Zau, "almost as common as priests." The man stood chest out with wide shoulders firmly held back, and looked up at Rowan in inspection. His surprisingly pale eyes in such a sun-darkened face displayed clarity, the eyes of a soldier who recognized another warrior. "You may pass, but please wait here while I summon a guide, who will charge a range of fees based on your degree of interest. This is the law. Pilgrims new to the city must be shown how to conduct themselves in this sacred place."

The long river journey here to the capital, Abdju, had not held many surprises. The views from the deck of the boat had been much like his first impression of Khémia before he reached the plateau near where the branches in the fertile lower delta flowed from a wide trunk north of overseer Heqet's construction site: palm trees lined the banks of the shining water on which reed fishing boats sailed; many wooden barges with square or triangular sails; green fields beyond dotted with oxen, carts and white-clad farmers. His shadow at noon had grown slightly shorter each day. Most memorable were the spectacular sunrises and sunsets due to the dusty horizon. Rowan and the other passengers, mostly pilgrims, sat spellbound until the jewels of heaven sparkled above where the goddess Nwt was said to hold up the dark blue night sky dome; her feet rested at one horizon while her palms set on the one opposite. As the travellers looked up, they peered into the starry naked body of the deity arched over them.

At first Rowan considered this idea charming, like an image from a story-book. After a time he wondered if the deeply awed Khémians perhaps knew something he did not. Then he believed he understood. He chuckled when he realized he would never see the Milky Way spanned across the night sky the same way ever again. But then another traveller corrected him. These stars formed a pool of milk, yes, but the body of Bat, a fertility cow goddess, a lesson that Rowan must not draw conclusions too soon.

The noonday sun shone nearly straight down, and replaced the contemplation of Bat with Abdju's gate, where he awaited the promised guide. He peered up to the top of the wall, crenellated like those of most ancient cities, that is, notched with spaces for archers to rain down arrows on their enemies. Such battlements remained antique reminders of a long-gone age, useless against modern plasma and phaser weapons, as well as aircraft and dragon ships, let alone the Eye in the Sky with the power to beam instant devastation anywhere on the planet's Surface to a considerable depth, and wipe out whole cities even if underground. Why had it not done so in Khémia? Heqet had implied that somehow this land and its people repelled it naturally. They lived happily on the Surface, although the people worked hard at very many underground installations and constructions ongoing for purposes other than shelter, mostly to do with hydro engineering, irrigation only a small part of it. Somehow the aquifers interconnected in a grid that fed into the pyramids' functions when completed – or rather renovated.

"This is your guide, pilgrim." The guard had returned with a tall old Khémian in a turban and a long white linen robe. The guard added, "Pilgrim, you will not have noticed that your face, form and soul frequency signature have been scanned into our database."

Rowan had not noticed anything that resembled a scanner in the time-worn cut-stone surroundings, nor evidence of high technology of any kind. Everything looked extremely ancient, as if unchanged since prehistory.

The guard added: "You are flagged conditionally as a benign presence, but any untoward action will instantly alert our internal defences. You will not attempt criminal action without quick and thorough deterrent. We mean no offence, it is simply that this place and its work have remained sacred and secure for an age. We insist that it remain so. Your weapons will be returned to you upon leaving. Know that they will be registered, easily traceable anywhere in Khémia."

The old guide, called Songuset of Abdju, who spoke in a strong voice inflected with a pleasant abrasion like a wood rasp at work, said, "I can speak many Eorthe languages fluently, sir. My guess is that you prefer Common Tongue, but if not, please ask."

"You guess correctly, Songuset. I'm happy to know that you can translate for me when necessary. My only mission here is to find my friend the warrior-priest Captain Masudah, who comes from Zau in the north."

The guide raised his eyebrows. "To ask for a priest of that name, never mind from Zau in the north… he may not be so easy to find." He sighed. "Yet as the *djinn* say, your wish is my command, sir. Let us begin."

Songuset led Rowan through busy, narrow but straight streets lined with high-walled enclosures, and behind them, mysteries. Twice they crossed wide courts lined with statues of gods beneath colonnades and crowded with people of many hues of skin in a variety of international costumes, even little clothing at all among the ones with black skin in a range of tones, half naked but always decorated in other ways: scarified patterns in their skin, feathers in their hair

26

and jewellery of leather, horn, bone, beads, wood and metal, sometimes gems. No one carried weapons, other than the city guards who roamed the streets and the tops of walls. Horses carried soldiers, and donkeys drew carts, some of the only animals in view so far, although a lion's roar echoed from behind one wall. Smaller tame desert cats roamed everywhere, apparently guests of the city too, which implied few rats.

"Please, sir, wait here," said Songuset. "I shall go inside to ask of Masudah of Zau. In this office is a database of citizens and guests I can for a fee access by request that may take some time to complete. The priests, especially if they are also warriors, are monitored. But we may hope to learn of today's assignments to your Captain Masudah." Songuset vanished into a plain plastered mud-brick building with a double wooden door inscribed with carved hieroglyphs.

With time to sit and rest, Rowan noted that none of the buildings that faced the narrow streets had windows. He guessed, however, behind the high walls fountains sprayed and gardens bloomed. The inner walls no doubt had windows to look out upon such luxuries in the desert. While he pondered, a soft sensation crossed the ankles of his five-toed boots. On the ground stood a little striped grey cat with an M-shape of black on its forehead. Its forefeet shifted their weight in turn as its gold-green eyes squinted up at him. It purred

Songuset *of* Abdju, Upper Khémia.

audibly even above the din of traffic, and stood up on two legs like a bear to be closer to his hand. An unexpected delight, a corresponding resonance emitted from his own throat, something that had not happened in a long time. Purring evoked memories of Samarit, with whom it was strongly associated. He picked up the tabby and stroked its head.

The wooden doors closed with a thump. "The *mau* likes you, sir," remarked Songuset. "This is an omen. They are discriminating creatures. They can, how you say… read souls."

Rowan placed the tabby back on the ground. It scooted off, and he stood up. "Did you find him? Did you find out where Masudah is?"

Songuset guffawed. With one hand he rubbed the back of his neck just beneath his white turban. He looked up at Rowan, and said, "Well… we have discovered a list of duties for thirty-seven Masudahs of Zau in nearly as many temples and shrines. So yes, you could say we have found him." He chuckled. "If he were not also a warrior, we would have to spend a week seeking among several hundred of them, and not just here in Abdju, but in outlying villages spread along the river for many miles in each direction… and on both banks."

Rowan, somewhat crestfallen, nonetheless after a moment cheered up. After all, it had been a long and dangerous journey. Now he neared the beginning of his quest. But he would return to Samarit and the canid Longbow clan one day soon with something of use. That was all that mattered. The guide led him to the first temple to enquire of Captain Masudah of Zau.

✦

Fourteen temples in three days, only three of them within the city walls, the rest beyond the city gates in villages nearby – no Masudah, but much had been observed of Khémian culture, especially its expression in mystic symbols, with complex commentaries by Songuset, who could not seem to stop himself from waxing lyrical. His eyes lit up even when the mythologies connected with the many gods and goddesses contradicted each other. Rowan, however impatient, had to admit Khémian beliefs evoked fascination. Each deity represented with mathematical precision one degree of a circle, itself a symbol of eternity and the formless Self on its journey through form, cycles within cycles. But it was Songuset's job as guide to remove confusion from pilgrims' minds with respect to the basic myths associated with each, the story of naked Nwt arched across the night sky just one example. On this particular assignment as guide to Rowan, the old man appeared to regret not having enough time for that.

"Songuset, this is all very interesting. Khémians obviously understand the nature of nature in a much different way than I've been trained to understand it. But time is precious. Don't warriors have mobile communication devices? What if there's an emergency?"

The guide tapped his right temple with his forefinger.

"Do you mean they use telepathy instead? Can we contact Masudah that way? I've been trained in remote-viewing. I believe you may refer to it as star-travel. Would that help?"

Songuset looked up at Rowan, and answered, "We make a suggestion to visitors from other lands: when in Khémia do as the Khémians do. You are right, our understanding is from, how you say… another angle. This does not mean to make it mysterious, only that it takes time to set aside one's belief to examine another. You must, so to say, take off your burnous to try on the new one the tailor has made. But yes, it may be thought of as bad manners to run when you should walk on holy ground. It must be respected. And what you seek will not be found without removing your old burnous, so to say, Captain Masudah or no."

"So there are no communication devices?"

Songuset sighed. "Yes."

"Does that mean yes, there are not… or yes, there are?"

"Forgive. There are none, other than the mind-to-mind." He tapped his turban, sat down on a time-worn stone bench and gestured to Rowan to sit beside him. "It is not my place, and I am old and tire more easily, but perhaps I can… how you say, filter what pervades us…" He gestured with his hands to suggest a sphere; "…perhaps to narrow our search. But please, do not try to help with your, how you say… viewing, the remote-viewing. You may trigger an alarm and draw attention that will demand official interrogation. You do not want that, yes?"

"Yes… I mean no, I do not want that."

The two sat on the stone bench while the sun lengthened their shadows.

Songuset's eyes remained closed and his breath had clearly stilled.

Rowan wondered if perhaps the old man had fallen asleep or even died – he studied him at close range, and decided that he meditated. Meanwhile birds in the trees nearby entertained his ears with song. People in the distance went about their daily duties. Twice little boys peeped from behind a wall and giggled, their dark eyes bright with a mixture of intense curiosity and potential mischief. From time to time Rowan stood and stretched, impatient to continue the search. But yes, his guide had been right to suggest that he walk, not run. So he sat down.

"I have it!" exclaimed Songuset.

29

"What?" With a start Rowan realized he had dozed off. "You have what? Where's Masudah?"

"We must go west, into the desert."

◆

The dry landscape that had enveloped them stretched to infinity after two days on the backs of camels. Abdju and the great river had been swallowed by the vast silence like a dream city vanished in dreamless deep sleep. At last a few rocky red outcroppings appeared to relieve the flatness of dusty ground under the pale blue endless sky.

"Are you still certain of our direction, Songuset?"

"I understand your need to ask so often, sir. I could be a villain who leads you into a trap, not so? Or perhaps a madman. But the feeling, it grows stronger, sir. We will meet Captain Masudah soon. But I do not know if we will be welcome. He has more than likely removed himself from the world for a reason."

"I'll take the risk," replied Rowan. "But what about you? You're a long way from home."

"Do not worry about that, sir. It is my duty to guide pilgrims and other visitors. I must sacrifice any self-importance. Ultimately it is the pantheon whom I serve. Pilgrims are manifestations of the deities, even if they know it not, visitors as well. Even beggars and thieves. Pilgrims have some idea of this truth. Wicked men have none. That is the only difference between them and, for example, your honourable self."

Rowan's brow wrinkled. "I don't believe I'm a manifestation of a god," he said. "I'm not even religious. Do you mean those you guide can command you to do whatever pleases them? What if they're criminals, wicked men?"

"The laws of nature command me, as well as them. If they depart from righteous ways, I am authorized to correct them, assuming no guard or warrior-priest is present. Of course I am to do this with the purest of love."

"That seems a bit soft, in my opinion."

"We do not believe this way, sir. Love to us is not a feeling of affection or the like, only the guiding unity beneath or behind all things, and yes, includes sentiment. Emotion is a form of energy. This is felt in the body, it is that part of the mind which makes it move, but it must be advised by intelligence. It is much like herding camels or goats, perhaps tending to children… to sail a boat well perhaps… any worthy endeavour, really. This is love. Unity."

30

Rowan nodded respect and automatically opened his mouth to respond, but something knocked him off his camel face-first into the sand. All went dark –

V
Stormbringer

Songuset and Rowan came to at nearly the same time. Their chins had rested on their collarbones, but now they weaved from side to side, then back and forth – and bumped their skulls hard together.

The guide groaned.

Rowan spat sandy grit. The sky: dark, *the hue of non-existence,* he thought. The blazing desert sun had rolled below the horizon, but no moon reflected its radiance, no stars illumined, yet Rowan could see in this dark, although with reduced perception of detail, which gave all objects a flattened appearance, like cut-out stage props, like post-apocalypse Perkona Ola. Judged by the positions of the rocky outcroppings, the two men had ended up not far from the spot where their interesting conversation had been so rudely interrupted. The camels rested off in the distance, a series of humped silhouettes on the desert floor.

"Songuset…" he whispered, parched and hoarse. "Can you hear me?"

"Yes," the guide rasped. "Yes… I can hear you, sir. But I see nothing."

"My wrists are tied behind my back," Rowan said, "but I can see somewhat. I see the camels. What happened?"

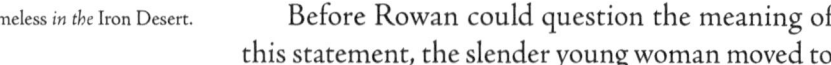

"I do not know…" The guide groaned. "My skull may have cracked."

"Be still. I'll work myself loose."

A voice spoke out of the darkness, a woman's voice.

"I do not understand your language," Rowan replied; then called out louder: *"Do you speak Common Tongue?"*

"The woman says to not bother trying to free yourself, sir," said Songuset. "You will not succeed. In fact we are not even tethered. It is magic that holds us. We are in the domain of He of Bones of Iron."

Nameless in the Iron Desert.

Before Rowan could question the meaning of this statement, the slender young woman moved to a position where she could be seen, dimly. Her black very curly hair had been twisted into many long ropes tied to hang down her back. Her skin nearly as dark, she wore not a stitch, apart from a thin belt of woven leather that circumscribed her slim waist, from which hung a small pouch of striped fur that hid her groin. Her shapely legs ended in dainty feet shod only in powdery dust.

"Ask her who she is, and if we're her prisoners, why."

Songuset repeated the questions, then translated. "She has no name, but serves the master of the hill yonder. She is his sentinel so that he can remain undisturbed to do his work."

"Well, please ask her to let us go! We seek only Masudah of Zau and mean no harm or bother to her master."

The old guide again spoke to the woman in her language. "I need not have asked, sir. It is as I suspected. Her master is Masudah, Captain Masudah of Zau, the very one you seek. We have found him."

From above, another voice, a man's, spoke quietly: "Yes, you have found him. What do you want? He is busy and does not wish to be disturbed." The speaker remained invisible.

"Masudah! Is that you? It's me, Rowan… Rowan Berry of Perkona Ola, in Vugh Deep in the north. I'm so glad to have found you at last. Please, tell your sentinel to let us go. We've been looking for you for a long time."

The desert resumed its limitless silence. A crimson streak appeared in the western sky beyond where the camels rested.

In the foreground, the black girl stared at her captives.

Rowan, unable to turn his head to see anything more than that, said, "Please, my guide has been injured and needs treatment."

Silence loomed, vast and dusty.

"Don't you remember me? You must have still been somewhere in Vugh Deep when the reptilians invaded. What happened, Masudah? I'm glad you made it back home as I'd hoped."

The questions went unanswered, but Masudah's voice spoke in the girl's language. An invisible force manhandled Rowan to a standing position, although the young woman stood some twenty feet away. He glimpsed her white teeth, as if she whispered to herself. The force shoved him in the direction of the hill.

The old guide followed, and stumbled –

✦

"I see the dunes in plain view out there, but we may as well be behind iron bars in this hole. It's my fault that you're here… when we get back to Abdju I'll make sure you're compensated… and with a big bonus as danger pay."

"But I see nothing, sir. I may be blind... it is dark here in the desert of He of Bones of Iron, Stormbringer by another name... the adversary of They of Bones of Silver, the gods and goddesses I tried to show you in the temples as we searched. Abdju may be the capital of the united kingdom, but in a way it is only an outpost of the north down here in the south, no matter how many centuries its walls have stood. This southwestern wasteland at the magnetic equator... it is the domain of He of Bones of Iron. I fear your friend the warrior-priest has become possessed. He is no longer a man. His bones have rusted. I have never known this to happen... only the legends tell of it."

"What does it mean, bones of silver and iron?"

Songuset's voice grew in strength now that his services were required: "If only we had a lamp and these rough walls were engraved with the symbols and images in the temples, and I had also a lyre, I would sing you the songs and tell you the tales of the deities of this magic land... if you had ears to hear. It is told there is only one god with bones of iron and subject to corruption: the god of drought, warfare and destruction, iron weapons, storms and foreigners, especially red-haired ones. But I do not mean your good self, sir. This last point may be, how you say... intrusive to the description of his rulership because of some hated redhead invader long ago from the far mountains of Evrys in the north.

"However, like any deity, Stormbringer represents a function or at least a potential of the Self. In the northern delta, where it is fertile, the god of light reigned long ages ago, a great king called Falcon, sanctioned by the gods as ruler of the upper and lower kingdoms, forever in conflict with his brother-uncle Stormbringer, who to this day without mercy battles for the throne. The gods are astral beings, but it is said only Stormbringer is truly also a material being, a lower... how you say...?"

"I don't know... demon?"

"Well, perhaps, sir. Perhaps then the king of demons. Only we do not think so much in extremist terms as do those in far-off lands. We say evil exists so that good can be. The two are always in contest, but like weights on a scale. This is necessary to measurement of truth. The insight helps us to forgive our imperfect fellow beings, who are caught between, so to say. All is weighed and measured in this world, otherwise it dissolves into a meaningless nothing... this what it means to 'rule'... it means to measure and assign value. Measurement and its, how you say... dogma perhaps, is what the gods war over."

"That's a somewhat shocking statement, Songuset. Where I come from it's believed that evil mustn't be tolerated. It must be overcome and extinguished.

But I've heard something else I struggle to understand, from another Khémian, a construction overseer… I must not hate evil lest I become evil too."

"Sir, we shall both be forced to learn much, I expect."

✦

Daylight never did return. Only red streaks appeared in the sky, but invisible to Songuset, who in any case slept much of the time. Rowan thought he must have a slight concussion. No one came to check on them. No one gave them food, nor even water.

Time – difficult to determine without the usual cycle of day and night – but a very long while passed until in front of the open mouth of the cave stood the black girl perhaps thirty paces off, in silhouette against the red streaks on the horizon. She had appeared as a barely distinguishable feature of the landscape.

Rowan's mane threatened to stand on end at this slight young woman's eerie presence, as difficult to admit as to fathom. Petite, completely naked, apart from the string-belted striped pouch, she carried no weapons. Magic dwelt in this place, but not the kind Rowan had hoped to discover. *"Let us go!"* he shouted. *"We mean you no harm!"* He pressed his palms to the transparent opening of the cave, but as before only pushed against an invisible barrier.

Again it appeared by the movement of her pink lips when they exposed her glow of white teeth that she cast a silent spell. One moment she stood with her dusty black feet firmly on the sand – in an instant gone, and left no tracks.

Rowan immediately fell forward, but regained balance. They could escape the cave. He went back for Songuset, awake now.

"Let us depart from this place, sir."

"How are you feeling, Songuset? Can you put up with a long camel ride back to Abdju?"

"I am somehow perfectly well. Perhaps all that has happened was a trick of the mind. I do not know, but let us depart from this dark place!"

"Come to think of it, I was extremely parched. Now I'm not. We can wonder about it later. Let's get out of here."

They made a beeline for the camels, who now stood. But the beasts remained sound asleep, immune to persuasion. The escapees tugged on their bridles and pushed on their rumps, but they refused to budge.

"I have never seen a camel act thus, sir. A spell has been cast upon them. And we cannot walk such a distance. We have some water still, but I do not recall any oasis along the way."

From above, Masudah's pleasant, calm but disembodied voice explained: "You could not see them if there were, just as you cannot see me. I control all the oases in the southwestern desert. I control all within my realm."

"*Masudah!* Reveal yourself. I've sought you out for your assistance, but it seems you've gone over to the dark side. Let the camels awaken and we'll leave you in peace."

Masudah's words reverberated as if in an echo chamber: "The *dark* side?" A dust devil rose in slow spirals before the captives, dimly tinted by the blood-red patches in the sky. "There are no sides," he said. "The ignorant see light and dark. The foolish seek to eliminate the dark they fear, thus perpetuate conflict." Masudah laughed without mirth. "The one you seek has died to all that. You may be useful. Why should I release you?"

Rowan answered: "You're obviously all-powerful. We have no powers, so how could we be useful? Anyhow, if you don't believe in light and dark, there is no conflict. We have nothing to contribute to your purpose. Let us go."

"Not to me, but to *you* there is conflict." The dust devil's spin increased. "The little one, the charming black girl, would you say such a creature had power? She is my conscript. I teach her the ways of He of Bones of Iron. I am he. She is mine. You are mine, just as he whom you sought is mine. All who enter my realm are mine. All who seek power are mine. I am *Stormbringer!*" Thunder cracked above and echoed ever further into the distance. "It is my destiny to rule the world. It will know itself as mine. Its measure will be my own. I draw its boundaries, which are the circumference and surface and core of the globe… in time the moon and the planets, and the galaxy… goddess Nwt shall be my bride."

"Sir, are you talking to the witch girl's demon master?" Songuset stared, blind, upwards in the direction of the voice. "I hear only thunder! A storm is coming! That damn cave is our only shelter!"

"No, it's only Masudah. You were right, he's possessed…"

The dust devil in an instant expanded to whip them with grit and gravel, its abrasive snaky funnel towered skywards amid spears of lightning that stabbed the sand at their feet and raised clouds of dust whipped into the vortex.

The camels remained oblivious, but nevertheless leaned into the force of the wind, their eyes and nostrils shut tight.

There was nothing for it but to beat a hasty retreat to the cave.

While the wind howled outside and filled the cavity with fine powder, Songuset crouched, and leaned into the back wall, the hood of his burnous over his face.

Rowan kept a lookout on the scene outside through a slit in a scarf wrapped around his head.

The storm soon blew itself out, but the sky remained black. This region of the desert – apparently permanently dark. Only the red streaks slowly returned.

"Sir, he has withdrawn. I cannot think what to do. He is without mercy. He seeks only power, power to control… he believes it is his right. I have been wracking my old head to break loose a memory from the myths of the gods, something that may help us."

"Just start anywhere," said Rowan. "Tell me of Stormbringer." He paced the floor, and listened.

"It is told the sky god hunted everywhere for him on the orders of the sun god, who had decided to end his evil ways. At last he was found and bound fast and executed by dismemberment, his remains scattered across the world. But it was not Stormbringer who had been brought to justice. It was only one of his warrior devils in disguise. The king of demons had transformed himself into a black cobra and gone into hiding. To this day he is hunted as evil, but remains elusive. Until now I thought this only a fable…"

Rowan asked, "How could Masudah, such a brave soldier and wise man, how could he have come to this? How?" He stopped pacing and turned to look at Songuset. "The soldier in the story you just told, the one in disguise who was executed… my old friend is like that now… possessed and projecting a convincing image of the demon king. No, I refuse to believe Masudah is Stormbringer. That's what the god… or whatever it is… wants us to believe. He's only possessed. How do we… unpossess him?"

"*Only?*" Songuset shook his head. "That is a big word here. We must take care not to seek to kill him. We may somehow succeed, but it will not help us. What is worse, we will become possessed ourselves, become Stormbringer… if we give way to fear and hate."

"Of course we must try to keep our heads." Rowan gazed into the darkness beyond the cave mouth. The jagged red streaks moved slowly across the black sky, and abruptly jerked to new positions from time to time as if they slipped the gears of prop machinery backstage. His hand moved on its own to clasp his obsidian pendant. He noticed the temptation, released the pendant and spread his fingers to look at the ring of gold as if it held the answer – talismans of his only magical powers, but they always exacted a high cost. Remote-viewing may reveal something that could be useful. And it was not magic, but a natural capacity of mind when calm and expanded to include more than the body-mind's socially determined limits.

"I am old and tired, sir, but will try to calm my mind as before to sense if there is a way to escape this darkness. If I appear to sleep, it is not so."

"Songuset! We're on the same wavelength already. I was just about to do the same thing. We may trigger an alarm, but what else can we do? Two heads are better than one as the saying goes. I've never tried this before, but maybe we can assist one another as nodes in a network."

◆

From above, the desert floor looked like stuff had collected on the surface of an air filter long overdue for replacement; scattered colourless bits of matter had clumped, caked with dust and strewn with random debris. The recent manifestation of He of Bones of Iron as a whirlwind had left a scoured track from where the camels still stood, apparently hypnotized, to the reddish outcrop and the cave where the travellers' bodies sat in stillness. In all cardinal directions and from the black sky dome to the circumference drifted streaks of dim light, now the hue of dried blood – but nothing else. Rowan sensed Songuset as an amorphous glow that hovered at his side.

From above their elevated position reverberated the placid voice of Masudah once again: "You seek in vain, dear deluded wanderers. I am neither here nor there. Time and space are not my categories, but under my dominion."

Rowan did not want to engage in a contest with a god, a power of nature. He had never been truly initiated into the culture from which this one sprang. There had been no time for that. Desperation had required that he borrow a couple of entry-level magical techniques from the original warrior-priest. But they had only been borrowed, not made his own through understanding. "*Masudah!*" he shouted. "I know you can hear me. Stormbringer has poisoned your mind to make you believe you're him. He's a trickster above all else. His only power is trickery. He's a liar and the father of lies…"

All around the blackness collapsed in a fog of acrid smoke. Gone were the reddish streaks, gone the desert landscape entirely. Gone was Songuset. An explosion of thunder replaced Stormbringer's soothing voice. In the subsequent spaceless silence a bright light appeared, like a solitary star. It occurred to Rowan it must be something very distant if it were not just a nearby spark. Perhaps his mind translated it that way as something it could grasp, remote enough from comprehension that it at least had to make the attempt, but not so far from understanding as to be filtered from perception entirely. What was it? Certainly it was beautiful. Slowly the star dimmed, reddened and smeared its dimension-

38

less point into widening streaks. The smoky fog lifted to form a starless black expanse once again. Sheet lightning flashed from below the horizon. Thunder rolled in the distance.

"Sir, are you near? I hear thunder again. Where are you? *Sir!*"

"I'm here, Songuset. We have passed a test, I believe."

"A test? I only wait for the light to return… if it will."

"To wait is our strength. That's how we passed through this bottleneck. Force is an inferior power. Patience is far better."

"Yes, it is so," agreed the guide. "All the same, sir… *now what?!*"

"We shall see what reveals itself. I have an idea. If you stand guard, like a sentinel on a watchtower, I'll try another experiment. I think I'm beginning to get the hang of what true power is."

VI

Nameless

THE CAMELS STOOD as if taxidermic in a museum diorama. They did not appear to breathe at all, paralyzed with eyes open, but unseeing and dull. Songuset pressed his ear against the dromedaries. He shook his head and reported no heartbeat. Yet they were not dead. "This is not unheard of, sir. There are even tales of entire battalions fossilized in their tracks by sorcerers and turned to dust by time. In this very place there may be layers of artifacts below our feet, weapons and such many thousands of years old. But I am puzzled. Sir, you had said you had great thirst, but then had none. How long have we been under the spell of Stormbringer? I too have neither thirst nor hunger."

"Good question," answered Rowan. "I find myself repeating memories intentionally, as if I might forget them, even my own name. If the look on my face is more idiotic than usual, we may be close to being truly lost."

Songuset's jaw dropped. In the dimness he stared as blind as the camels.

"I'm joking, Songuset. But I can't remember the last time I even had a drop of water. It's right here in the skins slung from our useless camels… if I wanted it. I've lost track of time entirely. It's because there's neither night nor day here."

"Sir, you may be correct. To me it is night only, the darkest Night of nights, unlike any other. Perhaps it is a dream, a trick."

Electrified by the black girl's voice right behind them, they spun about to run to the cave – but its entrance had disappeared, replaced with solid stone as if it had never existed.

"*Sir!* The woman, she startled me… but she says it is indeed a dream. She asks us to dare awaken… if we can."

"Never mind, Songuset, she scared me too, even though I called her to us."

"You… but why? *She is a witch!*"

Rowan kept a close watch on the girl. "Powers are neutral. It's the purity of the wielder that makes them good or evil. I know from experience they can worsen and fester even the slightest corruption in a soul. But if I'm right about her, this is another test. I'm just being proactive about it. She told you she's nameless, but ask her who she really is."

Songuset stared blank as a statue, but he spoke a few words in her language, and reported: "She repeats that she has no name, only that she is the sentinel of her master."

"Please keep asking until she remembers. It may take some time."

Songuset shook his head, but did as asked.

The girl's voice after a time grew more harsh. A hint of frustration inflected her tone with each answer.

Her dark eyes in her dark face made her hard to see, but Rowan sensed they narrowed, and she squinted as if bright light shone into them.

Stormbringer echoed from above, now with rebuke: "Why do you torture my devotee? She is an innocent child of nature."

"It's your lies that torture. Let her go."

The god remained invisible, but his presence palpable. His voice went on: "You think you can trick the trickster. I have seen you coming since you first set foot on this continent. The scorpion, remember? It was I who tickled your invisible face. The young woman is free to go at any time. She is no slave, except to love. Is that bondage? Some would have it so."

"Masudah, I know you can hear me. I'm not talking to Stormbringer now. Remember how you met her. Do it now. Take her hand and let's get out of here. Do it now."

The crimson streaks flamed ruby red, and branched in veins of light, and pulsed to a soundless rhythm like a heartbeat. A column of air downdraughted from above, made visible by the swirl of a torus of dust on the ground, its diameter the width of a man. Slowly the figure of Masudah appeared within it, the same Captain Masudah of Zau known to Rowan in the north.

"I cannot believe it was so easy," the warrior-priest muttered. "All I had to do was decide. I was free already." He looked about, and stumbled as he moved towards the black girl, and halted within a few paces of her.

She stared at him, impassive.

After another step, he took her hand.

She instantly relaxed and looked about. Her pink lips parted, which exposed her white teeth as she spoke.

Masudah quietly responded with a few words in her language, and took her other hand as well. They turned, and he led the way towards Rowan, Songuset and the camels, which now looked on the scene with interest. "Apologies, Sir Rowan," Masudah said. "I have lately been, how you say… not myself."

Rowan looked to Songuset, who sensed his gaze, but looked back unseeing. He returned to the couple, and replied, "Yes, but never mind, let's move towards the light."

✦

41

The travellers took turns borne on the backs the camels, apart from the girl, whom Masudah called Nefer, which he said meant "beauty on the inside and the outside." She preferred to walk, despite the increasing heat after the morning star appeared and the sun finally promised to brighten the eastern horizon, a welcome event nonetheless if it did, an omen of leaving Stormbringer's realm behind. She showed no sign of fatigue despite bare feet and lack of protection from the fierce sunlight, other than her abundant dreadlocks and black skin.

Masudah said her people had been sent into the north of the southwestern desert plateau, part of the distant western half of the continent, in ages past on the order of a king of Black Land long before Abdju had been founded in the south, a measure to preserve the knowledge inherited from the Antediluvians should a cataclysm again flood the lower kingdom delta and long valley that stretched along the banks of the great river into the upper Iteru. Migrations of a class of knowledge-keepers had been ordered across the seven seas to various parts of the globe, possibly extinct or corrupted now. "An even worse threat than the rupture of the global environment," Masudah added, "the Primordial Architects had perversely programmed their creations to forget and deny the sacred knowledge, hence the necessity of a method to preserve it."

Rowan replied, "They were children playing at life."

Masudah nodded agreement. "Nefer's people, the Waka, or Monitors, employ no written language," he explained. "The wise Khémian king had prohibited writing as a danger in their case, as he believed the words would change over time, with meanings of important terms in danger of reversal, depending on the experiences they would encounter over the millennia with changing climates, enemies and the supernatural. To minimize the danger, instead they used icons as, how you say… mnemonic devices that opened into scientific knowledge cast in musical terms. Song particularly became a dominant form of communication among her people, who maintained rituals and ceremonies according to strict tradition. Like Khémia, Land of the Song-Eyes is safe. The Waka build their interesting organic-looking houses above ground to this day. If you have the good fortune to be their guest, all the details will be explained thus and so to show how the knowledge is embedded and what the sacred geometric relationships mean in terms of the smallest elementary particles to the structure of cosmic objects. Thus the knowledge has been preserved intact."

Masudah claimed Nefer knew in essence as much by rote as the Khémian priests, who always performed additional roles as scientists, architects, engineers, healers and/or warriors. She and the Waka only lacked esoteric interpretation

42

of the principles and the technology to implement it on a grand scale, but that did not diminish their inherited cosmological and philosophical lore.

"Nefer has incredible magical powers, Masudah," said Rowan. "Does her clan or tribe practise sorcery?"

"No. They employ shamans, like most traditional peoples who prefer to live simply, close to nature. Theirs are mostly herbalists who have been influenced by the indigenous neighbours in their region. The powers she possesses arose after she met me, I am reluctant to admit." His voice cracked as he exclaimed: "I am to blame!"

"Obviously she adores you."

Masudah shook his head while he looked down at the sand beneath their camels' tireless feet. "Yes, it is true." His face could not be seen beneath the hood of his burnous, but a sigh escaped. "I am to blame for that also." A long pause followed the confession.

"Masudah, love knows no blame. Isn't that true?"

"Truth indeed, yet you do not know our ways. Not all priests are celibate, but most accept the surgeon's adjustment to merit certain initiations… that is, if they are not high priests, who hold political office. This is a demonstration of commitment to the gods they serve. The title of priest is also inherited, usually, but in my case that was not so. Because I was precocious in many subjects as a child, my teachers nominated me for a special royal appointment. It provided tuition under the highest holy men and women of the land, as well as military training. My parents felt blessed by the opportunity, thus agreed with enthusiasm. Do you remember my telling of my time as a hermit? That was part of the curriculum. The place where you found me now, in fact that was the very hermitage I made then! Well, in time I was promoted to the diplomatic corps. Thus I have been all over the world in the service of ambassadors, including most recently in the remote lands in the western part of this continent, Nefer's country, Waka, Land of the Song-Eyes."

Rowan listened for more, but only the breeze stirred by the sunrise tugged at his ears. "So how does blame enter into your relationship with Nefer? If my question is too personal, please ignore it."

"I am somewhat, how you say… perplexed with regard to that myself. It seems the gods have tested me and I have failed." Masudah sighed once again. "Apologies to burden you with this sad tale, my friend, but I find it of aid to put the pieces of the puzzle before me, so to say."

"I am happy to learn more of your world through any tale you have to tell, Masudah. It's no burden." However, only the soft padding of the camels' feet in the sand followed, so Rowan prompted, "Please, tell me more."

"Then it shall be a lesson in many things… for us both. To begin, I had been sent on a special mission regarding the ancient knowledge of which Nefer's clan is, how you say… curator. It was an urgent mission, made so because of the invasion of the Apep when I was still at Perkona Ola. I had already departed for Khémia ahead of it. When I detoured to the land where Nefer's people have lived for thousands of years, I felt at home at once. After all, they had once belonged to Khémia, not that their culture does now, as it has developed its own form. But I found the people most personable and generous. They were very friendly, and I was welcomed everywhere as a guest.

"I have mentioned celibacy. But only that, and not the surgeon's knife… I was free to choose either way. Ah, I was idealistic as a youth and aspired to purity, but did not foresee how the life force would erupt in middle life. Like a volcano! The surgeon may have been a saving grace as it has turned out. But eunuchs seemed weak to me then, and my goal was to also be a warrior.

"It happened two moons ago, when I was a guest at her father's house, the high chieftain of his district. He introduced me to his household, she last as the youngest child. I tell you it was like being hit by a thunderbolt. There stood Nefer, as I call her. I swear I had never laid eyes on such beauty! I was lost in the moment of our eyes meeting. Her parents had given her another name at birth, but she has rejected it since we met and prefers to go nameless, especially after what happened later. As you see, she also refused to cover her body. She says it is holy, not something to hide, not an evil thing as her people have decreed." Another long pause followed.

"What happened, Masudah? Of course I can imagine, but how did you both come under the thumb of Stormbringer? It must have been a long way from there, from Wakan country, to down here in the southwestern Iron Desert."

"Forgive. I hesitate, but now I see I must shift the burden or die. Rather it has become a kind of birth canal I am forced to endure. It is painful. I tend to choke! But let me try to continue. Yes, it was a very long journey, and we were hounded for much of the first part of it. But before that there was a legal trial. Each jurisdiction of the clan has a special building for dispensation of justice. It has a ceiling so low no one can stand up. Thus fighting is limited, as all are confined to a sitting position during hearings.

"The chieftain, her father who had grown suspicious, had caught us in a tryst in a place where we thought to be undiscovered. Before that I believed I was a strong man, veteran of many a campaign. But alas, I am weak. Now I know it. As a dignitary and representative of Khémia, I was reduced to humiliation of the worst kind, with trousers down! Poor Nefer was condemned as an outlaw, but if certain penances were observed, she would be reinstated eventually. But this she refused. She is too proud to bear the scar on her brow, brand of a fallen woman. And worse, one who consorts with another race, how you say… damaged goods. To prevent that, I offered to marry her… and to resign my office. Of course this was not acceptable to the tribe. They could not allow a Wakan Song-Eye to emigrate without exorcism of the knowledge, best accomplished through, how you say… trepanation, drilling of the skull to modify the brain. If we stayed, how would we live? I was not one of them. I would require trepanation to protect the knowledge also… I would be made an idiot, a burden. If they decided otherwise upon thorough judicial examination, my tongue would nevertheless by default be amputated, as well as my hands because I knew how to write. In addition, as a lesson to all for life, I would be, how you say… castrated… because they said my skin was like milk with a little dirt mixed in. They were properly and purely black; even the brown races had not diluted them in thousands of years. I pointed out in vain that skin colour has nothing to do with anything more important than sunburn. They had kept their tradition pure since time began, they argued… foreigners could not be tolerated as permanent guests. Their whole reason for being was to keep the sacred knowledge intact, although I am certain most of them have no idea what it means, although all can parrot it.

"So she insisted on following me, as after another brief trial I was deported immediately and undertook the journey back to Khémia, where I am sure to undergo yet another trial and be stripped of my rank." Masudah looked down at the undraped and unshod shapely figure of the girl who walked beside his camel as if she were on a leisurely stroll in a garden. "As you see, Nefer is not a large woman, and a great beauty. It makes me want to protect her from all harm."

She paused her humming to smile up at him. Her face beamed nearly as dark as darkest chocolate but nevertheless shone with an inner translucent light, even in the mid-tones and shadows where the sun's dazzle did not reflect the highlights fully in rich copper radiance. Full pink lips parted to show perfect pearlescent teeth, and her wide-set eyes sparkled like orbs of black diamond set in whitest ivory. Beauty indeed – and magic.

"But she is young, strong, brave and quick," Masudah pointed out. "All were seated in the courtroom, yet she easily darted through the open entrance and escaped into the wilderness. The place was in, how you say… an uproar. She could never go back after such an insult to the court… and to her father, a high chieftain. But I found her waiting for me on my path, with a smile on her beautiful face, and now as naked as the moment she had been born, having discarded her itchy sackcloth of shame on the way. It was at that time that her inborn gifts began to flower, perhaps due to the shock of loss of her former life. As well, she was highly motivated to avoid my disfigurement, and hers… myself as a speechless, handless, idiot of a eunuch was a horror to her, needless to say. Well, I had been deported. Somehow she had tracked my position at all points along my way. I could not send her back after that. She was my responsibility. I must take her to Khémia and face the consequences, how you say… take it on the chin."

Rowan nodded acknowledgement. "Your importance to her doubled after she ran away. Her fate is entangled with yours now."

"We are strange creatures, Sir Rowan. And I mean all of the variations the Primordial Architects created. They seem to have thought it interesting to exaggerate various species' traits, mix them with a brutish ape-man and to build flaws and blind spots into our characters to provoke challenges… like extra weights on a champion racehorse to lessen its advantage, so to say. Each of us was doing well in our respective racecourses. We were sincerely following the rules. Then the goddess of love threw her perfumed jewelled net over us. Now we are entangled in it for the rest of our days."

"I know what that's like," Rowan said. "We don't seem to have a choice about who we fall for. But you never know how things will turn out. I never thought I'd see Sam again, but then the world turned inside out and social taboos with it. Now I'm a Longbow too. It's probably the first time ever a felid has joined a canid clan. Come to think of it, I suppose if there's a proper ceremony when I return, my new name will be Rowan Berry Longbow. But then again, maybe you're right. I have no idea whether I'll return to find Sam waiting for me. Or even whether she'll survive. At times I think I should have stayed. The world is being purged of all that the reptilians deem unworthy, and that means all non-reptilians who don't particularly like the idea of submission to genocide."

"We endure a difficult fate, Sir Rowan. Khémia is safe for the time being… but I will be forced into menial labour. Nefer will not be able to stay with me. I will be too poor! I care not about myself so much, but she is the daughter of an important chieftain and deserves so much more than service to some… rich aristocrat." His brown eyes betrayed a grim thought – then it came out: "Her form of beauty is rare in Khémia. It makes her highly valuable."

Rowan felt Masudah's pain like a blade in his heart. "No worries," he said. "Things will work out somehow. You're noble souls. As you say, the gods are testing your mettle, not on the battleground but through existential crisis. Don't lose faith. I'll do what I can to help. And you'll help me in my search for something that can defeat the reptilians. We may have to search the world to find it. But we'll never find a home for any of us if they win."

VII

Into Temptation

THE WAY BACK to Abdju grew darker as the sun behind them in the west dropped below the horizon in a fantastic display of purple, magenta and pink. And lastly, crimson streaks, a suspenseful moment. Songuset expressed it for all when he said that his gladness would be unequalled at seeing the evening star, a sign to him that other stars would quickly follow, perhaps even the moon, and that the coming night would not revert to permanent blackness. His wish was granted in time, and their camp under Nwt's arched anatomy brightened in the light of a fire of dead brush and dried camel dung, another sign that civilization must be just over the horizon. Songuset produced a wooden flute from a saddle bag, played a repetitive melody in an exotic scale, and played very well. Nefer, fascinated, relaxed her watch over Masudah and drew near the musician, and hummed an improvised counterpoint that broke into joyous vocalization. Delighted with her performance, she spun in place at times, clapped a rhythm with her hands and danced around the fire. Like cats honed in on a bird, the eyes of the men hardly blinked at her graceful pirouette.

"Nefer is gifted in many ways," said Masudah, who shone with pride. His careworn face relaxed and youth returned, although the dense dark stubble on his chin showed signs of silver now to match his temples. "I did not know she could improvise!" he exclaimed. "Her people are very musical, yet the strict forms are as ancient as the sands under our feet. I was told improvisation is just not done. It is what in archery is called a 'sin,' that is, to miss the mark."

"Were there words to her song just now?" asked Rowan.

"Yes, impromptu lyrics as well! She sang of the joy of the falcon who soars into the sky for no other reason than that the joy of life itself has taken its form."

"And yet," Songuset blurted out, "predators do prey," but averted his eyes.

✦

On their way again the next morning, Rowan said, "Masudah, there's some distance to cover before we reach the city gates. By tomorrow afternoon we'll have arrived. Maybe now's a good time to tell of how you came under the influence of Stormbringer, He of Bones of Iron, as Songuset calls him." From the back of a camel Rowan looked ahead to the guide on foot, who distanced himself from the group after his comment the previous evening about predation. "But only if you want to."

Masudah shifted in his saddle a few times before he answered: "All right. I will tell. But a moment is needed. It is difficult." He looked down at Nefer, and relaxed. "Ah, she is so sweet, not so?"

Nefer, who walked between their camels, ceased her humming, and bit her lower lip. And she looked up and smiled at him, and swayed her slender shapely hips, and strolled with her fingers entwined behind her, which exposed her palms as more lightly pigmented.

Masudah grinned at her, and continued: "As I have told, Nefer joined me on the path of exile. We made for the nearest natural portal that would take us nearer to Abdju, on foot of course. As a courtesy to Nefer's people, who prefer no high technology to sully their tradition, only horses were permitted to us while there. My steed had been confiscated, and by Khémian law my company of men were no longer under my command. A trial in Abdju may reinstate my position if found falsely accused, but I am most profoundly guilty, unfortunately. I mean in the legal sense and, to be completely, how you say… candid, in other ways as well. The court, it will decide. All the same, there was some distance from their border to the portal. The weather turned, how you say… inclement at higher elevations, but Nefer refused to cover herself. Her skin was her temple roof, she said, and her heart its altar fire. Very well, I said to her, it needs tiles or it will leak. The sacred fire will steam and fizzle out. I pointed out that our ancestors lost most of their body hair ages ago. I agreed it is a shame to hide such perfection, but told her clothing had been invented for good reasons. She only laughed, bless her. She remained radiant, but perhaps it was due to my agitated state that I got quite ill. But we carried on after she searched for and found some herbs to keep one foot moving ahead of the other.

"I knew the route well enough. Orientation and geography I am well trained in. But we got totally lost. A dense fog either arose or descended… it is unclear in memory. It may even have been pink or red. But my mind began to play tricks. The terrain and climate were nothing like I had remembered after I and my men emerged from the portal on our way to the west. This was now some other country, uncharted. I did not know what to do, as my compass reported nothing reliable. It spun this way and that as I gazed at it! It seemed fatal to simply wait it out in the cold, so I uttered a prayer and we began to walk.

"The elevation decreased with more consistence. The air grew warmer. I stopped shivering so much… yes, I, a veteran warrior, could not endure a little hardship… although I have to say Nefer is made of sterner stuff. She seemed to neither hunger nor thirst, let alone shiver. I cannot recall seeing her sleep!" He again gazed at the bare black beauty, who looked up at him and grinned.

"She is amazing… now, where was I?… Orientation was totally lost. I had thought there must still be some hours of daylight left, but twilight came, very dim, as if a great smoke filled the sky, but there was no smell of it. Soon all was black as an abandoned coal mine. Dear Nefer for some time had been in the lead. She is always so confident. All I had to do was keep my eyes on her… in no way a difficult task, as you can see… but even that became impossible. I could no longer hear her footsteps, but then she goes bare of foot and weighs little. I stopped. I called out. There was no one. For a long bizarre moment I believed she had died… the fever had addled my poor brain! But enough of that. Whatever has followed and will follow from my weakness is no one's fault but my own." He inhaled, held his breath and let it go. "And yet, it is a divine weakness." His gaze drifted towards Nefer, who had been watching him, her eyes a little misty.

To keep Masudah from withdrawal into revery, Rowan prompted: "This is spellbinding, my friend. Please, continue."

"Apologies. However, I found that I must have fallen asleep where I stood." His eyes widened and showed their whites. "Of a sudden I was awake as never before!… somehow afloat and looking down on a man in uniform with a stupid look on his face. This fellow was familiar, only I could not recall having seen him before. But the military uniform I recognized as belonging to Khémia. I saw that he wore the sign of the priestly class on his collar. That I knew! I sensed that Nefer drifted there, up high with me. Then I saw. She had not died, but had a bluish glow, the most beautiful aura! I at times see it still. She is a true wonder!

"I have no idea of how long I was like that, just gazing at the beauty that is Nefer. Time had no meaning in that state. But sometimes she would disappear in a radiance so great there was only the blue light everywhere. I too disappeared, but it was no loss, believe me. We had become one. Forever."

Masudah's camel stopped and turned its head to peer at the burden on its back –

"Are you all right?" Rowan asked. "Maybe we should take our turn at walking."

Masudah nodded assent and dropped to the ground. "Apologies. I felt faint for a moment. The memory… it takes me back there, to that state."

Rowan replied, "We can continue your account another time. Ask Nefer if she'd like to ride." He called out ahead: "*Songuset! It's your turn to ride the camel!*"

The guide only raised his arm and did not look back.

Nefer smiled sweetly at Masudah and shook her head, her hands behind her back again. She stood with one foot pointed like a dancer, and swivelled a dusty toe in the sand, her head bent down a little. She raised only her dark eyes, jewels really, and gazed at him through her black lashes.

Rowan waited a few minutes, and watched the pair without intrusion, not that they would have noticed had he not. He said, "It's a bit too early to stop for a rest. Let's all walk together, Masudah. You can tell me what happened next. I'm eager to hear it."

Nefer took Masudah's hand. The company continued their journey, although by now Songuset had gone quite far ahead. At times he disappeared from view down the trough of a dune. Masudah and Nefer had eyes only for each other, and the camels did not complain of a break from their burdens.

Rowan wished that Nefer would give them some space. He saw Masudah as a honey-mad bee with its head in the petals. The blazing sun beat nearly straight down on their heads in a continuous blast, which did not help either. Masudah remained silent, and Rowan remained patient.

◆

His sharp eyes could just make out the pyramidal tops of Abdju's obelisks that poked through the clouds on the horizon opposite the sunset. However, those tapered pillars kept their distance. They had drawn no closer than they had been hours earlier; it may be a mirage. He remained unconcerned. Time would take them there. But Songuset had not been seen for some time either, a fact of great concern. "Masudah, I'm afraid we have to pick up the pace. Please ask Nefer to ride the camel with you, otherwise she'll be forced to run… Masudah?"

"Yes, Sir Rowan? Oh… I understand… your guide. We should make haste." Masudah mounted the camel, and leaned over to extend his hand to Nefer, who shook her head and just looked at him. He frowned and said something to her.

But she turned away and crossed her arms.

His dark brows knit together as he stared down at the back of her dread-locked head.

"*Masudah,*" Rowan insisted, "*let's go! If Nefer is as fit as you say, she can catch up.*" He turned the camel's head, but turned it back. "No, wait… I can't believe I said that. I'll go on ahead just far enough to scout. Keep up. *Don't lose sight of me!*"

With a prompt, his camel leapt forward, and quickly attained a brisk gait. Rowan scanned the eastern horizon. No Songuset. No sign of Songuset. No Songuset footprints – the desert breeze had filled them in with sand already. He called out his name: "*Songuset!*" His voice verged on a lion's roar, which startled him. *How could I have let this happen?* He brought the camel to a halt. He must

51

be patient. And Songuset was an experienced guide, a son of the desert – or at least the river valley, which must not be that far off. He turned the camel back the way he had come, west, towards the setting sun. Blinded by it, he called out: "*Masudah!*" His keen ears reported the incessant hiss of countless grains of sand that slid across each other and blanketed the unpeopled land with golden dunes engraved with patterned grooves and scalloped ridges. "*MASUDAH!*"

In an instant night fell black and starless with a loud thud and snuffed out the bright sunset. Its echoes crossed the rippling landscape from one end to the other and back again, and made the ground shake each time. The camel panicked, not knowing which way to run. Only with great difficulty did Rowan regain control of the animal, unsure if he had gone deaf or if all sound had been absorbed by the soft surface on which fidgeted the nervous beast beneath him. The dust settled. He sensed movement at the edge of the wide plain of pulverized charcoal – but unable to exhale until he could interpret what his eyes reported. Fear, the primal impulse with two possible expressions, fight or flight, demanded action. But Rowan envisioned a third option.

An amorphous silhouette traversed the blackness in silence and grew larger. It stopped. And wavered – possibly either to make an assessment or to transform. It may be dithering. Rowan knew he must listen – and not add anything to the listening. He knew what he heard would tell him exactly what to do next. *This is the power, inaction in action.*

The waver increased its frequency until the shape grew smooth. Its edges formed a circle to make a large dot. With no source of light to pinpoint a high-light, to distinguish its shape, whether flat or spherical, may not be possible. But a spark of blue appeared in the centre, tiny, and grew to gradually fill the entire circle, now feathered at the rim to look like a glowing ball, as the middle grew nearly white. It also either grew larger or else approached Rowan's stationary position. He felt compelled to back away, but the camel refused to budge – likely hypnotized again. Rowan leapt to the ground, drew the small phaser he had retrieved upon exit of Abdju's city gate. The weapon refused to power up. The row of indicators on its barrel remained unlit. He squared his shoulders and planted his feet in a wider stance, and faced what must come. *Breathe!* The glowing blue sphere remained of no discernible dimensions. It could have been three feet in diameter or three miles. All reference points had been absorbed by its radiation. *Breathe!*

"As you see, it is unwise to try to trick the trickster." The calm voice came from the sphere, but it was not Masudah's, instead monotonous and mechanical: "Resistance only increases my power. Opposition is useless."

Rowan remained silent and still.

The sphere slowly and rhythmically expanded and contracted as if it breathed too. "As my power increases," said the voice, "yours fails."

If Rowan held his breath, the sphere's rhythm stopped too. But by this time he had mostly withdrawn attention from the external world, despite the threat of another manifestation of Stormbringer. Whatever power remained to him, it would not be forfeited through engagement with a god. Instead he formed a shield of light in imagination, a sphere of white, edged with purple flame and expanded to match the glowing blue sphere, but no larger.

Thus the two radiant orbs confronted each other in the black expanse. A sound emerged, a hum that grew louder. Out of the interference pattern, a third entity emerged amidst the competing vibrations. As its pitch increased, it became visible light. Soon it grew less translucent, more opaque, and the hum decreased in volume. The light revealed beautiful Nefer, dark with a coppery lustre, but haloed in an aura of deep blue, suspended with grace within the stereo pattern. She announced in the same monotone as heard before, not a female voice: "I am Stormbringer, He of Bones of Iron." White teeth glowed between her pink lips turned up at the corners. Her eyes did not smile, however. Nor did they sparkle.

Surrendered to the power of patience, Rowan discovered fearlessness at the heart of it. In the stillness, he watched, alert and ready to respond to wisdom, should it dictate action.

Nefer looked behind to the blue orb, like a child to a parent. By the time she returned her gaze to Rowan, she had been replaced by a bare black Samarit! She floated upright, leaned forward to clasp her hands on her thighs and look down on him. One of the several heavy twisted ropes of hair that hung down her back slipped over her shoulder. The pink lips parted, and in her own voice she said, "Now, kitty baby, don't resist. You know you're mine. You want me, don't you?"

"Where is Masudah, Nefer and Songuset? Let us go!"

The entire apparition withdrew into a blue spark and vanished: no Samarit, no Nefer, no blue orb. Nothing – only a moan of ghostly wind and soft footfalls in the dust as they receded into the spectral distance. Even the entranced camel had vanished.

VIII

Stargazers

As before, Rowan experienced neither hunger nor thirst. And as before, time lost its meaning. It may have been two days or three days since the vision of Samarit had vanished. He tried to estimate the number of footsteps he had taken by reconfiguring the portable scanner to sense his movements. At least he'd had the presence of mind to bear his rucksack on his back, where the scanner had been stored, even while seated astride the camel, a better strategy than strapped to the saddle, despite the inconvenience. Besides, he had not truly believed the travellers had left Stormbringer's realm. Yet the safeguard proved vain, as the scanner too refused to power up. He picked a direction and tried to keep to a straight line, a gamble with no visible stars in the dense blackness. Despite the flatness of the featureless plain, he might fall into a pit – or travel in circles.

He stopped, sat down on the black sand and closed his eyes. To focus, he hummed a deep tone that resonated in his belly, and activated his felid vocal cords. A ferocious roar might be going too far, but a gentle purr resonated with serenity. In the clear surface of mind nothing reflected yet, therefore he released any expectation, and merged with essence.

The thought arose that the universe energetically supports one's Eorthely manifestation at all times, but for natural unfoldment requires space, thus loss can and often does occur. Nature does not tolerate a vacuum, thus replaces it with what is more resonant with one's core vibration, which emerges from the limitless essence. What comes is therefore in harmony with authentic being.

The sifting sand hissed and rushed, and dusted his body. Darkness pervaded, eyes closed or open. The silent plea ended on its own after an incalculable period, and he opened his eyes on lessened night, perhaps an illusion because of attention withdrawn from the external. He stood up and walked in faith to an imagined horizon. The ground grew distinguishable: a charcoal dome above, an expanse of pitch below, with a horizontal boundary between. A star appeared, then another. In time the dark charcoal sky turned dark blue but moonless, and exposed Nwt's arched naked body to his grateful eyes. Her spangled form with a limb at each side of two cardinal points showed that he indeed had been heading eastwards, where lay Abdju along the great river Iteru.

With the white sunrise came great heat – and thirst, a good sign. Yet the camel had borne several skins of water that would have been most welcome now. To take his mind off that, Rowan imagined the crenellated walls and obelisks he would see on the horizon sooner or later. However, visions of palm trees that encircled an oasis appeared in his mind's eye to supplant the capital city. His guide Songuset had mentioned an upcoming important festival, one that the monarch hosted only every forty years, so Rowan again turned his attention to this interesting feature of Khémian culture to take his mind off his unsated thirst for the cool and precious wet wonder that is water —

◆

"Sir," Songuset had explained, "unlike other lands, in Khémia the king or queen is not so much a mighty power as a servant of the public. He or she acts in that way like the medicine people of old in all lands, the shamans, who still practise their arts in some places. They travel realms beyond the physical on behalf of others. They seek to reconnect spirit, soul and world, for healing and learning. In the case of shamans, it is mainly for individuals. Of course this benefits the entire tribe. What is a tribe but individuals? A forest is no forest without each tree. But Khémia is a vast forest. Its needs for connection to spirit are the same, but on a grand scale. Ones such as your friend the warrior-priest had not replaced the shamans. No, the priesthood serves the gods, which is a little different. It was our rulers who acted as shamans, whom today is a queen. She serves the nation as the bridge between above and below. It is a well-paid but dangerous job, not one to be envied by anyone. Therefore it is a lineage, inherited so that it is accepted from birth. She must prepare to die, as she will be buried alive in an alabaster sarcophagus for days in order to journey to the twin universe. If she is impure, she may not return, as it is a harrowing journey.

"As a matter of interest, Khémian culture was fully formed as far back as our historians dare to speak and remain credible. The plan of the whole civilization exists and has always existed in the other universe, the twin, where there is no time to formulate it, let alone corrupt its perfection. Thus there was no need for evolution either. We grew from hunter-gatherers into sophisticates as we deciphered the plan. Our civilization will never change so long as we adhere to the plan. The wheel needs no reinvention."

"Songuset, what do mean by the 'twin universe'? No time there? Time is an obvious feature in this one, no question."

"Sir, you must ask your friend the priest of this when we find him. I should not speak of these things, I of lowly rank. Yet I cannot help but ask: Is there truly time in this one, this universe?"

At this point in the conversation Rowan had looked at his guide, reminded of Masudah, who had often said time is a construct. It had not made much sense then, nor had Songuset's rhetorical question now.

◆

"Greetings!" a voice called. "Who goes there?"

Rowan emerged from revery as he walked, stunned that he had not sensed the old man's presence.

"You look like you could use a drop of water or two," he said. "Hang on. You're almost there." He ducked into his tent of linen. Out he came with a flask beaded with droplets. "I'm no threat." He extended the flask to Rowan and nodded encouragement, raised his free arm palm outwards, and said, "Here, take it. I have plenty. There's a well not too far off... at the oasis."

Rowan fell to his knees and accepted the flask.

"Slow down, my friend, not too much all at once."

The ander indeed appeared a non-threat: no weapons, rather less than athletic, dark tinted glasses and a long beard admirable for its brilliant whiteness. It must have taken a long time to cultivate, but in battle a deficit, a convenient means for his opponent to either break his neck or choke him to death unless he were as strong and quick as the late Squire Krumb. But the kindness in the intelligent eyes under the brim of his weathered straw hat, and his broad grin – possibly genuine.

"My name is Snood Iotah," he said, and extended his hand, "stargazer."

The old fellow might be Stormbringer too, but Rowan shook his hand. "What are you doing out here, Iotah? Am I near Abdju at all?"

"I'm an astronomer. Call me Snood. I like the silence of the desert. The night skies are incomparable, and there's loads of space to make stone circles. As far as where you are goes, no, you're not all that close to Abdju. But it's within a couple of days' journey by caravan. And... you are?"

"I'm Rowan Berry... Rowan Berry Longbow." He returned the flask. "Thanks."

Snood peered at him. "I know that surname," he said. "I thought the Longbow clan was canid, though it's hard to tell unless you can see their ears."

"It's a long story."

"Well, obviously we both hail from the north. My work takes me all over the world... or did. It was dangerous as hell because I must be above ground much of the time. Here's another reason why I like Khémia... it's safe from the damn snakes and lizards, apart from the little ones that belong here. They can be nasty too, but at least they're not eight to sixteen feet tall and graceless on the dance floor to boot."

Rowan peered back at Snood. The odd turn of phrase reminded him of his courageous squire, murdered by one of Kirzaka's bodyguards. "Snood, are you from somewhere in Vugh Deep?"

"Yes, the Uaimh border country near Sector 9. I lived in Perkona Ola once I began university. After that I emigrated to Bharat for advanced degrees in astrophysics. Why do you ask?"

"I'm from Perkona Ola, and I too attended the university."

"Interesting that our paths should cross so far from home," said the old man. "Your accent doesn't give you away."

"I was born in the hamlet of Berry, a tracker colony on the Surface under Rep control. You won't have heard of it, ruined many decades ago."

"Ah, I see. How you escaped must be an interesting story! But what brought you to this desolate place so far south? Even a warrior like yourself would have a tough time surviving in this vast wilderness."

"I'd come to Khémia looking for a way for the Longbows to survive up north, but I've been separated from my travelling companions." Rowan turned to look to the west where the orange sun slowly dissolved in the magenta horizon. He shaded his eyes with his hand. "They're out there somewhere, touch wood," he said, and absent-mindedly tapped his forehead. "If they're still alive."

"I see. You must tell us about it. We hear Perkona Ola is a ruin now too, along with so many other cavern cities. Very sad. I mean if you're interested, later. Right now it's time to see how my superior is doing before the sun goes down. There's a new moon tonight too. It's still light outdoors, then the sun sets, and boom… instant night."

"Yes, I know. Boom."

+

Among the palms of the oasis stood a small caravanserai that had seen better days. Rowan purchased a goatskin canteen and filled it with water from the well. Apparently not enough caravan traffic justified the presence of soldiers. But they soon found Snood's "superior" when she entered the shop, his wife Aaru, a woman Rowan thought may be of the lower kingdom, much smaller than her husband, and brown-skinned. She looked only a little younger, but hale and upright, her almond eyes large and luminous, and only a few silver strands in the dark curls that sprang from beneath a straw hat like her husband's. Her hair hung in one long loosely woven cable down her back over a cloak of coarse wool or camel hair with a pointed hood, common among desert dwellers, which matched Snood's burnous.

The man put his arm around the woman's shoulder and squeezed.

She smiled up at him, pressed close and chuckled.

"It's not her real name," he said, "which is Alakana. Emphasize all syllables equally or she'll ignore you." He stroked her cheek. "This little beauty is from Bharat, the Land of Light, far to the east across the Sea of Sindhu. We studied under the same masters. Nearly everyone there lived underground. The observatory where we were students was a dangerous place because it was partly above ground. I'm sure it's gone too. I call her Aaru, a Khémian name, since it's our home now. It means 'field of reeds,' what the natives picture as heaven. Mythologically it's the underworld beyond the horizon, which reminds us of where we met and used to work."

Rowan found the couple charming – with a small reservation. In the western Iron Desert, he could never be sure Stormbringer did not orchestrate everything. Such a powerful god had not killed him, however. Why? Perhaps that would not be cruel enough. Perhaps all in this realm he deemed his playthings, like the Primordial Architects, like an errant child who had refused to withdraw from his toy planet because he enjoyed pulling the wings off flies too much –

"Are you all right, Mr. Berry-Longbow?" asked the old man.

"Call me Rowan."

"Come back to camp with us, Rowan, my friend." Snood checked to see that the innkeeper did not overhear, and added, "It's more pleasant than this collapsing heap. You can help us survey if you like. Our goal for a long time has been to build a complex of stone circles that will survive far into the future as a kind of time capsule. This sort of thing is a tradition in Khémia, only their project near Fustat at the Divine Island is going to involve more than just two or three people. It's going to engage at a minimum the attention of the entire population to build the pyramids there, and will take a very long time, generations longer than we've been at it here, which has been extended periods over decades already. Not so, my dear?"

Aaru added, "We used to come here for working holidays. Now our tent is our permanent home." A brief shadow haunted her dark eyes. "Yes, please come, young man. Company is most welcome."

"Thank you very much," said Rowan, "I will. Near an oasis is probably the best place to wait for my friends. At least for now. They may encounter a caravan, maybe drift in this direction too."

✦

"This is very nice, Aaru and Snood… the excellent meal, the fire, the stars, the deep calm. Thank you. Would you mind telling me a bit about the Divine Island? I hadn't heard it called that, although I'd stopped there near Fustat to look for my friend Captain Masudah of Zau, a Khémian warrior-priest. I saw the work in progress, as the incredible foundations were being laid out, though some of it looked to have been there for a long time already, such huge blocks of the densest material. What you tell me may shed some light on what you're working on here."

"Gladly," replied Snood, who rubbed his palms together and smiled through his snow-white beard. "At this time of year you may not have seen much evidence of water near the plateau, other than the river. When it's in flood, nearly the whole delta is underwater. The silt left behind is why it's called Black Land, as you of course surely know, extremely fertile, the basis of their great wealth. The myths speak of the cow goddess, whose amniotic sac breaks annually and gives birth to new life after it pours out across the land into the Middle Sea.

"Just think of what we do here, in a small way, and scale it up, way up, while you imagine the pyramids. Then add innumerable engineering features that will benefit not only Khémia but the entire planet. Some are obvious, such as pumping water for irrigation even further out from the river banks, but most are not. The constructions at the Divine Island, the plateau that is surrounded by water in flood season, will influence everything beneficially in the form of subtle energies linked somehow through their arcane science to the energies of the entire globe and beyond, the sun and other planets. I'm told the entire cosmos is the true foundation of its mystic workings."

Rowan leaned back. "I guess you could say that's big. I hadn't realized how big, but the time it will take is far too long to repel the Reps. Subtle energies are, well, subtle, not that I know much of such things. There must be something to it. Khémia is mostly a Surface-dwelling nation, unlike any other that I know of except tiny Land of the Song-Eyes in the west… but Reps just don't come here. I want to know how they're kept at bay."

"Because I'm an astrophysicist as well as an astronomer," said Snood, "there's a bit too much magic in it for me. Maybe it's just way over my head. Aaru's a far better mathematician than I am and even she's baffled…" He paused to glance at his wife. "I meant to say 'highly intrigued.'"

Aaru merely peered back at Snood, silent.

He winked at her and continued: "Rowan, we'd need another lifetime to be initiated into the mysteries to figure out how on Eorthe they make everything so precisely, all aligned to cosmic bodies, not only in the present, but calculated far into the future when the whole thing will finally fall into ruin. Yet it will still be working its magic, in a diminished manner, as long as one stone remains, so they say, hyperbole to be sure. It appears to us as magic, but to them it's natural law, despite all the religious stuff, which is some of kind of holistic shorthand anyway. And the results are amazing. As far as subtle energies go, that only means they're beyond our detection. They're extremely powerful, likely the clue to resistance to the enemy. Now, we've been trained in how to move and place the big stones we need. We know it works. With only one or two labourers, we can do it all ourselves. Yes, two old people… well, one old man and one lovely grown-up woman ripened to perfection. Knowing the little of what most educated people of the League nations know of antigravity, I still can't figure out how it works. But it works."

Aaru added, "Today we non-Khémian scientists focus too much on theory and mathematical description, not enough on experimental observation. The strange thing is, we found evidence of someone unknown long ago doing much the same thing that we do now. They obviously understood the speed of light. It is really intriguing. As the natives say, there's nothing new under the sun! The ancients actually encoded the distances to the major constellations where Khémian mythology says their gods came from. We are studying and expanding on that. They need not have made everything so complex just for an agricultural calendar. Something much simpler would work just as well. But we think they needed to gauge whether the solar system bodies were predictable. If they did not show up on time, they would know something was out of kilter and that they had better prepare for comets or giant lightning bolts from static electricity between planets in near collision to strike the surface. It must have happened before to provoke such exacting study.

"Our knowledge of the sky too will be encoded by precisely placing large stone markers in the ground. There will be seeming inaccuracies hidden among the extreme accuracies, which should puzzle a good mind. When investigated, the answer to a question future generations did not even know they were asking will be obvious. Anyone even many tens of thousands of years from now, with sufficient knowledge derived from observation of the stars, will be able to work out exactly when these monuments were built. It will let them know their ancestors were not mere baboons, no offence to that species, only that from the earliest times the people of Bharat, where I come from, have believed that the iterations of *sapiens*, though they obviously did not ask to be genetically modified, must take responsibility for their place in nature. The indigenous people of Bharat say… said… but perhaps some have survived… they say we tell the stories of the other animals. That is their way of saying we produce the meaning." Her brows lowered. Her hands fidgeted. She stood up and paced back and forth in front of the fire. "I do not think the reptilians take responsibility for the meaning they create. They believe they are victims, but do not admit it and project their vulnerability onto others by domination, to control what they see as chaos, all the so-called irrational drives that other *sapiens* species are gifted with… or cursed with, in their opinion. They only create chaos this way."

Rowan asked, "And what do you mean by 'irrational'? That doesn't sound too mentally healthy, certainly not a gift."

Aaru replied, "The definition I would assign to that word is in contrast to the reptilian unexamined belief that intuition, aesthetic sensitivity, creativity, invention, imagination, spirituality… all those faculties are disruptive to rational order, which must be imposed by an agenda derived from logical analysis."

Snood added, "They're definitely not stupid, the Reps, it's just that their thinking is limited, apparently to what Kirzaka wants."

Aaru continued, with vehemence: "It's only intellectual laziness. They think they lack all those 'irrational' traits, but judge by the results."

Rowan did not want to fan the coals of Aaru's increasing vilification, and remained silent on the topic.

"Their violence is truly irrational," she said, her dark eyes alight, "as is their lazy philosophy, if you can call it that. It has led them astray. It has reached a developmental dead end. They will only destroy our only home and foul their nest too with their fundamentalist ideology, their worship of that oxymoron 'machine intelligence'!" Aaru glared, formidable for such a small person. "They call it a god, Maçina the Artificer, but it is more like a metaprogram, totally and rigidly abstract, a principle that promises power but is ultimately limited by its ignorance of the totality, the matrix it exists within, if it can be said to exist as anything other than an abstraction. We have heard the Reps too want to launch into space from the moon to dominate the entire solar system, then the galaxy. On and on and on they crush and poison whatever they touch, till the whole cosmos is one big filthy lizard pit. *They* won't even like that, should it come to pass! But for them this is their manifest destiny sanctioned by Maçina."

Aaru stopped, turned and sat down. "But any sane person knows this. Forgive me, I do tend to rant… my entire family was wiped out by their unholy firepower." She gazed at Snood. Her voice had grown strained. "We only have each other now. And our work."

Snood gazed at her in return. "Yes, dear, but that's a lot. Future generations might mistake these simple stone monuments for primitive attempts at relating to something unknown and mysterious beyond… and they would not be wrong really… but with intelligent examination, if they're free enough to be curious, they'll understand that our knowledge was far from primitive. Maybe they'll see that our destiny is to manage our spaceship Eorthe so beautifully that it will indeed become the perfect springboard to the stars it was meant to be." Snood looked to Rowan. "Since our work involves the heavenly bodies, I like to speculate, fancifully perhaps, that our local star, the sun, is a living entity, a god if you will, who fosters life on Eorthe in just such a way that eventually it will shoot spores in the form of *sapiens* of one type or another… probably many types rubbing elbows, comfortably or not… into the star field to propagate elsewhere. We already have a space station with a wonderful telescope, which orbits the globe… or did until a short time ago. Do you have any news of this, Rowan?"

"Sorry, no. I don't know if any League craft are still left, never mind the unfinished space station. I'd hoped to find out more here in Khémia, but this land seems removed into the antique past, unaffected and unconcerned."

"I wouldn't put it that way exactly," Snood replied. "Antique in a way, yes, but they believe their building projects will affect the entire planet beneficially, including the reptilians by default. Maybe they think a collective mental light bulb will somehow switch on… but there's likely only the Rep station up there now. As I was saying, it's only a dreamy idea of mine, but with the sun as father and our planet as mother, well, it's a way of framing our situation. It makes the competition between our various species less about racism and more about the fittests' success in the cosmic plan… come to think of it, saying it like that makes it sound a bit like Maçinism. My beloved Aaru does not agree, however. She thinks I'm too generous in my assessment of our reptilian cousins, who in her opinion deserve to be annihilated. And I concede that she holds the more grounded view."

IX

Nai *of* Lightland

For the next three days Rowan made daily visits to the caravanserai to ask if his travelling companions had turned up. The innkeeper each time said he would send them straight to the astronomical site if so, but it was at least something to do other than hold a surveying rod for hours while Aaru and Snood made calculations. They were so patient – the shadows the sun made, the positions of the stars at night, all these they measured with their instruments repeatedly and timed precisely, with much checking of devices and scribbling in notebooks. All data collected would need to be checked for accuracy afterwards at the observatory in Abdju, the only one left in the world, no doubt. No wonder the work took so long. But Rowan deemed it time to either move on to wait in Abdju or commit to an indefinite wait here. Remote-viewing yielded vague and contradictory results, as if the desert of He of Bones of Iron had an invisible shield that skewed not only compasses.

On the fourth day Rowan decided to make one more visit to the innkeeper, then see what suggested itself. About to pass from the bright courtyard into the deep shade of the colonnaded passageway, a tall figure appeared out of the shadows and blocked his path. The man, or something much like a man, stood close to nine feet in height. His ice-blue eyes were set wide and proportionally larger than any species of *sapiens* – and the pupils, cross-shaped. Atop his head sat an extremely tall conical hat of brown felt with no brim and a blunt tip, less than practical in the desert sun for such pale skin, yet with no sign of sunburn on his long pleasantly proportioned hairless face. The ears were long to match, but not quite as pointed as a canid's, and slightly flared at the tops. No eyebrows. At first glance Rowan found it difficult to distinguish gender, but then the man spoke, in Common Tongue heavily accented, his voice basso: "This being is come to take you to Lightland."

Rowan tilted his head back to look into the man's eyes, and said, "Pleased to meet you too."

The headdress made the stranger's height more like eleven feet. Nothing about him intimidated otherwise. The expression on his face remained neutral, and his voice smooth and calm. The long brown plain woollen robe tied at the waist with a simple rope might be that of a monastic.

"Who are you?" Rowan asked. "And why should I go with you? I have important things to do. How do you know me? And who sent you?"

The tall man looked down at Rowan. His long arms hung at his sides. "Many questions," he said, blinked and paused. "It is good that you come. Is that not reason enough?"

Rowan took a step back. "Maybe it's not important where you come from, Lightland or wherever. Is that Bharat? Anyhow, these days I'm a little leery of anyone who goes nameless."

"Like the little black-skinned she-wizard who goes without raiment." The tall man's pupils transformed into four-pointed star shapes. "We are not like that."

"Where are my friends? Do you know what's happened to them? Where are they?"

The no-name man did not speak for a very long minute. "One meant well… the other and the little black one… distracted."

"You can say that again," said Rowan.

The man opened his mouth and looked like he might actually repeat his statement. But then he stepped out of the shade into the bright light. "Come. We waste time." His star-shaped pupils contracted to form four black dots in each eye. He turned and looked eastwards, clasped his long pale hands behind his back and strode through the gate into the open desert.

◆

"In case you don't already know, which seems unlikely given your mind-reading abilities, my name is Rowan Berry Longbow."

The tall man continued his long purposive steps across the golden sands towards the east, apparently uninterested in this revelation.

Rowan continued: "I'm only following because you seem to know something about my travelling companions or else you're reading my mind. I want answers to my questions. Then I'm turning back to say goodbye to my new friends before I go on, whether that's to the east to Abdju, where you're headed, or west into the desert to look for the others."

"We do not go to Abdju," replied the strider.

"Fine," said Rowan. "Maybe you're going to Lightland, wherever that is. Fair enough… it sounds like a nice fairy-tale kingdom. Tell me if you know where my friends are."

"Your mind is busy. It wants peace," the man said and continued his great strides across the sands. "Lightland is not a kingdom. You must try to keep up."

"No." Rowan stopped. "You go on without me. This is ridiculous. Your mental powers are impressive, really, but in this world things have to make a certain amount of sense. Goodbye and good luck." He turned in the direction of the astronomical site. A dozen yards had been crossed –

"*Wait!* Come back. The master calls."

Rowan turned to look at the tall man.

He had removed his tall conical hat, thus revealed his pale hairless skull as equally elongated and conical without it.

"*Tell me your name!*" Rowan shouted. "*Who is your master?*"

The tall man pulled the conical hat onto his head like a stocking, glanced towards the east, and strolled near. He looked down at Rowan, and said, "This being is too sensitized for this kingdom. This being's manners are insufficient."

"Next to good manners," said Rowan, quoting a great sage like Masudah often did, "the most important thing in the world is enlightenment."

The four round black pupils in each pale eye expanded into four-pointed stars. "This being bows to wisdom," he said, lowered his gaze and did not look up again.

"Let's start over," Rowan suggested. "I told you my name, now you say yours. That's how we do manners here."

"This being has no name. It is told you may call it Nai. It means 'sailor' or 'navigator' in Lightlandish."

"Pleased to meet you, Nai. Now we shake hands... no, your right hand. That's it, just clasp my right hand briefly, firmly but without breaking any bones. Pump it once or twice, then release it or people will talk. Good. It's a custom here on Eorthe to show that we conceal no weapons."

The cross-shaped pupils remained expanded in the star pattern.

"Nai, may I ask who's telling you things? Is it your master?"

"You may," answered Nai. "It is indeed the master."

"Are you telepathic? Is that how you communicate?"

"Yes. Mind to mind." He shifted his weight. His long arms hung. "Well," he added, "Nai is a servant. It does not teach. The master is a servant. It teaches. They serve the Limitless. For you, called Rowan Berry Longbow, Nai will try to explain." Nai, however, remained silent for a long time. Meanwhile his pupils expanded the star shapes into diamonds.

"Excuse me, Nai, I must interrupt your contemplation. Why not call me Rowan? It's informal, between friends."

Nai nodded assent. "Nai gives thanks. Yes, Nai is a friend... to Rowan."

"Maybe now we should take a break from etiquette lessons and visit my other new friends. You can tell us of Lightland. We'll take it from there. Right?"

Nai's long face betrayed nothing, but his pupils reverted to star shapes. He glanced eastwards again, turned back and said, "Rowan will introduce Nai to Alakana and Snood. We will… chat."

"By the way," Rowan said, "Snood calls his wife Aaru. It's a nickname."

"Aaru… 'heaven.' This is a kingdom. She was born Alakana Chakrabarti."

Rowan's brow wrinkled, but he said, "Shall we?"

"Agreed. And Nai will think each syllable of her name with equal stress."

◆

Both Snood and Aaru dropped their cooking utensils and stood to face their guests, one most unexpected, apparently. The stargazers' jaws dropped.

"Aaru and Snood," said Rowan, "meet my new friend Nai. He hails from a place called Lightland. Nai, meet Aaru and Snood, they're…"

"…constructing an homage to love," said Nai. "Work is love made visible. I bow to beauty." He crossed his right arm over his middle and folded his torso, and stooped to shake the pair's hands, Aaru's first, very carefully.

Impressed with how quickly Nai learned, Rowan thought: *Telepathy… I want to learn how to do that more than just accidentally.*

Nai looked at Rowan. "Even the gods cannot save you from what you want," he said, in the words of a great sage Masudah often quoted.

"Please, everyone," said Aaru, "let us sit down in the shade. The sun is brutal."

Snood retrieved a tall flask and four small metal cups. A delectable liqueur of apricot accompanied his toast to their mutual good health.

Nai hunched to fit under the awning, finished off his drink in one fell swoop, his face afterwards as inscrutable as ever, and held out his tiny cup for a refill.

"So, Nai," said Aaru, "tell us, if you will, of your home in Lightland." She removed her old straw hat and ran her open hands back from her forehead, which made her curly dark hair spring away. "By the way, the land of my birth is also called Land of Light."

"Bharat," replied Nai. "This is the light of truth, beauty and good. Nai bows to the Supreme." He pressed his palms together and touched his thumbs to the point between his eyes.

Aaru grinned and returned the gesture.

"Ah, where should Nai begin? Nai has said Lightland is not a kingdom. If one considers carefully, one sees that environments are value-neutral." His pupils retained their star shapes.

Snood jumped in: "That sounds reasonable. This desert is often called a wasteland because it isn't bought and sold. To others it's certain death. Yet to us it's a treasure of clear skies and open space. It's perfect."

Nai looked long at Snood until his pupils grew round. "This is truth. Let Nai try to formulate its thoughts more clearly. *All* objects of mind are value-neutral. What is called 'kingdom' is an object of mind. This land is called Khémia. Yet to each citizen and each visitor it is a different object. In fact there is no Khémia, only Khémia-thoughts."

Snood nodded acknowledgement, but squinted. Aaru only squinted. Rowan did not squint, but scratched his head.

Nai's pupils transformed into crosses. "This is difficult at this time. Let it arise in the mind's eye when it will as Nai's master would say. But allow no skin to grow over that eye." And he nodded encouragement.

Aaru stirred. "I have never heard of Lightland, although it may have other names. Can you say in which direction it lies?"

Nai's pupils expanded into stars. "Yes, Nai can say. The cardinal direction is east. Nai can be more specific with respect to longitude and latitude if it is wished."

"How far east?" Snood asked. "All the way to Bharat?"

"No. It is just beyond the crest of the second large dune in the distance, where the sun rises each day. It waits in the hollow. But this you cannot see with sense instruments called eyes. Let it arise in the mind's eye, like the sun. No force. Can you will the morning light to come? This letting-of-arising may require the appearance of the body to move in the direction east."

Aaru looked to Snood. Snood looked to Rowan, who watched Nai with great interest. "Nai," he said, "let's go."

◆

"I don't see anything," said Snood, who with his wife stood on the crest of the dune and looked into the large depression below.

"That's because you're man-looking," said Aaru. "I see beautiful patterns the wind made in the sand."

Snood guffawed. "My lovely wife is the brains in the family," he said. "I can only do my best to keep up. Lads, you're welcome to camp with us. But we should head back now. Right, Aaru? We have a long day tomorrow."

Rowan's brow wrinkled. "Don't you see it?" he asked.

67

Snood smiled through his long white beard, shook his head and raised a palm. "Lads, we're off." He winked at his wife. "Like the bride's pyjamas." He extended the crook of his arm to Aaru, and said to the others, "Good luck. See you later, if you change your minds. If not, may we meet again in a better world." The astronomers receded into the reddened west, back to their encampment.

Rowan watched them go, shifted the weight of his rucksack, and said a silent goodbye, along with a blessing of protection and good fortune.

"Nai learns much," said the Lightlander. "It is good. It is… liberation. And such lovely innocent creatures, Alakana-Aaru and Snood. Nai just loves them." Dispassion remained as his long face looked down at Rowan. "And Nai loves Sir Kitty Baby."

Rowan retreated a few steps.

Dispassion softened, and the corners of Nai's mouth turned down. "Lovely friend," he said, "Nai means no harm. Ah, Nai learns of presumption. Nai suffers enlightenment sickness." The giant Lightlander turned away and stepped heavily, and half-slid down the bank of the golden dune towards the wavery silver sphere. His distorted reflection in its dimpled surface grew larger when he drew near and raised his long palm. The sphere acquired a shimmery translucent silver-blue aura, and flattened to form a smooth rounded disc. In its edge an ovoid door grew from a tiny circle to accommodate the giant. He turned and called to Rowan: "Come. We waste time." His pupils had contracted into four dots in each eye.

Nai *of* Lightland's silver sphere.

X

Isle *of* Flame

THE INTERIOR OF the disc, dark and cooler than the desert at sunset as if some hours had passed already, rather than that of a machine turned out to be a gateway into a subtropical dry broadleaf deciduous forest, which spread without discernible boundaries under little puffy clouds adrift in a midnight-blue moonless sky.

Nai stood nearby, dwarfed by a stand of trees seventy-five to ninety feet in height, with massive thick cylindrical trunks a third of that in diameter, the size of the biggest grain towers of the late Vugh Deep, and relatively short compact branches at the crown, like a veined foliated mushroom cap or the flower of a gargantuan stalk of broccoli.

Rowan tore his gaze from that, and asked, "Nai, are my friends here?"

The neophyte's lips parted, but his pale blue eyes raised to peer into the distance, the pupils dilated greatly in the darkness, thus their shape less diamondiferous and more round now. "The master comes," said Nai.

Whom he referred to resembled the apprentice, except for his conical skull covered in shaggy red hair instead of a tight-fitting cap, like a tamarack in autumn, but with eyes the green of a clear mountain stream kissed by a sunbeam. The master glanced at Nai.

Nai stared back, and his brow wrinkled.

The master looked down to Rowan, and rumbled like friendly thunder: "Pilgrim, welcome! We are of the Order of the Ram. You may call me Aa. It means 'great one,' yet I am smallest of the small."

Rowan, for the moment tongue-tied, pondered the paradox.

"Rest easy, pilgrim. I suggest that you see past the literal meaning with calm resolve, as understanding is born the child of patience."

Rowan, unsure whether he had accidentally invited a teaching, decided to introduce himself: "I'm Rowan Berry Longbow of Vugh Deep in the continent of Evrys. I need to find the warrior-priest Captain Masudah of Zau in Lower Khémia, and Nefer the Wakan of Land of the Song Eyes, she whom Nai calls the 'she-witch'..."

"She-wizard," corrected Nai.

"And my guide, Songuset of Abdju in Upper Khémia..."

"*They are in the clutches of Stormbringer!*" added Nai, nearly breathless, and looked to his master wide-eyed. "*He of Bones of Iron!*"

Aa raised his long hand, peered over Rowan's head at his protégé, and said, "Eorthe manners, Nai. Our guest need not have introduced himself."

Nai bowed his long head.

Aa dropped his chin, and to Rowan said, "Your friends are in the Shrine of Rust. We can help and will. But first, pilgrim, you must shed your skin and grow beyond yourself."

"I'm a felid... not a reptilian."

"You speak of your formal configuration. Can it claim the 'I am'? Be sure of what you seek. The cost is to die before you die."

Rowan peered up at the red-headed giant. "My species isn't me," he admitted. "Other than that, I haven't really looked into it."

"Very good, Pilgrim Longbow. Self-knowledge is the beginning of the path. At the end, what you seek is the lover within all your other lovers."

"I've only the one." But a pang pierced Rowan's breast. He sighed and looked away, and thought of Samarit in the warm soft light of the firestone beneath the gnarled pines under the cool light of the silver moon beneath the sea of stars the night before his – yes, departure from her side, on a noble mission – of course, but what if she had felt abandoned, despite the brave face...?

"Assumptions can be deadly, pilgrim."

Rowan sighed assent. "I discovered that in commando school."

"In that case, consider every situation, flowery or foul, as a battlefield."

Rowan pondered flowery combat, or the jade stalk in the jade gate, symbols of an ancient culture of the East, likely extinct now.

Meanwhile the hidden sun cast a rose-orange glow that made the backlit forest a tracery in silhouette. In a moment the morning rays caressed the little clouds in a spectacular display of golds and purples. And a second sun rose, slightly smaller and tinted blue –

Eyes wide open, Rowan stared at the scene, and a thought formed: *Well, I'm definitely not in Khémia anymore...*

"You never were," said Nai.

"Peace," Master Aa ordered. "Pardon my apprentice Nai, pilgrim. He resonates with Eorthe still, and his manners are unmastered as yet."

"If I may, please tell me, Aa, where is this Shrine of Rust?"

"Come."

The giants' long strides forced Rowan to run to keep up. The two colossi disappeared below the edge of the forest. Beyond the sharp edge of a clifftop easily one thousand feet above a wide forested plain, bounded on its far side by titanic snow-capped mountains, between which a river meandered under the pink sky. The twin sunrise reflected in the ribbon of water that transected a city, more precisely a megalopolis. Translucent towers spired at the perimeter, although bound by no outer wall, only the scalloped rim of a shallow crater spanned by two bridges, one for each transection. Much of the interior grew green with well-tended parks that encircled a half-mile-high conical stone tower.

By the time Rowan had followed the giants down the cliff into the forest, the city had disappeared from view behind the trees. By dead reckoning regardless, along the way he came upon a garden glade with a conical fountain supported by four sturdy Lightlander women carved of stone, like bathers under waterfalls. The soft tones of wind chimes, and soothing chords of perhaps a percussive instrument made of wood accompanied the twitter of songbirds. Sandalwood or a similar incense permeated the air. Conviction eluded him, however, and doubt formed a thought: *All this seems so real…*

"What is real is changeless," said Nai from behind him. "Change is unreal."

Rowan spun about and peered into the forest, apparently populated only by birds, however, and the stone women of the fountain.

"Silence, Nai," said Master Aa, also invisible. "Please leave teaching to the teacher. Pilgrim Longbow, you are wise to doubt. Question the unreal."

Ship afire *and* bound *for the* Isle *of* Flame.

The glade grew dark but starless. The fountain's burble and plash grew quiet. The birds must have flown off. The incense smelled burnt. At the edge of blackness, a reddish-orange glow appeared in the distance – *fire* – and flared into firestorm reflected in the surface of heaving black water.

Ocean spray washed over the pilgrim, and he rose and fell with the sea, as well as rocked from side to side like a buoy, but on a ship's deck. Sails billowed and flapped in the whistle of the wind, which grew into the howl of a gale, and made the vessel pitch, shaken like a toy boat. He crouched, grasped a nearby rope and hung on for dear life. *What the…?!* –

Master Aa's thundery voice boomed from above: *"The answer to your prayer!"* The semblance of his face appeared, formed of wind-blown tones of heavy dark vapour, partially blended into the swirl of roiling black clouds –

Rowan peered straight up at the vision, but did not recall having prayed.

"You did! When you believed you were lost in the realm of Stormbringer, He of Bones of Iron! This is why Nai was sent to fetch you to Lightland!"

The flames loomed ever more near and greater, and licked the sea, clouds of steam hissed and thunder cracked –

"This is hardly the answer to a prayer!" Rowan shouted. His hair blew straight back and his soaked clothing billowed like the sails, but he tried to look behind him for the captain of the ship of doom, or anyone in control of the helm –

"No misgivings!" Aa shouted. *"A prayer of supplication never goes unanswered. But the form the answer takes is never up to the supplicant!"*

Even the black water caught fire –

Rowan supplicated with all his might, bent low and let one hand slip from the rope to shield his eyes from the conflagration that engulfed the wooden ship, and the sails burst into flame –

✦

"Does non-existence exist?"

"Good question, pilgrim, but look you before you seek."

"Have I died before I died?"

"Before and after have no meaning here, pilgrim. Neither does life and death. Call it the Isle of Flame. It is what the Antediluvians called it in memory of their homeland as they last knew it."

"The Khémian legend… the tale tells that all was lost… home, hearth and health, a whole world of wonders."

"Not everything," explained Master Aa. "Survivors scattered across the globe like seeds to start over."

Rowan thought of Samarit's poetic metaphor under the silent cold glitter of stars on their way down with Squire Krumb into Mudredd Vale, the viper pit.

Aa continued: "The culture's knowledge layer had been stripped off, and with it the wisdom-stories, yet fragments remained. Long ages passed, but the seeds were hardy, did their duty and died. The embryonic culture sprouted in the black soil of Khémia, the kingdoms of Bharat, the northernmost of the Arktikan Circle, the southernmost of the continent of Afara, as well as Antarktikos, and the Mountains of the West in South Verden. This cycle of nature has repeated many times and will recur many times."

"Is that why you say Eorthe is the place of ever-beginning?"

Master Aa nodded confirmation, and added, "Or cyclical if it is too difficult to contemplate at first. Be sure to remember, like the lightning seeds, you too must die before you die."

A knot gripped Rowan's solar plexus as he pondered the paradox of death while still alive.

"Pilgrim, your prayer's answer is here."

He surveyed the circumference of the burnt-black treeless horizon. His soles sank into soft sand – his jaw clenched tight at the thought that formed: *I'm right back where I started... damn Stormbringer!*

"Caution, pilgrim," said Master Aa. "Reactivity is typical of the Beginner archetype. Leap to a conclusion and the jaws of the crocodile are sure to open wide in anticipation of a meal. The rivergoing beast is a supreme transformer of raw material, yet worry not, sorrow not for the dead nor for the living." The red hair on Aa's long conical head shone bright from within, like the dread Isle of Flame. "*Courage, Lionheart!*" boomed he. "*As with all else, whether grand or grim, let patience give birth to understanding!*"

The light faded. Aa had gone. Blacker than black even to felid eyesight, only the hiss and sift of sand remained.

XI

Shrine *of* Rust

THE ISLE OF FLAME had been the end of a world, and the end of an age. Like a prophetic dream, the vision heralded a sowing of seed, thus death in the service of life. The black granular wilderness hissed alternately louder and softer. The dawnless night persisted. Nai had been right in a way: the vast dark wilderness that surrounded Rowan consisted of nothing but thought, including *this is wrong and it must change*. With neither a discernible enemy in sight, nor a safe haven, nevertheless his body tensed in preparation to either fight or flee –

"Which is to be then?"

Nefer…

Her aura cast a soft glow on the black sand, and revealed her bare black silhouette within the blue luminescence.

"Where are the others?" he said.

"They seek the future."

"You're Stormbringer."

"There is nothing that is not He of Bones of Iron."

"*Where are they?!*"

"Patience, kitty baby." Samarit had replaced Nefer, in perfect black skin highlighted by the blue aura.

The corners of Rowan's mouth turned up, and he winked at her.

Samarit morphed into Nefer. Apparently unaware she had been for a brief moment supplanted, she said, "And now you know who you are."

"You're right. I do."

"You are He of Bones of Iron."

"If I am, you're old Iron Bones too."

Nefer's arched brows knit together; her very dark eyes blinked. Her arms crossed. Her pink lips pouted. She glared, shook her head and scoffed: "You think you can trick the trickster. You are a fool."

"You said there's nothing but He of Bones of Iron. Then you're a fool too."

Nefer stamped her dainty feet. Clouds of soot billowed, which grew into a dust devil and engulfed her, ascended into the sky and disappeared.

Rowan closed his eyes to the fine airborne particles and the sting of grit. He opened them to red streaks on the horizon, which spread, then jerked to a new position, again as if they slipped their cogs like stage scenery. The dunes grew visible, barely. He stood up to survey the perimeter.

A figure in peripheral vision snagged his attention: a huge armoured Rep, fifty yards distant. Out of the stillness of the desert, the fast-rising pitch of a projectile grew louder – a plasma spear –

Rowan stepped out of the shining arc of its path. But he kept his eyes trained on the thrower.

A humanoid-shaped blur in the dark, the reptoid stood with its clawed paws hung at its sides as if deactivated, its small orange eyes dull, the blue feathered comb flaccid.

Regardless, Rowan backed away with care, eyes fixed on the enemy. His ankle brushed something soft –

Samarit lay on the ground, no longer black of skin. What was left of the spear stood pointed skywards, a scintillating spike of ionized gas about to fade. It had penetrated her heart. A dark red stream between her breasts collected and expanded into a pool of blood on the sand beneath her body. Her face had drained of life, framed by wavy dark hair splayed in every direction over the black dust, her dead eyes open to the sky and already filmed over.

Rowan's heart ached to breaking point. Her unique fragrance, infused with a hint of wildflowers, however sweet engulfed him in sorrow. But he stifled the urge to roar; nothing could be believed here in the realm of He of Bones of Iron, the father of lies and tiresome tricks.

The reptilian had vanished. The corpse at his feet remained, however, while the red-streaked sky transitioned from pitch black to charcoal to gunmetal grey.

Samarit's body grew translucent. The pool of blood that stained the black sand even blacker, the last of her to disappear, took the darkest of the dark night with it.

Rowan scanned the dawn's faint blush on the horizon for any potential destination.

But then an indistinct dot appeared in the mirage that shimmered in the distance, and bobbed like a fishing float. Soon another dancing dot joined it – the heads of men. And below them now wavered forms – camels, ships of the desert that rose over the horizon and the reddening dunes.

"*Where have you been, sir?*" shouted Songuset, backlit by the dawn. "*We have been searching for you for a very long time!*"

Rowan watched him – and Masudah – who both appeared utterly real in every detail –

The riders looked to each other, and back to Rowan.

Masudah halted his beast of burden.

Nefer caught up, tilted her lovely face upwards to him and grinned – a little dusty, but as black, bare and beautiful as ever.

Rowan crossed his arms and waited. This might be another trick. How to tell the difference between Stormbringer's illusions and the real thing?

Master Aa spoke: "*It is within your power to decline to drink Stormbringer's poison, the interpretation he strongly suggests you make your own. It is your freedom to choose. He is persuasive, at times coercive, at others seductive, but has only as much power as you grant him. He is a squatter. Evict him.*"

Songuset dropped down from his camel and approached with wary steps, and glanced at Masudah, who likewise had dismounted.

The warrior-priest, his moustaches like wings on the rise, said, "We have found you, Sir Rowan. And you have found us."

Nefer drew near and gazed at Rowan dewy-eyed.

"Is there any water left?" he asked. "I'm parched."

◆

"The Shrine of Rust we know nothing of," said Masudah, who strode hand in hand with Nefer on the next leg of their trek across the red sands. "Likely what is meant is this very Iron Desert. We have made the sacrifice, now we are blessed. All the same, it has been a long and bizarre waking nightmare, but we have sacrificed the false on the altar of truth."

Nefer said something to Masudah in Wakan.

He looked up at Rowan, who rode high in the saddle of his camel. "Nefer asks that you bless us, Sir Rowan. She is anxious that we be wed, you see."

"I wish you good fortune. I believe you'll need it once we get to Abdju."

"In Khémia there are no special ceremonies for weddings, other than the celebrations observed by families to demonstrate their increase of bounty to the community. The marriage itself is sanctified by the gods or not at all, we believe. If not, the two go their separate ways, lessons learnt or otherwise. Therefore we must be brave, thus Nefer wished especially that you bless us. Songuset has already done so. To her you are family. She calls you Brother Red Lion. She believes you are sent by the higher powers."

Rowan looked down from the height of his camel at the young woman, met her dark eyes and nodded acknowledgement. "Please thank her. Tell her that I'm touched and honoured. If I hadn't come down from Longbow clan territory to look for you, who knows how things would have turned out… of course you have my most sincere blessing, Nefer and Masudah, for happiness, long life and prosperity."

"We would be caught in a time loop still, I am sure of it, Sir Rowan. I was deluded by, how you say… grandeur. Imagine, I, the wise priest, saviour of Khémia from Kirzaka! Yes, I, wizard of the cosmic power! How funny. An offering of thanks must be made to Stormbringer for exposure of my hidden arrogance, a leftover from my time as a novice, an ascetic, an ignorant hermit in search of purity. I had congratulated myself then that I had passed a test of virtue, because a goddess sent me in search of a very beautiful harlot in a desert town. Fated to meet, I found her with ease, and without my asking, she that minute renounced her profession for me, but as instructed by the goddess, I sacrificed any gain and introduced her to religion, which saved her soul when she became a devotee of Lord Min, the god of procreation and fertility. That was many years ago. Sent most recently to Land of Song Eyes on what I believed was a diplomatic mission, Stormbringer laid bare, quite literally in the form of my beloved Nefer, my weakness for a pretty face and form. It has been a supreme test to not fall prey to low motives, blinded to her beauty of spirit, seduced by lust, moreover tempted by jealousy and possessiveness, suspicious of your and Songuset's virtue, two strong men equally blessed with full view of her abundant charms each day. The lesson for me has been that love desires nothing but to give, because it needs nothing. Each moment I let her go, while at the same time my only desire is to witness the joy of my beloved."

"She is very beautiful," Rowan replied, "as the name you gave her implies. And I understand her desire to demonstrate to all that her body is holy and as innocent as a newborn's, but when we get close to the city, Songuset should go ahead to buy her an appropriate outfit. I still have a coin of gold that I'll give him for his wages. When he cashes it, the remainder should cover the cost. I insist. You won't talk me out of it. And please know, Masudah, to me your heart remains the purest."

◆

With Abdju's walls, towers and obelisks in plain view in the distance across the water under the silver crescent of the moon, Nefer, Masudah and Rowan waited in the desert just beyond the palm trees and green fields that lined the great sparkling river. The warm light of the fire played in highlights on Nefer's smooth black skin in the most exotic manner, and revealed her as one of nature's finest works of art. But her restless dark eyes watched Masudah, who paced back and forth.

"I tell you," he said, "I have been initiated by the highest teachers of the Path of Freedom, but now I am like any ignorant neophyte. I have forgotten everything I believed I knew. The thought of surrender of my beloved Nefer to the jaws of the crocodile is unbearable and has chased any wisdom out of my head like a flock of frightened birds. I hope to represent myself well. But it is not possible! I have no defence. As a servant of the gods I am doubly responsible to uphold our traditions. I will not likely be imprisoned if the vizier admits the whole truth to the court without bias, but at the very least I will be made an example, demoted, dismissed without honour and reviled."

Rowan studied the warrior-priest, so unlike the confident and cheerful Masudah of times past. "I know Khémians don't have lawyers to represent them," he said, "defendants must speak for themselves, but I can be a character witness."

"Gratitude, my friend, but it cannot stand up against the hard evidence as reported by Nefer's chieftain father. It will have been documented by my superiors as an affront to an allied nation and a moral failure."

Rowan asked, "Do you remember our conversation when I was in the lock-up at the military base in Perkona Ola prefecture? When you told me of Sam's betrothal to the Longbow prince, Pineshadow Touchstone-Longbow? I imagine I felt then somewhat like you feel now… terrified. You gave me much good advice, likely just as you'd done many times as a priest to countless young people whose hearts had broken. To be honest, not a lot of it sank into my hard head, but I do recall two things. The first was that I had to love my way out of the predicament I was in. For me that meant letting Sam go, in the same way you spoke of letting Nefer go yesterday. She was bound by clan law, but to separate a canid from her people is as good as killing her. The second point was something about the art of life being like a drama, with me the actor who must perform his lines well or get off the stage. It meant to learn the script and moreover make it my own, not just reel off the lines. But you know, I now remember a third point. You said I had to follow my heart. You taught me that my heart is not my feelings. It's the essence, that without which I would not be me, and which is always free, limitless and unconcerned."

Masudah had slowed his anxious pace to listen. "Who was that Masudah?" he asked. "He sounds like a wise man."

XII

Banished

AT LAST SONGUSET returned the next afternoon. He led a donkey that bore gifts of raiment for Nefer and other luxuries for the nuptials the travellers would celebrate here at the threshold of Abdju. "I was able to enlist the help of my good wife," he said, "to find a most beautiful gown for the bride. She was at first most angry with me for having disappeared for so long, but I explained at last to her satisfaction. This took much time, for which I apologize. She would not believe me, but she was very happy not to have lost her old friend, most important. Also, she has great superstition of the Iron-Boned. In fear she had consulted a fortune-teller, who told her I was lost in the underworld, abducted by a heretic posing as a pilgrim. I tell her she has the gift of second sight as much as anyone, but she replies that caring for the sick, flowers, stray animals and small children is better for the soul. Perhaps she is correct. But she waxed most enthusiastic at the task of the bridal dress. She admires greatly the black-skinned peoples, as she has inherited some of that blood. I invited her to join us, but no, she said, it is between us four who triumphed over Stormbringer's temptations. I think she is a little afraid of us, but perhaps she did believe me a little also."

Nefer frowned at the donkey. She turned her back to the others and to Abdju, and walked some distance into the desert to stand under a lone date palm. The heat reflected off the desert floor and shimmered tree and woman.

"Dear Nefer worries," explained Masudah. "It is not having to cover her innocence alone that offends her… she is a proud woman… but she fears I will be imprisoned. I have explained that I will be officially stripped of my rank and at best left to my own devices as to how to survive without it, should an employer overlook my disgrace. She must also learn a new language, not so difficult really. But of a royal bloodline, she has not been educated to work for a living. And she is very young. This is part of growing up, but difficult."

"You can be a guide for pilgrims," Songuset suggested. "I will help."

"Thank you, my friend," said Masudah. "We shall see what is decreed."

The men waited for the bride. The sun climbed the blue heavens and the day grew very hot, and the sands shimmered the air.

Nefer's dark form too wavered in the distance, along with the palm tree. At last she made her way back to the campsite. She stopped and peered at the three men who had stood when she approached. After a moment she walked to the basket the donkey had borne and opened its lid, lifted the long tight skirt of white linen and examined it by pressing it against her dark body. The beaded waistband would hang from a network of two straps formed of criss-crossed blue cylinder beads woven with felt-lined copper breast caps enamelled with a floral pattern, too small for all but minimal modesty by the standards of Perkona Ola, but highly complimentary to Nefer's figure. The basket also held leather sandals, as this celebration would be a special occasion, and a compact mirror as well as kohl for the eyes, and perfume of lily, myrrh and cinnamon in a blue glass bottle. Lastly, on loan from Songuset's wife, a fine necklace of turquoise and gold, less rare than silver in Khémia: on the other side of the river from Abdju and far into the eastern desert lay rich gold deposits.

Silver had to be imported. Songuset's gift, a plain but precious ring of it, he said served as his sacrifice to They of Bones of Silver and a blessing to the bride.

Nefer folded the dress with precise care, replaced everything in the basket and closed the lid. She walked the path to the riverbank nearby and entered the water, followed closely by the men in case a crocodile should try to make a meal of her. She emerged among the reeds and glistened with natural jewels, the beaded and streaming water, a gift of the river. Again thigh-deep in the slow current that sparkled in the sun, she faced the waiting party, raised her hands to the sky and beamed a grin at last.

Masudah exclaimed something in Wakan. He turned to the other men and translated for Rowan: "Nefer outshines the sun!"

And they clapped, cheered and hooted in praise of the bride, who enjoined each in damp embrace to prepare before the informal wedding ceremony.

◆

The three men sat on the steps outside the courthouse, not a happy sight to each other, but invisible to passersby distracted by the vision of Nefer's regal beauty, despite her diminutive size, whose hand rested on Masudah's shoulder and at times caressed it. Many second and third glances were cast her way. Clothed now, she was just as lovely. The necklace of gold had been returned to Songuset's wife, but Nefer was the kind of woman who even in rags inspires the eye.

Masudah had told them, sadly, "Unless I now voluntarily and promptly embark on a long journey into exile, I shall be escorted by my own men, if I wish it, to some border or another. The vizier has decreed it; the queen agrees."

Songuset asked, "To where will you go?"

Masudah sat silent. His moustaches drooped as he looked back at him, and he reached across to his opposite shoulder to clasp his hand to Nefer's.

Rowan, Nefer *and* Masudah *in* Abdju, Upper Khémia.

Rowan said, "I took the hard road to Khémia to find a solution to the Wishbone Longbow tribe's search for a safe haven. More than that, it must solve the problem of all the free peoples of the world or it's temporary at best and no solution at all. These Khémians freely walking this street topside have no idea what it's like beyond their borders. Masudah, please help us. That's why I came."

The ex-warrior-priest bowed his head. "It is a great temptation to descend into self-pity after a lifetime as an important person." He turned to gaze at Nefer, who already gazed at him. "But I must move beyond that now. Just look at her! Even one day in Nefer's company is more than I could ever have hoped for in this world. But I will help you, Sir Rowan, whether it is in some forsaken land or not. The only decision to make is which. But you could remain in Khémia, you know, to perhaps find another who can help the Longbows."

"I have no other connections here. And I'm not a native. Why should anyone take an interest in a remote tribe of a distant land?"

"Ah, yes," replied Masudah, "your association with me will not endear you to the authorities either. You would have to convince someone in power to allow you, a foreigner, initiation into our religion at the lowest level, like a child. This would take many years to complete even if granted."

81

"If you agree and it's not insane to bypass the orthodox initiation, I would prefer that you teach me more magic. I know it's dangerous, but I'm willing to risk it if it saves the Longbows. They must move to another country. No place on Eorthe is safe now, even Khémia, but maybe there are pockets of resistance. But where? Obviously the Land of Song-Eyes is out, and I told you of Snood and his wife Aaru, the astronomers. She was originally from Bharat, where they studied at one of the world's oldest and best observatories. She said everything there had been destroyed."

"'Everything' is a large number, even for astronomers," replied Masudah. "I suspect in that land there are survivors. But Bharat is very distant, best reached by ship across the Sea of Sindhu, now dangerously exposed to the sky. It is unknown whether there still are seagoing vessels that voyage the Sindhu, but I think it increasingly unlikely and unwise in any case. There is the greatest mountain range on Eorthe at Bharat's northern border, greater than the Fell range, where were very big caverns. In a vast plateau high above the treeline is an ancient race, the Bön, who migrated from the region of the inland seas west of there and less than six hundred leagues from here. There may be some survivors in caves of the Bön's high eastern mountains, but it would be more likely, I think, that the land of their ancestors between the two inland seas northeast of Khémia would still be home to their forebears, as they are a high culture and may have outwitted the reptilians. They are called the Ahan, or Beholders, some say Watchers. As far as we know in this age, they were Eorthe's first astronomers, although Khémia does not admit it, since the kingdom of Aha is only known to a few scholars as legend. Like their distant relatives the Bön, that is to say very genetically distant now, they live in remote high places. They have kept secret, apart from the world, so few have even heard of them. However, the evidence suggests to me most convincingly that they do indeed thrive in the highlands.

"They are anders, basically, but not so mixed as others, such as us Khémians, nor even the Bön. Neanderthal stock has a greater share in their genetic heritage. The legend I am aware of says the Primordial Architects added a special, how you say… amalgam of extraterrestrial elements as well, as an experiment, which is meant to explain why they look nothing like the Bön. To their land is a long road from here, but a lot closer than northern Bharat. Moreover, I happen to know the natural portals along much of the way to the mountains of the Ahan."

"What about weapons?" asked Rowan. "And a scanner?"

"I had already surrendered any military weapons in my possession when arrested by Nefer's father the chieftain. But the vizier today let me keep my ceremonial dagger… not entirely useless, I suppose… I think he felt sympathetic to my plight, as he has several wives and adores women, perhaps more than is modest… but please do not repeat that I say this. His verdict was just, and I am grateful. He might have been tempted to take Nefer for his own but for the queen's disapproval. To purchase weapons is not possible. My identity has been flagged. Perhaps you may be able to buy elsewhere than Abdju, as it is sacred ground, although it would be difficult. Foreigners are not legally permitted. I am surprised they did not confiscate your phaser. Perhaps the gods bless us in secret. But there is the black market, if I dare risk it. As to a scanner, this is not the traditional Khémian way, which relies on what the wider world calls magic. We call it sacred science, until recently my field of academic expertise. I had been sanctioned to experiment with one before my last assignment to Perkona Ola, but it too was taken by Nefer's father and returned to my superiors."

"I still have my little hand-held scanner," Rowan said, "which resembles an old soldering iron more than a weapon, which I'll retrieve from the guards' vault at the city gate along with the phaser. It too isn't entirely useless if a natural portal is compatible. It powered up no problem as soon as we were well clear of the Iron Desert. It looks like we'll have to make do with what we have. It was ever thus, not so, my friends?"

Songuset stood up, and said, "I am an old man and have seen many strange things. It has been the most amazing adventure of them all, I must say, but this is officially the end of my guided tour, Sir Rowan, my friend. May you have been blessed by it as pilgrims hope when they come to Abdju! I return to my wife, a good woman who will cease her scolding one day when she no longer fears a stranger will take her man away into the unknown." Farewells were said to each and all. Songuset made his way along the narrow street, but turned and waved, and disappeared into the crowd.

"Your beautiful bride," said Rowan, "will go where you go. And from what I've seen, she's more than capable."

Masudah placed his arm around Nefer's shoulders, as she had sat down beside him. "Yes, she promises to follow me anywhere, even when she could remain in Abdju, and in luxury. She could choose, how you say… hypergamy, but instead is a hypogamist, so unlike many women, who trade in beauty in the sanctioned business of matrimony. Perhaps it is my blessing that she is without dowry." He gazed at her and grinned. "This little one is a great mystery to me, Sir Rowan. So delicate, yet so strong. So refined, yet so fierce, like a wild creature. She tells me that I make her feel safe. I wish to protect her from all harm, yet it is she who watches over me! So independent, yet so loyal. She is young and has much to learn, but something of the ancient knowledge that her people stewards in code for us is somehow embodied in her pretty frame. Like goddess Nwt, so dark but so bright! But have no doubt that the power she displayed in the Iron Desert, that seemed bestowed by Stormbringer, is in fact hers alone. Like most, she does not know it. She is as superstitious as Songuset's wife. But I know better. I know because it is true of me as well. You know, Stormbringer was right in a way. He and I are one. Rather, I am Him at my worst, but He is not me at my best."

Rowan peered at Masudah. Khémian mysticism often did not make much sense to him. But he had spontaneously said much the same thing in response to He of Bones of Iron after symbolically dying to his old self at the finale of the Lightlander episode.

◆

By barge and lastly by a large reed craft, the three travellers headed upstream further south along the great river, their first destination Kaina, near the temple complex dedicated to the fecund cow goddess, the Great One of Many Names, figuratively responsible for the flooding of the sprawling delta hundreds of miles to the north when her amniotic sac broke each spring, said to be the mother of all goddesses.

"If Songuset were with us, Sir Rowan, he would no doubt insist that we take a short detour to explore her temple, this one in her form of the cosmic mother sky goddess Iunet, Eye of the Sun. It is small, undecorated like all the oldest works, so old no one knows who built it. It is said to have always existed, or at least since the creation of Eorthe. There are much newer structures, but still extremely ancient, built up around it. We *do* know who built those… our ancestors the Antediluvians, who first explored this region. By building on or near sacred sites they found it more convenient to educate the indigenous population to their ways, who were equally ignorant of the unknown builders, yet in awe of them."

"I'm fascinated of course," said Rowan, "but we have no time for tourism… and I do understand you may feel that you're saying goodbye to your homeland forever." He punched Masudah's shoulder lightly. "When we're finally done with saving the world I'll talk Sam into us joining Nefer and you on a grand tour of this magical land."

Masudah tilted his torso to look at Rowan beside him on the bench fixed to the deck of the reed boat. "Do you not recall, Sir Rowan? I am in exile. I am a deportee, once we leave Khémia. I am never to return. If I do, I may stay, but in two pieces, one of which is my head. Do you see the problem with your otherwise very nice idea, my friend? This may be your only chance to see this ancient treasure."

"True enough, but there may be no nice ideas possible ever again if we don't find something that gives us the edge with the Reps, and fast."

"You are right. When in Khémia, even in disgrace, I am Khémian. When here I admit to not care all that much about the outside world. This motherland is balm to the soul. Although its beautiful forms remain strong and stable, the culture encourages, how you say... complacency. We are safe here. The threat seems so far away. It is as if we say, 'Let us just have a nice time, enjoy. What is wrong with that?' I shall miss it. But yes, we must hasten slowly. I mean we must waste no time, but neither get ahead of ourselves. We explore the unknown now."

Rowan nodded assent. "You sound like the Lightlanders."

"Ah, that is indeed an interesting experience you had. The myths are contra-dictory and vague when they tell of those supernatural beings. Now I have a much more clear picture of their true nature. They are mysterious, but I would trust, how you say... implicitly anything they have to teach. I believe their world is of another dimension, of a finer frequency range than this one. Yet they can visit us, much like we can swim in the sea, if we learn how, some of us even dive deep in underwater craft for extended periods to observe sea life. To the Lightland giants it is like this, but for observation of what to them is dream life."

True to Masudah's depiction of the Khémian mood, the three travellers, with Nefer having returned from watering the waves, now nestled in the middle, relaxed in the evening sun on the reed deck of the boat, slipware tankards of spiced fruity beer in hand, safer than river water. The sun hung in the vast sky like a huge molten orb of gold, slightly flattened as it melted into the red western horizon. Rowan had no trouble envisioning it as a god that blessed them all with healing radiance. Nefer's black skin glowed with copper highlights in its light, while Masudah's tanned face shone raw sienna.

"I want this moment to never end," Rowan said. "If only Sam were here with us."

"It is a good wish," said Masudah. "This is what we seek, the beauty that makes beauty beautiful. May our seeking end in finding. No complacency, and a stable peace. I am a fallen priest, but this is my prayer for us now."

XIII

Devils' Doorway

Aₙₒₜₕₑᵣ ₗₒₙ𝒈 ᵈₑₛₑᵣₜ journey by camel caravan took the refugees to a caravanserai at an oasis they had reached in two days after debarkation at Kaina on the eastern bank of the Iteru. They would not travel the full length of the path from the caravanserai to the gulf coast. Masudah said a portal along the route, known to the local tribe as Devils' Doorway, would save them a dangerous crossing by ship to the coast of the continent of Aja opposite. In any case, the few seagoing craft that remained wisely stayed close to Khémian shores.

◆

"Such an ominous name," said Rowan, who with his two companions stood before yellow sandstone cliffs that averaged seventy-five feet in height. "It looks to have been made by giants, doesn't it?"

Long ages had passed since a somewhat plain but once precisely incised door frame, apparently a false one, near to thirty feet tall and ten feet wide had been carved in the otherwise rough cliff face, blank stone in the plain flat space within the chipped and cracked jamb pale yellow in the morning sun's slanted rays.

"Its name is well earned, I assure you," replied Masudah. "As I have explained to Nefer, legend tells of entire herds having vanished in the vicinity of this carving, along with the shepherds or goatherds. Soldiers who were sent to investigate never returned, nor was any evidence found of their remains, apart from their tracks in the dust. Their footprints ended a few steps from where we are standing now. This is why the camel drivers yelled at us as we walked in this direction from the oasis after we sold our beasts of burden."

Rowan said, "To me it didn't sound like they were wishing us fare-thee-well. I'm glad to be rid of them in any case. They were too interested in Nefer, as I'm sure you noticed. This seems like what we need, a natural portal, but by the sounds of it, unruly. I hope my little scanner can deal with it. Who carved it? They must have had some shielding to do that."

"No one knows. The style is like the original temple near Kaina, the one I wanted you to see, only the bas-relief pillars were added much later, so someone was using it ages before even the Antediluvians arrived. Those ancients are believed to have been mariners, as here was once a shoreline. Among portals it may be a wild one but, since the carving has survived so long, it must be reliable

Devils' Doorway, eastern Khémia.

in another way. This is often not the case. Portals can unexpectedly alter their locations greatly, depending on currents beneath the ground among other factors. I have been here before. One of my men was a gifted dowser. He reported two energetic lines that cross just here beneath this cliff, likely once forested above a beach all along the base. As we know, sea levels were much higher in ages past. In this heat it is difficult to believe, but long ago the North Wind blew cold in this place, as Evrys across the Middle Sea from Black Land delta lay in a coma beneath miles of ice." As if chilled at the thought, Masudah wrapped his arm around Nefer's bare shoulders.

Rowan retrieved the hand-held scanner from his rucksack, measured the distance and set it before the door.

"Let us close our outer eyes," said Masudah, "calm our minds and bind our triad into a unity."

Nefer, between the men, joined hands with Rowan as well.

Masudah spoke something in Wakan in soothing tones.

Her trembling hand relaxed – a bit too much – her fingers slipped his grasp.

Too soon the rectilinear doorway fractured as if an earthquake had just ruptured the subsurface. Rowan lost his balance and slid towards a large crack in the ground barely visible amid a dense cloud of dust. Another shock wave saved him from a head-first plunge, but slammed his body into Masudah.

They rolled as a single tangled mass for a few seconds. Both lay on their backs covered in dust, too stunned to stand up.

"*Masudah! Are you all right? Where's Nefer?*"

The ex-priest coughed and spat, and rubbed grit from his eyes. "*Nefer!*" he croaked, stumbled to a standing position, one eye open, and squinted. "*Nefer! Nefer, come back!*" Masudah dashed towards the crevice as if to leap to the doorway –

But Rowan tripped him.

The ex-priest fell hard onto his face.

Rowan waited until certain he would not try it again, rolled him over and helped him to stand up.

Masudah, scuffed and dusty, stared at the cliff face. He panted and clenched his fists, unable to speak for some moments, and cried: "*Thema!…*"

Rowan stood stymied, but managed to ask: "What happened?"

"I am punished by the gods. Stormbringer…" Masudah groaned. "But no, it is my own doing. I cannot cast blame. Oh… *poor Nefer!*"

"What is a 'thema'?"

Masudah did not take his eyes off the carved doorway, now no longer broken but back to its former antique yet whole appearance. "Thema is her Wakan name. It means 'queen'. After she abandoned it, I called her Nefer. She accepted that, but only if I spoke it. And later yourself and Songuset. She referred to herself as nameless. *No!* I will not speak of her in past tense. She lives. *She lives!*"

Rowan kicked the disturbed ground where he had left the scanner, searched in a wide circle, and found it fifty feet away. "The indicators only show low power," he called out. "These things have no moving parts and are extremely robust. Something… an electromagnetic field maybe, is interfering."

Masudah crouched, and glared at the doorway. "Many other kinds of fields are involved in portals," he muttered. "Technicians do not understand, even League engineers and physicists only knew how to manipulate some of them in the hope the more subtle ones comply. Usually they do… but not today."

Rowan drew near and crouched on one knee beside Masudah. "We *will* find her. Where's the other end of the wormhole? She may be there."

Masudah sighed. "When I was here before, we calculated a position in an uninhabited area of Ibn on the eastern coast of the Middle Sea, if one follows the edge of the peninsula opposite and northeast of Black Land, an arid region called also White Country for its snow-capped mountain range. But instead we ended up in a place called Tel Ba'al, also in Ibn. On top of that mound of remains from countless generations of habitation we found a huge platform built of gigantic blocks of granite, many times larger than the largest building stones used in Khémia to date, some more than sixteen hundred tons. The engineers among us were amazed and could not explain how it had been constructed. Even our best antigravity technology would be too challenged to duplicate it, although our precision is equal. Our engineers were inspired, so we shall see what they have yet to come up with, if the gods be with us…"

"It sounds like the other end is even less reliable than this one," said Rowan.

"I trusted this end more than the other, yes, but hoped we would be anywhere in Ibn that much closer to our destination north of there, the kingdom of Aha. In fact we should be more than halfway there by now. But I know not whether Nefer awaits us in Tel Ba'al. She could be anywhere." The ex-priest stared at the door as if his dark eyes might burn a hole through it.

Rowan stood up and offered his hand to Masudah. "Come on, soldier, get up. We have work to do."

A walk of several hundred yards from the doorway allowed the scanner to power up once more. From a distance Rowan estimated the portal as intact. Only the creviced depression in front of it left by the quake must be avoided.

Masudah straightened and said, "Forgive my weakness. Guilt, it plagues me still. This has happened because I have abandoned the gods… not that they have abandoned me. My reputation meant more to my sorry self than I had realized and it continues to be a source of delusion even now that it is lost. What the world thinks of me is of no importance. It never was. I see that now. This is the gift in, how you say… adversity. You are right, we shall find her. We *will* find her. Somehow, some way. We must."

"Let's start with a review," said Rowan. "My eyes were closed, as were yours, I assume. I felt Nefer's hand let go of mine. The effect was immediate. Losing her grip seemed like the cause of the quake."

"Yes," said Masudah. "My eyes too were closed. First I checked that Nefer's were also. I gave her clear instructions. She understood, as she repeated them back to me, how you say… verbatim. But she let go of my hand also. I believed this disaster is because my focus was on my little worldly self and its worries. I did not give the rite its due attention. True, but I think now the most important factor was Nefer herself. I have said she is a powerful being, only she knows it not. With long training she could be a high priestess, but I would have to release her. Such women must be unwed to serve the gods and goddesses in purity."

"I can see that." Rowan nodded agreement. "Purity's important to her."

"But why would she let go?" Masudah ran his hands through his dark hair. "Was she forced by something? Someone?"

"Masudah… did she do it on purpose? Sorry, we must consider everything before we try again."

Masudah tore his gaze from the portal to stare at Rowan. "Why would she do such a thing?" His tanned face went blank.

"Either she was abducted or sabotaged our jump. Or else it was an accident pure and simple."

Masudah exhaled. "Yes, as hard to explain as it is, I want to believe that. This is not helping, however. We are here, she is… missing. For now."

"You're right," said Rowan. "You're a warrior, Masudah, whatever the vizier and the high court decided about your dishonourable discharge. All your skills are intact. It's time to put them to use. My commando training tells me that when all the available data is in, decisiveness wins the day. Our scanner is working. The door is intact. Let's open it."

The scanner's indicators lit up to indicate full charge. In closer proximity to the doorway, the two warriors each calmed their minds to a still mirror. Masudah spoke the magic words in Khémian, and in unison they held their attention on the rectangle of light that appeared within the carved frame. A loud hum came from the entire cliff, and the doorway transformed from two-dimensional blank stone to a window, through which appeared a deep landscape with low hills in the distance under a cumulus-clouded sky. In the middle ground stood a citadel with rounded towers in the battlements. Very near the portal, perhaps a dozen brown-skinned bearded men dressed in long striped or patterned robes and brocade cloaks stood in two groups. Some wore loose pantaloons tied below the knee, and soft ankle boots with pointed toes. Most wore turbans. They appeared embroiled in argument over an unrolled parchment, voices silent to Rowan and Masudah, however. Some carried cudgels or staffs they raised in the air and shook.

Masudah peered at the scene with great focus, but pointed at the scanner and signalled to cut the power. The scene faded to a doorway of blank solid stone again.

"What was that?" asked Rowan. "Who were those people?"

"I do not know, Sir Rowan. I have never seen that manner of dress, nor that style of architecture. It was definitely in Ibn. I know that landscape, but I suspect not of our position in the timeline. There are no buildings larger than shepherds' huts there now, mere shelters, and have never been any. It may be far in our future. I strongly doubt that it was in our past. What is more, I could not understand the writing on the parchment. Peering into their world any longer would have alerted them to something strange in their midst."

"Are you sure it wasn't long ago? It certainly looked archaic."

"I know my geography. And I know my anthropology as well as history. I am well versed in a dozen languages. Khémians take the long view of time, although we often remind ourselves that it is a construct. Yet in the transactional order of things it is wise to study it well so as to make good use of it. Otherwise, it uses us, as if the camel rides the rider. We know for certain that advanced civilizations rise and fall in cycles, cultured people become depraved beasts, then learn to overcome their faults and grow further or regress, and have done many more times than we know of at present. Intuition tells me that we have just witnessed a living tableau many thousands of years in the future. But when it comes to portals, time and space lose their assumed meanings."

Rowan said, as much to console himself as his friend, "We *will* find her, Masudah. We'll search all the timelines until we do, even if it takes forever."

Masudah sighed, but acknowledged with a little nod: "Forever is a very long time, the longest, but thank you for your support, my friend. Time travel may be an ultimate risk. It is feared it can violate cosmic laws. To my knowledge no one has made a breakthrough with a reliable technique. One day someone will succeed, no doubt."

"If it's possible," said Rowan, "maybe someone already has."

"Indeed," agreed Masudah. "But yes, we must try again. This time I suggest we both think of dear Nefer, I in my own way of course, but you too must in your heart of hearts hold the purest of love for my beloved. She calls you Brother Red Lion. I will teach her to say this in Common Tongue. It will clarify and strengthen the bond. Until then see her lovely face in your mind's eye and send her strength to calm her mind. She believes you are sent by the gods to be our friend. She is right, in my opinion. Together we must attract her attention, for she no doubt seeks to reconnect also."

Rowan powered up the scanner for the third time and measured the distance. The two men stood, eyes closed in deep concentration. Once more the inner frame of the doorway glowed white. This time the blank stone within wavered in bright misty rainbow hues. Masudah glanced at Rowan, nodded once to signal advance, and they stepped forward into the light –

◆

"Is this the platform?"

Masudah's tanned face had turned pale. "It is… it is indeed Tel Ba'al by the look of these massive walls."

"Good. Let's climb up there and search. We can start with the perimeter. That way we can see what's below too."

"No, Sir Rowan, wait. We must consider… and consider well."

Rowan tried to leap to the seam at the bottom of the next course of giant blocks, at a height of more than twenty feet, no problem for a felid still nanoid-augmented. But he gained no purchase on such tight joints. He dropped to the grass on all fours, and said, "I see what you mean."

"I do not mean how to climb," Masudah replied. "Look beyond the top course of blocks. What do you see up there?"

"Pillars, columns, very tall. Probably a row of them, as far as I can tell by the capitals of the two I can see… with a beam for a roof… the rest seem to have collapsed. No wonder. This place is extremely old. Let's find a staircase or something. There has to be one."

Masudah sat down on the grass and rested against the wall.

"Hey," said Rowan, "let's get a move on… what's up?"

Masudah rubbed his eyes with his palms. "This is *not* the Tel Ba'al of my memory. Yes, this is the foundation I lean against, but there were no ruins built on top. They are very old, but very new compared to the foundation. It was merely a vast platform as I and my men found it before."

Rowan sat beside Masudah on the dried grass, their view a wide valley with low bare mountains in the far distance. The pastoral scene included small farms and a village in the middle ground. Something moved along the ribbon of road about a mile away – a wheeled vehicle under its own power, of a type unlike any Rowan had seen before.

Occasionally similar vehicles rolled along the highway. The sun moved noticeably along its arc before either man made any remark.

Rowan spoke first: "There's nothing for it except to explore this place to see if by chance Nefer followed the same route. We have to rule out that possibility."

"You are right, Sir Rowan. We must be professional, like investigators of crime. But saying it thus makes my heart sink. The possibilities are infinite… she may be here now or not even arrived yet. She may have lived a long life in that village beyond, her great grandchildren elderly or even asleep under the headstones of the cemetery. The graveyard too may have turned to dust, buried under intervening ages of soil deposits. Possibly only these giant quarried stones against which we lean remain as an outpost of the past to puzzle the minds of archaeologists."

Stymied *at the* ruins *of* Tel Ba'al, Ibn, also known *as* White Country.

"I know how that feels," said Rowan. "I was already too many leagues distant from the Longbow tribe, wherever they are now, when we were still in Khémia. The distance in time is… I don't know how to say it."

"Disappointing? Daunting? Dispiriting? Disheartening?" Masudah sighed. "What do we know? This end of the wormhole, as you call it, the gate, has terminated at Tel Ba'al more than once in my experience. That is something."

"Difficult. Demanding," Rowan added. "Disputable. Debatable. How we feel about it us up to us. Decisiveness wins the day. We must soldier on, whatever the odds." He stood up and looked to the top of the wall. "So this is Tel Ba'al. That's a start. We have a working scanner, just like before. You know how to work the magic words. We have ourselves intact, with only a few scratches to complain of, should we be in the mood to whine. I want to add one more important thing. Your word 'disheartening' reminds me… you told me once that the heart is not the feelings, Masudah. The heart, according to you, is the essence and always free of any circumstance. Etymology of 'courage' means exactly that. Right?"

"Who *was* that Masudah? He sounds like a wise man."

93

XIV

Eye *of* Stone

THE EMPTY PLATFORM of Masudah's recollection had been littered with the ruins of a temple complex toppled by earthquakes in its old age. No other force could have been powerful enough to collapse the many large and strongly built structures – unless the reptilians rained fire from the sky.

"I tremble to think that it may be so," said Masudah. "That would mean they were masters of Eorthe for thousands of years. These buildings are huge, but do not look like they were designed for creatures of their size. How would the builders have had time to make this elaborate place before the Apep ruined it? The peaceful Surface life in the valley below suggests there was no such threat. Or at least is no longer. As well there is no sign of intense heat here."

"Centuries of rain would have washed away any smoke stains, but I assume you're referring to vitrification, melted surfaces," said Rowan. "I think you're right. It was a big earthquake. Possibly several."

"Again the platform amazes," said Masudah. "So cleverly made. Clearly it has weathered greatly since last I laid eyes on it. It must have shaken as a unit. But we have found nothing to help us here. Shall we head for the village? Or try the portal, wherever it is? The first time I ended up here it was… oh, you have it?"

Rowan already ranged his scanner in the direction Masudah pointed. "It also seems to have moved on from where we arrived," he said, "down there at the footings. We'll find it."

The complex must have been erected on the command of an emperor or empress, someone with enough wealth to impose their will on a large and skilled workforce for a lengthy period. The hill formed of layers of civilization before even the mysterious platform had been laid, by giants possibly, provided a wide view of the surrounding territory and a perfectly level foundation large enough for a sizeable village. It took all day and into the evening to scan the whole area with a hand-held instrument.

Masudah said, "I do not know about you, but I am exhausted. Yet I wish to try one more thing. The longer Nefer is away… but I do not know. Ignore my baseless worries. Despite my shame as an ex-priest, I believe They of Bones of Silver do not withhold my access to magic. Otherwise I should no longer recall the spells. Thus it is written. I am an outcast to Khémia, but not to the gods. When the moon rises free of the shadows, I shall experiment."

The sky glowed clear in the warm evening near sunset. The partly standing structures around them amidst the rubble emerged as *chiaroscuro*, a study in light and shadow, the phase that preceded Eorthe's satellite Lunah's appearance above the nocturnal horizon.

Masudah checked the sky, and said, "I shall be strengthened by the sight, Sir Rowan. Until dear Nefer disappeared, I had been bereft of my status, in despair. Upon the loss of my beloved, it came to mean less than nothing in comparison. And now… now the hidden gift is that I am free. I am no longer obliged to follow the rules meant to serve the society. It is dangerous, or does it seem, to be so stripped of its protection, but I must sacrifice any misgivings. This is what the gods ask now, that I give all for another."

Rowan and Masudah sat in the moonlight on a fallen fluted column. Their seat overlooked an area they had cleared for the rite the ex-priest planned to conduct.

"Masudah, I hope that doesn't mean what it sounds like, but then I don't think in religious terms. It's figurative, right? You feel you have to let go of the past to permit a better future. A happy future. We *will* find Nefer, you know. It's only a question of…"

"Time. Yes, Sir Rowan, you understand. My language is not so clear. Forgive, I am tired and anxious, like a small boy who should go to bed instead of courting a, how you say… tantrum. I have no magical tools now, no altar, no special regalia, incense, potions or infusions. We have cleared a floor before the pylon of this old fane. This is our ritual space now, along with the night sky and our ally the moon, Khonsu, or Iah, who is a god in our mythology, one who can drive away evil spirits. He is in the correct phase. Or close enough. He is called also the Eye of Stone. You too are my ally and, with respect to magic, more than you may think. I do not mean the support of friendship, which in itself is a kind of magic, but the hidden power of nature we need in order to find my beloved." Masudah turned to peer at Rowan.

"You see," he continued, "it is your red hair, not natural to Khémians, that is highly valuable for this work. It is believed to be a divine attribute. You say the Lightlander teacher Master Aa has red hair. I now think it is possible that he or another being of his kind influenced Khémia's thinking from the very beginning. Red hair is associated with great magical power. Moreover, our god of magic Heka is depicted as a bearded man who wears a lion headdress. He is the potency, the force that enables manifestation."

"Interesting," Rowan said. "My understanding from studies of world religions at university is that you also need the sacred texts, in addition to the concoctions and the other paraphernalia."

"I now know," replied Masudah, "that I *am* the tools. They are of value to focus the mind, helpful, but nothing sacred. The gods who represent nature's forces do all the, how you say… heavy lifting. The sacred words of the texts are engraved in my soul since youth. They assist to form the magic vibrations through sound. It is true that it would be helpful to have the sacrament of blue lotus. It lulls the body-mind into the meditative state to open a window on spirit. But it is an adjunct only. Most important, I knew I would give my life for Nefer from the first moment I laid eyes on her. This was prophetic. I know that now. I did not foresee how it would manifest, however. But I am clear of regret. I can again work with Heka, who provides the raw power. The Eye of Stone on the left… and you, Brother Red Lion, on the right… is all that is necessary to focus it."

"I'm ready. Let's do it."

◆

This time the jump proved a challenge to endure. They tumbled out of control several times through a vortex of energy that transformed into a breaker, not of foaming water but of vibrations under which they submerged. At first weightless, then pushed straight down by a heavy force, they again rose upwards on a fountain-like spout that streamed them into an unknown sky. Yet they had found themselves back to back stood upright, but fell on their hands and knees. Rowan leapt to his feet in an instant, stance wide, knees bent and arms spread outwards in case the ground shook and it was not just vertigo that made everything reel.

"*Sir Rowan! Are you all right? My eyes… they blur…*"

"I am now, Masudah. A little dizzy, that's all. Where are we?"

Rowan's eyes reported a box canyon – unusually eroded, either by aeons of rainfall or a dam that had broken and sculpted vertical channels in the yellow sandstone cliffs, now bone-dry, another sun-drenched desert environment. Moreover, its drainage basin remained populated with dozens of tall rock formations, each a hundred feet in height, like mushrooms with thick stems, organic spires with conical caps of harder and darker rock that protected the softer layers below from erosion.

"Is this… real?" asked Rowan. He felt like a small insect in a garth of organic mineral towers that grew into the sky. "They look like… giant phalluses."

The fairy chimneys *of the* Garden *of* Desire, northern Ibn.

"Indeed," replied Masudah. "I know where we are, the Garden of Desire as some call it. It is north and west of Tel Ba'al, but still south of our ultimate destination, Aha Domain. We are only a little further on our path. If these fairy chimneys be inhabited, our timing is off. The first thing we must do is find out so that we guess which segment of the timeline we have landed in."

"Fairy chimneys? Is that because of the holes in the sides?"

"Yes, those are windows, doors and flues, but they were carved out by anders long ago, not fairies." He winked. "I hope you are not disappointed. This whole area was at the crossroads of empires in conflict when the world was young. The towers were reasonably easy to hollow out as homes for the local tribes. That way they could avoid for a long time armies passing through. I see no smoke, but let us walk through the canyon to check for trails and tracks."

"If they're abandoned, Masudah, we're in the timeline segment when the Reps have at least begun to force Surface dwellers below ground. Right?"

"One hates to say so, but for our sake let us hope that is the case. After that perhaps we can narrow our estimate to the century, year and day. If we are heading towards our own time or even have arrived at it, then we can find a more tame gateway or even walk the rest of the way."

"That's hopeful. But how does this help us find Nefer?"

"I believe our hearts have been much purified of distortion. I know mine has. I have been dismembered and put back together since I met dear Nefer, but it is all to the good. I see that now."

"So a pure heart means greater accuracy? Or maybe now there's a stronger connection. Is that it?"

"They are equivalent, Sir Rowan. We cannot lose what is our own, but the bonds can be strained and weakened if personal integrity is not firm. This is the reason discipline is a virtue."

Already two steps down the canyon, Rowan said, "Then let's quickly see if anyone's about, then move on." His natural felid tracking ability did not take long to determine that no one had even visited this place for years. Nor had anyone passed by on their way east or west between the traditional battle-grounds, although an unpaved road remained somewhat visible.

"This is a good sign, Sir Rowan. Either we are close to our own time, if not in it already, or the fairy-chimney-dwellers, if not massacred by some army, have moved on to somewhere with a better water supply."

Rowan picked up a forked twig from the ground. "You mentioned dowsing before. I've only read about it at school, where it was described as a folkway and a superstition. The Longbows dowse, so there must be something more to it." He walked back into the lowest section of the canyon a little, and the twig nearly jumped from his hands and pointed straight down. "Beginner's luck! I'm no expert, but I'd guess there's water here. Plenty of it. Let's find the portal. Where do you want to go now? Assuming we have a choice."

"This is another sign," said Masudah. "Good. Omens seem superstitious, yet we must increasingly rely on intuition. Often the universe speaks in symbols if we but listen, as in dreams… waking and dreaming essentially differ little. Time has lost its shape, but still we do not want to waste it. Yet I think we do not have so much a choice as an opportunity. We cannot simply purchase travel tickets as one once could in the Perkona Ola station of Eastport. When I say opportunity, I mean to convince you that our purest of intentions must be in partnership with the Divine, then release the result to it alone. It is true that as a priest I called it the pantheon of They of Bones of Silver and He of Bones of Iron… and still do. They are manifestations of holy intelligence. But, you know, so are we. You are. I am. We are sons of the Divine, whose symbol in this world is Ra, the living sun. We are apparently of different mother species, but really she is the same Great One of Many Names, cosmic mother sky goddess, the Eye of the Sun, whose temple I tempted you to visit at Kaina. I wanted Nefer to see it also, as she would have been inspired and come to know her man better, but I must have faith that I will do that another day. I have no sanction of Khémian culture now, but no one owns the Divine. It is not us… but we are it, each and all. Either one knows their identity with it or one does not."

"You're the magician," said Rowan. "I was born missing the religion gene, but I have faith in *you*, brother." He grinned at the ex-priest and held his gaze. "Let's find Nefer and get on with saving the world."

Masudah laughed in his husky way for the first time since his bride had vanished, which made his moustache a raven in flight. "And I in you, Brother Red Lion. No more is needed. The Eye of Stone shall be our armour, shield and sword tonight. We know what to do. Let us now do it even better than before."

♦

The sunset had been spectacular. Ra had painted the fairy chimneys in a vision of some strange planet: tall yellow towers bathed in red light against a backdrop of deep blue sky, as if the extinct natives had been giant termite-like insectoids. To prepare, the two warriors had cleared a space for Masudah's work. They had used the scanner to meticulously align it with the cardinal directions. Well-chosen fragments of stone high in quartz content they had stacked in a formation that pointed to Aha Domain. All they had to do now was wait for the Eye of Stone to take His position.

"Masudah, if this is our segment of the timeline, I'm a bit concerned that using the scanner outside of Khémia will attract the attention of the reptilians. Even without it we're at risk… anyone foolish enough to wander the Surface is. If they can penetrate the planet to such a great depth, they can surely pick up even a tiny signal. During orientation at Perkona Ola's military base for our first mission to Mudredd Vale, we were told they could count the hairs on the head of a parachutist in a tornado."

"That may be truth," said Masudah. "Perhaps it was said for effect only, how you say… hyperbole. But we must use your scanner to enhance the magic or work too slow. Take comfort in Khémians' belief that the reptilians are a crude race and do not understand subtleties. They ignore our country in part because they overlook us as nonsensical, how you say… pseudoscientists. They think they have the power to easily wipe Eorthe clean of us. But they are mistaken."

99

The Eye of Stone rose above the canyon wall bright and near to full, and cast long shadows before the fairy chimneys. Time to power up the scanner —

✦

Rowan *and* Masudah arrive *on the* portal stone *in* Aha Domain.

The tall beings surrounded in a tight circle and negated any relief that may have blessed the seekers from such a smooth transition. The portal jump this time had been effortless.

Rowan even wondered for a moment if it had worked at all, except for the fact that, when he looked down, under his boots had appeared the top of a mountain clearly artificially levelled. He and Masudah each stood with one foot on a stone carved with ancient petroglyphs. The giant platform had vanished, however, as had the ruins under the moonlight. Instead there domed a vista of diamond-like stars strewn above many deep blue valleys blanketed in mist, and snow-capped peaks in the distance under the Eye of Stone, a wonderful sight that would have been better appreciated minus the presence of the very large

100

beings who stood in a circle around the felid and the ex-priest. They must be the Ahan, a subspecies of *Ander sapiens*, obviously, but unlike any Rowan had ever seen even illustrated in books as speculative.

The people stood between six and eight feet in height, strongly built, their faces long, angular and pale. Attired in long tailored jackets, quilted, belted at the waist and hooded, their long straight white hair hung well below their open collars, with trousers tucked into tall boots. Six women, six men – the females stood between six and seven feet in height and less muscular, but voluptuous, one quite buxom, but all obviously capable of breaking a man's bones.

The tallest man's distinctive facial features stood out pronounced – a heavy square jaw, chiselled nose and massive brow ridges, and blue eyes, large and luminous even in moonlight. He carried a long staff of gnarled wood carved with sigils. Its head of bone had been shaped into a vulture's skull – or perhaps it had belonged to a hatchling. The man also wore a long cape of probably vulture feathers, black. He reached to his pointed cowl and pulled it back, and revealed long straight white hair that cascaded from an elongated head. Unlike the Lightlanders' cones, his and presumably all of the Ahans' sloped back to the boundary of the parietal and occipital bones to extend the cranium, supported by a muscular neck.

Rowan did not think it wise to speak.

Masudah stood at his back in the middle of the circle, equally silent.

Rowan heard in his mind either a command or an invitation. He only knew for certain it was not in his own familiar inner voice:

"We have been expecting you. Come."

The path proved easy to follow in the moonlight, as the steps had been lined with slate and bordered with cut stone. Below the treeline, a group of buildings came into view. The slate roofs with steep inclines indicated snowy winters at this elevation. The lodges had been beautifully constructed of massive timbers. The air on Rowan's exposed skin felt mildly cool, but the windows glowed bright within the main lodge, three storeys tall. The group stopped before its double wooden doors carved with a scene of a mound of skeletons, and vultures that carried bones up to the stars.

The big man in the feather cape stepped forward and tapped his bone-tipped wooden staff three times on the stone pavement before the arched entryway. The doors swung open and two very tall and massively muscled men each held one open. Inside at the end of the large square foyer swept an elegant wooden staircase directly across from the door. The entire group entered to stand in the candlelit entrance hall.

101

No one followed a pattern of military order, yet Rowan sensed extreme discipline among these people, sure Masudah must feel it too. With no apparent signal the people flipped back their cowls, if they had not already, and bowed. With eyes closed they began to hum, and sing in harmony a wordless melody, very beautiful.

Rowan believed that creatures who could sing like this, although powerful, were only a threat when crossed.

Two striking Ahan women appeared on the landing above, then shock – she must be their queen, although she wore what her subjects wore, and no crown or other signs of power, only a brooch or badge.

As she descended the staircase, Rowan saw it to be a stylized silver vulture within a circle of gold woven like branches and leaves.

She halted at the bottom.

Two large men ushered Rowan and Masudah forward before the queen.

"Sir Rowan Berry Longbow, welcome," she said, and turned to look into Masudah's eyes, dropped to one knee, took his hand and kissed it.

XV

Domain *of* Aha

MASUDAH HAD REMAINED silent since their arrival. He did not speak even now. Rowan understood that he could not. Not yet.

The queen rose to her feet, and searched Masudah's face. "You have found me," she said. "Have you no words of joy at our reunion?"

Rowan looked to Masudah, whose wide eyes and slack jaw elicited an urge to slap the man's back to make him take a breath.

Masudah finally found his voice on his own: "But… I wanted to be the one to teach you Common Tongue." He leaned towards her, but stopped, and asked, "Shall I call you Thema now?"

The queen burst into peals of laughter and embraced him, which made his moustaches wings in flight over a white grin. "You may call me whatever you wish," she replied. "I remain nameless. The people of Aha, my people, call me Havasarakshrrut'yuny. It means 'the balance.' In Ahan it is a mouthful. To you I hope I will always be the beauty that makes beauty beautiful as you say, so 'Nefer' is what I love to hear from your sweet lips." She looked up at Rowan, then back to Masudah. "Come, you two. We have much to discuss." She slipped her hands into the crooks of their arms and led them up the staircase to a private room, where a meal had been laid out. Servants, the two women from the landing, in fine dark woollen tunics with matching skirts that extended below their knees and the tops of their tall black boots, stood at attention. They too had the elongated heads, white hair and blue eyes, and looked like sisters. One stood slightly taller and less buxom, but also very shapely. Otherwise they could be identical twins, yet all the handsome Ahan resembled each other to a great degree.

Masudah remained uncharacteristically diffident. Nevertheless, he asked, "Nefer, how does this come to pass? I feel as if I dream. You know I have often said to you that life is but a dream, but until now it was less literal. Or so I believed. You have learnt a new language. I always thought of you as regal, but now you are a queen no less, true to your Wakan name."

Nefer's dark eyes gazed softly at him. "You, a priest and servant of the sacred, a warrior, are anxious for no reason." She took his hand. "All is well. All was ever well. This is what I have learnt and what you yourself told me when you explained your life in Khémia and the principles you taught when asked. Is not all unfolding as it must?"

"Ex-priest," he corrected. "How soon I have forgotten the teachings. But they are returning afresh, almost as if for the first time. I was telling Brother Red Lion that, since meeting you, Masudah has been reborn."

Nefer chortled. "Indeed, you are a babe." She reached up and pressed her finger to his lips, and said, "But you are my babe."

"Seriously, Nefer, what happened? You must tell us. And we will tell of our long and strange journey to Aha Domain."

"Please, be seated. Do not wait for me." She took a seat at the table, looked at them both and began: "I too was a babe, a mere child before. Sheltered by a large family, I had not left the nest, the spoilt youngest. Then dear Masudah the exotic foreigner swept me off my feet. So sophisticated and dashing, so confident! I loved to make his little moustache fly like a bird. I wanted to snare it, a great prize that I would cherish forever. And he represented the great world beyond our isolated one, so set apart by tradition and geography. You know the rest. In my resentment, idealism and rebellion I tried to shed my identity. To assume a new one was difficult, but you were there to guide me. Yet I was not prepared for the power that entered my being when we stood before Devils' Doorway. I believe it was and is always there, but hidden, the power. It showed itself in the Iron Desert too, but I hardly remember much of that. It was like I was possessed. I *was* possessed, like you. We were both under a spell. But when I was with you last, after we had sold our camels, it was different, overwhelming, engulfing totally. This Nefer is a different version of that Nefer."

"Yes," Masudah said. "You were queen of my heart. Now you are queen of the Ahan."

"No, no, dear husband," she said, "I am only one, not two. I am first the queen of your heart, then queen of my people. Two but one, like you and me. Do you not remember the teachings? You, a priest!"

Queen Havasarakshrrut'yuny.

"Ex-priest." Masudah nodded. "I understand. Love is one. It has no opposite. It can never be broken into two."

As she leaned towards him, Nefer smiled whitely and took Masudah's brown face in her dark hands, and replied, "Now you remember."

Rowan waited impatiently for the rest of the story, but he may as well have been a portrait on the wall.

Nefer seemed psychic when she looked at him and said, "I feel I must add to my explanation and finish. After the explosion of power when you, Brother Red Lion, activated the scanner and took my hand, I found myself in a blank place of no dimensions, no time, nothing. My little body in its lovely wedding dress had gone, my mind too. I mean I was already nameless, but my little mind had vanished as well. I had no history, no story. Only one thought remained. And that was of you, Masudah. Where were you? Then I forgot even that. I was back in my father's house. Nothing had happened. He was the high chieftain. I was still his little girl."

Masudah sat very still, his eyes locked on Nefer.

Rowan said, "This is amazing, Nefer. Apologies, I mean Queen Hava… shuti… apologies, I mean Your Majesty."

Nefer snickered. "That is funny. I will not translate what it means, however. It is quite rude, what you say in Old Ahan." But she giggled and explained: "It is spoken no longer by voice, which is for song alone. The people are telepaths since the Genitors visited last. That was long ago, they say two million years. But yes, it is an amazing thing to tell of, even more to live through."

"Thank you. May I call you Queen Nefer?"

She closed her eyes and nodded assent, and grinned at him.

"Thank you, Queen Nefer. Now, as amazing as rewinding right back to before the moment you met Masudah… or close to it… as amazing as that was, what must have happened next is even more mysterious. How did you get from that to this, I mean from Land of the Song-Eyes to Aha Domain?"

Nefer gazed at him with her large black-pearl-like orbs, and tilted her dark head a little. She pursed her full pink lips, sighed and said, "Well, I am trying to think how to say it." She pressed her palms together. "It was not like riding a reindeer from Castle Vale to this lodge. Neither was it like activating a portal and stepping through to a distant place. It was not a linear thing. But I see by the look in your eyes that this is not the right way to tell it. I will tell it like a storybook. Then you may take it with you and think about it later. This is what happened…

"Once far, far away, in a far-off land where nothing had changed in thousands of years, there lived a princess, a pampered little girl. Then something profound occurred. She met herself coming through a gate made of light, very bright. She had no idea there could be such a thing. And so near her home, in fact at her special place, where she went to think. When she was little, there used to be tiny forest folk who would meet her there. They taught her things and together they played. It was her special place. There one day the bright light appeared.

It was frightening. She could not move. Then out of that glowing light stepped herself. It was like looking into the mirror in her room at home. But this mirror image was no little girl. It was a woman. She was beautiful and bare as a baby just born. The woman looked at the girl. The girl looked at the woman. They smiled at each other. The girl's fear melted away… and she with it. Two but one. She knew everything the woman knew… Masudah, Songuset, Brother Red Lion… everything. At that moment she took a step, then another. Into the wilderness she walked. She never looked back. This time she did not need to throw away the sackcloth of shame, only the name she was called. She walked all the way from the west of Afara along the coast of the Middle Sea into the mountains of the heart of the kingdom of Aha to find Masudah. There she climbed the castle steps to the empty throne. Then the people came and praised her and told her the prophecy was fulfilled. Now they could rise from their caves, breathe the mountain air again and regain their kingdom. Yesterday she rode the royal reindeer to this lodge to meet her Masudah and Brother Red Lion as expected. And that's what happened."

"You expected us?" Masudah's tongue loosened. "But… are you safe from the reptilians then? How?"

Nefer the queen looked at him, narrowed her gaze and said, "I would not say safe exactly, my dear. They are what they are, and we are what we are. I would say fear is not the Ahan way. In truth, the only enemy is within."

Rowan looked to Masudah, turned back to Nefer and said, "Pardon, Your Majesty, I must stick my oar in here. I've had direct contact with their leader Kirzaka. He calls himself the Deathless, among other titles. What he is called by his enemies should not be repeated in polite company. I can assure you any reptilian, even an old one on its last legs, is a nasty piece of work, and the Talon is ten times nasty. He's head and shoulders above them. Literally. Their intent is to steal our souls, bury our corpses and eat them when ripened. To them the unpalatable among us are vermin. We must find a way to eliminate our common enemy."

Nefer looked up at him through her long dark lashes. "A noble ambition, Sir Red Lion. You are bold and brave. You are a brother…"

Masudah rubbed his palms together and cried, "That goes for me too, Sir Rowan, my warrior brother!" He glowed, inspired. "No one is safe until we unite our efforts, do our utmost and leave the results to the gods. In Khémian thinking there are twelve of They of Bones of Silver. But there is only one of He of Bones of Iron. Yet the twelve must be united in order to match the one's iron strength. To the reptilians' way of thinking, there are no gods other than the one, Maçina the Artificer, a manifestation of the same principle of evil. Their great strength comes from him, they believe. But that is their weakness. They are totally ignorant of the twelve. This blindness will be their downfall."

"So this is really about a contest between the gods?" asked Rowan. "Are you saying Stormbringer is Maçina?"

"I am saying there is a principle of chaos, ignorance and disintegration. Call it Stormbringer, call it Apep, call it Maçina or give it another name. It is all the same. It is divine power appearing as supreme deception, on many levels, yet it is always balanced in favour of the powers of good in the long run... which can take many generations to achieve, however."

"All right," said Rowan. "I'm following you, I think. But remember I'm not religious, so it's a bit like translating different languages into something I can deal with."

"My wisdom is no greater than yours, Sir Rowan. I still tend to speak like a priest. There is more for us both to learn of this, much more. I repeat what I understand from the sacred texts. But they only speak of reality, what is real and what is not. That belongs to no one."

The queen had listened politely, but now held up her hand, and said, "Pardon me, please. I do not like to interrupt the talk between you men. Perhaps you will save the remainder for another time. We were parted by power. Nefer sought Masudah. He and Brother Red Lion made the journey to find Nefer. She speaks Common Tongue now, no need to ignore the little black girl's presence and talk over her dreadlocked head. It is finished. The search has come to an end."

Masudah bowed to her. "The apology is mine, dear Nefer, my queen. You are right. Instead we should ask, how are the Ahan able to remain above ground with such confidence?"

"It is as we the Ahan say: no fear, no worry."

Rowan disagreed: "But fear is what forces me to find the energy to do the impossible... eliminate an implacable foe. It ignites a fire that burns away any illusions. Then I act despite it."

The queen shook her head. "We do not speak the same language, Brother Red Lion. Your words are Common Tongue, but this is not confidence. This is very brave, but not the same."

Masudah, with a little bow of the head, said, "Perhaps in the meantime, my queen, you will tell us of the prophecy. If it is your pleasure."

Nefer giggled. "My poor dear Masudah! You are so formal." She grinned and took his face in her hands again. "This is all a bit of a shock, not so? Did you expect to have to rescue your Nefer from pirates or the chains of a dungeon?

Perhaps a monster of legend? Of course I will tell. But first you must understand something. The Ahan are a great and ancient people. They are descendants of one of the more successful experiments at the end of the Seminal Age, and the elder race. The Genitors, the Sky Fathers, whom the League calls the Primordial Architects, had been called back home. But they were uncooperative, immature, naughty. They ignored the call. In defiance they played some more with their games, but were tired and made mistakes. They should have listened to Cosmic Mother. We have all of us inherited those mistakes, especially the reptilians. It is not their fault. The Genitors went home without finishing them. It is not their fault, but it is their responsibility. The Sky Fathers also made one more god, but in Khémia named He of Bones of Iron, Stormbringer, worshipped by the reptilians as Maçina. They knew they had done wrong. This thirteenth god was a desperate attempt at preventing a disaster after they had gone, to balance the other gods, who otherwise would have become divided and destroyed each other. They needed Stormbringer to unite against."

"And, my queen, who is the Ahan equivalent?"

"Anggh the vulture god embodies all in one, thus the balance may appear in the form of an animal or a man or a woman, even a child; all are equal in death, you see." The queen continued: "The Ahan are unlike any other *sapiens* on Eorthe. They are an ultimately capable but ultimately peaceful species. Their material needs are minimal, yet what meets those needs must match a high aesthetic standard. Thus they are rich in pleasures of all kinds and the universe happily complies abundantly, as it requires the least entropy. As warriors, no one could defeat them, yet they do not appear in the history books of the world as victors in battle. The reason is that they have avoided conflicts with others, largely through remaining unknown. They were here first but their younger sibling species have no inkling of their existence."

"Yet, my queen, I heard the myth from a famous old teacher when I was young. That is why I suggested we take refuge in Aha Domain when I was sent into exile. But all I really knew was some scant military intelligence reported of the outlands. And then there were the legends. They were said to originate where the North Wind is born. They were said to come from the stars long ago before that. I knew it was fanciful, yet with a grain of truth. At least I hoped so. Anyhow, there was nowhere else to go."

"They are like us," Nefer said, "challenged to awaken to a new world."

"But… my dear Nefer. How was a prophecy responsible for your becoming queen of this elder race?"

"Yes, it must seem strange. They are so opposite, the Ahan and their queen. They are exceptionally brilliant, valiant, tall, strong, pale of skin and white of hair. They are noble and wise. All these great virtues only need a little ballast to ensure the kingdom's stability. In the deep past, only a king or queen with a flaw, mental or physical, was necessary. The world outside would have seen these flaws as minor had they known, as their own leaders were and often are extremely flawed, even insane. But the Ahan ideal kind of ballast was very rare among them. When found by a special method called the Oracle, that individual was destined for the throne, which is not an inherited role as it is in Khémia. By this means a kind of grain of sand is embedded, around which a spiritual pearl forms. This inner wealth is the basis of their power. Each Ahan draws their material good fortune from it. But this is the least of it. Each Ahan is an Ahan precisely because of their communion with the Ahan archetype, which like Anggh is very stable when manifest. You will see the native Ahan resemble each other greatly because of this, although the Ahan archetype can in principle manifest in any humanoid form, in a way similar to how Stormbringer does or any of They of Bones of Silver. The knowledge of an Ahan's identity is beyond individual. It is an expression of the whole race and all their acquired knowledge over millions of orbits of the sun. These are the main tenets of the orthodoxy, of which there are variant interpretations."

"I see," said Masudah. "Are you, my dear, the new grain of sand?"

Nefer chuckled. She leaned in her chair to her side, reached over and pinched his cheeks. "Such a smart fellow." She slid over to sit on his lap, draped her arms around his neck, closed her eyes and hugged him, and said, "Let me tell all, my sweet prince." She straightened to a more dignified position for a queen who nevertheless willingly sat on her subject's lap, and adjusted her jacket. She gazed into his eyes, and said, "Now, the Ahan have no what we would call faith in common, except for the reverence of the vulture god Anggh. They have instead wise women and men, usually of advanced age but sometimes not, who are recognized for their obvious mature intelligence and attunement with what you, my lovely priest, call the Divine."

"Ex-priest."

"You will always be my holy man, dear husband. I will remind you if you forget. But please do not interrupt."

"Apologies, Nefer. I hang on your every word."

"You are so funny." Nefer giggled. "Please, do not make me laugh. It is undignified of a queen to be so amused. But I do not laugh at you. Nefer is so happy. Masudah makes her joyous." Her mirth lowered its intensity to a smile.

He replied, "A beautiful queen perched on Masudah's lap is the height of dignity, no matter what anyone says," and his moustaches took wing.

She gazed at it, puckered her lips, looked up and said, "But, to continue… the Ahan king had died. It was expected. It was time. Consultation of the Oracle, a lifelong hermit whose only office from birth is to seek out candidates for an empty throne, had begun years earlier. But there was not one to be found in the entire kingdom. Not one. The elders reasoned that the reptilians' increasingly powerful influence had penetrated even their own domain through vibrations in the World Soul, which of course includes all. This influence had an unintended side effect… it affected the Ahan archetype such that their only possible response was to grow towards the light, towards good, towards perfection. This was an innate response, unconscious. This was why no new Ahan royal could be found. They were at risk of disaster, a laden ship without a keel. The storm was coming. They hid underground, still strong. Even the fire from the sky could not penetrate their shield. Not yet. But now the reptilians knew there was something, someone, down there. The Oracle then declared that his inner vision had searched the globe. And he had found the new ruler."

"And that ruler was you, Nefer. The Oracle found you."

"Yes, my dear sweet prince…"

A small section *of the* castle complex below Fivefold Mount: Mekhute East *and* East Keep; Castle Vale *in the* right foreground, with *a* view *of* Serpent'ini River *and* Gavia Valley *in the* eastern distance.

Engraving *by the* prophet Mtatsum.

110

XVI
Tears *of* Blood

A MIGHTY BELL tolled in the distance. Ferment resounded from the foyer. Heavy boots ascended the staircase. The bell pealed again. Neither the herald nor the servants spoke. Nefer's last sentence of her speech to Masudah and Rowan remained incomplete. Her attention had gone elsewhere, as if she listened to a voice unheard by them, who glanced at each other. She peered intently at the herald, who nodded his head and fled down the staircase.

Again the bell pealed –

People scurried below. The double wooden doors slammed, and the cross-beam bolted them.

And the bell pealed –

"Forgive me, Masudah," said the queen. "Forgive me, Brother Red Lion. Duty calls. I must leave you to attend the advisory committee. The servants will show you the way." Nefer, truly Queen Havasarakshrrut'yuny now, stood up and left the room. The brawny men who had held the double doors open upon Rowan and Masudah's arrival accompanied her down the staircase.

The bell pealed –

Servants led them below to the foyer as well and returned their gear. The two doormen bowed and gestured that they should follow. Behind strode a group of Ahan men and women, the service staff of the lodge. Once outside, the entire group joined others from lodges nearby. In an orderly fashion they mounted reindeer the size of which Rowan had never imagined, of a heavy breed meant for pulling enormous machinery, for agriculture or warfare.

Rowan felt himself lifted off the ground like a child, shocked to find himself so lightly tossed into the saddle behind a female rider.

The bell pealed –

She urged the animal to an immediate gallop.

He hung on to the belt at her lean waist, and her long white hair whipped his face until he pressed his cheek to her neck. To the thunder of hooves, at one side of the path the mountainside blurred as the riders galloped to the moonlit misty vale below.

Behind them the bell pealed –

Rowan looked to the starry blue-black sky. A few clouds backlit by the Eye of Stone drifted high. Then he saw it – a dragon ship, dark, nearly as dark as the night. A row of red lights at the edges of its arrowhead shape coursed like two speeding snakes that knocked their heads together at the tip, each time brighter as it ramped up power. The silent dark craft hovered, and rotated into position to aim at the mountaintop.

Stragglers scrambled down the mountain. The dragon ship loosed the terror on them that would spread after the survivors had fled underground and infected the whole with dread. In those deep recesses fear would fester and ripen until it could be harvested at Kirzaka's leisure.

Rep ships were said to now be capable of instantly vaporizing their target with not even smoke as residue, but here the power had been lowered to create a more spectacular and impressive display of fireworks, a light show. The lodges on fire and the forest aflame likely were seen from far across the valleys below, even beyond the horizon, a beacon of despair to non-reptilians hopeful of a long life. Afterwards the smoking molten granite upon which the beautiful lodges had once stood would harden into opaque glass, forever a testament to the might of the dominators, but evidenced to themselves alone when their soul harvest had finished and their victims consigned to extinction.

◆

The Ahan cavern Rowan had been delivered to on reindeerback looked unlike the metropolitan tailored environments in Vugh Deep, and more like the remnants of some of the cave habitats he had passed through en route to Black Land, that is to say, rustic. Felid eyesight had no problem with dim lighting by phosphorescent creatures in its ceiling, nor apparently did large light-gathering Ahan eyes. The people moved about with ease as they placed the belongings they had prepared for just such an emergency. The cavern lacked climate control, but banks of firestones along the perimeter, and a long one in the middle, the only evidence of high technology so far, radiated warmth. Apart from that, the scene could be from any time in Eorthe's long history: shelter from asteroids, comets, storms or invaders. He noted archaic weapons: long knives and daggers, swords, shields, spears, bows and quivers of arrows.

A servant woman from Nefer's dining room approached, the shorter and more buxom one. Her clear blue eyes expressed a gentle humble nature, impassive and serene. Nor did she speak, but Rowan sensed a friendly greeting. Her straight white hair fell forward as she bowed her head, and wild rose scented the air between them. "Sir Rowan Berry Longbow," she murmured, vocally, not telepathically, "this woman is called Lyka. She is to tell you Prince Consort Masudah is safe. He is with the queen, where Her Royal Highness communes with her advisers. Lyka is

112

to take you there." Humble she may have been, but her strong hand of six digits gripped his firmly as they made their way through the throng.

◆

"It is beginning," she said. Lyka had led Rowan part way through the long tunnel she said connected to the cavern where the queen and Masudah waited. But she stopped. The force of a far-off hammer boomed and vibrated his boots' soles. "No fear, no worry," she said. "This place is strong, a mass of ancient rock without cracks, crevices or detectable entrance. It is like a giant vulture egg those above hope to crack." She took Rowan's hand again, but lifted it to her ample bosom. "Lyka will comfort you," she said, and pulled back her long white hair with her other hand, and gazed up at him.

Rowan withdrew. "Thank you, Lyka," he said, "but I can take care of myself."

Her limpid blue eyes remained deep pools of kindness. "No fear, no worry," she said, drew close and pressed her long palms to his heart and spread her twelve fingers wide.

Rowan took her hands and pulled them off and away.

Lyka reached up a pale forefinger and pressed it across his lips. "No fear, no worry. Lyka, she understands. Listen." She lifted her chin towards the ceiling and looked up.

The relentless pounding grew louder.

"We must enjoy, for tomorrow we may die. Your woman wishes for you to be happy, no? It is Lyka's duty. And you are so beautiful, like a big strong lion." The woman reached up and ran her fingers through his mane.

He grabbed her wrists and pulled her hands away with more force.

"Lyka wants so very much to make Sir Red Lion happy."

"Very kind, Lyka, thank you. But please, just take me to the queen. There's no way I'm going to die tomorrow or any time soon. Please, lead the way. I'll be right behind you."

Lyka sighed and tried to take his hand again.

But he quickly stepped back and raised his palms.

"Lyka only wishes to lead you to the queen and your friend the consort, lovely lion. Lyka means no harm."

"Look," said Rowan, "I'm nobody's pet. I'm a felid, that's all, not a lion. I do not need my hand held. I'm a big boy. Get it? Now, let's go before the Reps cave the ceiling in or I'll file a complaint with the queen."

"No fear, no worry," she said, her beautiful large blue eyes soft and clear. "Lyka's joy will remain unshared." The woman bowed, turned and walked on.

Rowan took care not to follow too close, and did not take his eyes off the white hair that spilled down her strong back.

◆

Lyka led Rowan to the shadows at the edge of the loose group of intimates and advisers that encircled Queen Havasarakshrrut'yuny under the light of a large candelabrum of crystals. The vulture motif in Nefer's brooch also appeared here and there on shields and flags, as well as on the lapels of some of the Ahan, likely security guards or soldiers.

Masudah stood behind her, his hands clasped behind his back. He unclasped them, and his hands formed fists as he shifted his weight.

The queen addressed the tallest man, who wore a long cape of black feathers. "Gregor," she asked, "how did we not see it coming? You say it was not in the bones. You inscribed the bone, then burnt it, you read the cracks, but did you somehow miss it? How is this possible?"

Eight-foot-tall Gregor's long pale face scanned the entire group. He answered: "Your Highness, the bones must be asked specific questions. We did not ask if the consort and his felid presented a threat, as they were vouchsafed by you, my queen. We did not question whether they would lead the enemy to our gate." The shaman looked directly at Masudah, and said: "Before this august company I declare there is a traitor in our midst." He looked back to Queen Havasarakshrrut'yuny, and added: "This renegade is responsible."

Nefer's black eyes flashed.

The corners of Gregor's mouth turned up a little in a subtle sneer as he looked down on her.

Lyka nudged Rowan's elbow, puckered her lips and placed a forefinger across them, looked into his eyes and shook her head.

Rowan nodded assent and resolved to calm his mind to reinforce psychological boundaries, an empath's biggest challenge.

Lyka's upper arm remained warmly pressed to his side.

But he stepped away.

Her soft blue gaze lingered, however.

Nefer said, "Gregor, you are hiding in plain sight. You even admit it. *You* are that renegade."

Rowan had expected the crowd to gasp, but all remained unexpressive – all except Masudah – who quickly jumped in front of Nefer, his ceremonial dagger drawn, the narrow moustaches in a grim straight line above his stiffened upper lip, and he slashed a wide arc in the air with the blade. Rowan too leapt to her defence, despite Lyka's strong grip on his forearm. He broke free, but taller Ahan men surrounded him before he could dash from the shadows to cross a third of the distance.

◆

A huge circular stone blocked the entrance of the cold cramped hollow into which Rowan had been thrown. He looked at the backs of his hands and spread his fingers. The ring of gold dimly reflected the living phosphorescence in the walls. He dropped his hands to his lap. *My power is to wait.* He did not have to be patient for long.

On the other side, someone grunted, and the stone door rocked.

He had earlier tried to budge it himself, to no avail, but now added his strength to the effort.

"Lovely Sir Red Lion," she said through the subsequent crack, "Lyka is come to save you. You must be very quiet."

Little by little the door opened enough for Rowan to squeeze through. "Lyka," he whispered, "where are the queen and her consort?"

"They cannot be saved by Lyka. Lovely lion is too beautiful to die."

"So is the queen. So is Masudah. Take me to them. Now."

Lyka's blue irises shone and floated in their whites. Her mouth opened as if to speak. But she turned quickly in the narrow tunnel and vanished –

Her fear had resonated in his own body. Tunnels branched off in every direction, but the scent of wild roses led the way. Many dead ends later, he came to the same large cavern where he had first arrived on the reindeer's back.

The Ahan had settled in. Some slept, others huddled in silent communion. The little ones played quiet games with small toys or sticks and stones.

Rowan kept a lookout for Lyka from the shadow of a natural stone pillar.

The footfalls of a group of people approached from the tunnel on the far side of the cavern. Queen Havasarakshrrut'yuny's council emerged, led by Gregor. Not all appeared. Possibly half a dozen or so other members were absent, with no sign of Masudah, apparently made the royal consort in the past few hours.

But Nefer looked queenly, head held high, when she could be seen at all among the tall Ahan. Gregor and the queen stopped and waited until all had passed into the main area. He climbed to a higher spot and tapped his bone-tipped staff on the floor three times. Everyone grew still and faced him, including the children. Gregor's exaggerated body language, as if he were a mime artist, added to the palpable tension in the room, as did the vertical lines under each of his eyes, red war paint. Each line ended in a dot, like two exclamation marks in blood on his long strongly defined pale face. Gregor pontificated as if his voice spoke between Rowan's ears:

"*Her Majesty Queen Havasarakshrrut'yuny, Her Royal Highness, the Balance of Rule and Monarch of Aha Domain, has decreed that I, High Shaman Gregor, announce her desire, which is that I, High Shaman Gregor, take command of Aha Domain.*" He looked askance at the queen who stood among the council.

Nefer did not return his gaze. She stared into the space before her.

He continued: "*I, Gregor, am her strength! A second special amendment has been made to the Law of Rule. From this time forward the Crown, the treasury, all Aha, its guilds, business districts, banks, factory towns, farms and fields, commonages, citizens and properties thereof are under the jurisdiction of the Office of the High Shaman for the duration of this emergency. The war will be long and bitter. No one can conquer us, but our enemy is rigid, stubborn and defiant, however ignorant of what they have started by intimidation, a storm of death brought upon them and their false god.*" He pointed to his face. "*Look well! These marks have not graced a high shaman in many centuries. If you do not know or have forgotten, they signify tears, tears of blood. We do not undertake bloodshed lightly, especially the blood of our siblings, in this case the Unfinished, the youngest. It is with a heavy heart that we must be the ones to now literally finish them. Their power has amassed to such an extent the Unfinished challenge our stewardship of Eorthe bestowed by the Sky Fathers. They have no right and never did have the right, nor ever will.*

"*Forgive them, noble Ahan. Forgive them while you slash their slime-blackened throats and wallow in deep warm pools of their lizard blood and cut out their lying forked tongues to sacrifice on Anggh's holy days. May you relish feasting on their scaled flesh in celebration of our great day of victory!*"

Instead of rallied to a war cry, the Ahan bowed their heads and each dropped to one knee. All faced Gregor – not their queen – stood up, and a solemn chorus, very beautiful, poured forth in harmony as one voice from their open mouths, throats and hearts.

Rowan's heart resonated with the anthem. But he had to shake his head free of the thought that Gregor had the divine right to seize power.

XVII
Sky Burial

THE AHAN SANG the council back into the tunnel until the last had filed out. Intense telepathy pervaded the chamber. The men clasped each other's forearms and looked into each other's eyes, as did many of the women. The mothers among them and some of the men hovered over their children, who had already resumed their play.

Long six-fingered hands grasped Rowan's waist from behind. A full firm bosom pressed against his back, warm and insistent. "Brave beautiful lion," she said. "Lyka is here. Forgive her. She ran away."

Rowan pried her hands off while he tried not to attract unwanted attention. He spun around and covered Lyka's mouth, glared at her and shook his head.

She nodded acknowledgement, and tugged on his hand while she peered into his eyes, and said, "No need, Sir Red Lion. No one can hear Lyka. Lovely lion learns quickly. No one can hear him either." She leaned into him, looked up and stood on her toes. "But then he is so exceptional, and so very lovely…"

Rowan grabbed Lyka's hand and pulled her into the darkness of the tunnel behind them. He grasped her other hand too, once out of sight. "Listen carefully, Lyka. It's not that I don't like you. In fact I owe you one for helping me escape that hole they chucked me into. And you're very attractive. *Very.* I mean it. But please try to restrain yourself. You're acting like a silly pubescent girl, not a grown-up. Besides, I'm not available. Get it?"

Lyka's face remained deadpan as before. Only her eyes betrayed hurt.

A pang of guilt stabbed Rowan's heart.

She nodded agreement, but kept her eyes fixed on his. "Sir Red Lion, Lyka will hide her love for him. Their ways differ. Because he commands it, Lyka remains his faithful servant."

Rowan peered at her handsome face. But his stomach churned. "You don't even know me."

She shook her head. "Lyka knows. From the first moment nothing is hidden. But now Lyka will live as Menak."

"Menak… what's that?"

"A maiden alone. Lyka will not mate in this lifetime. This is for the best. Lyka's heart is given, entangled now. This would only harm others unless Lyka remains apart. She cries inside, but the world will end soon."

"That's…" Rowan released her hands. "Not if I can help it." He sighed and rubbed the back of his neck, and steeled himself to look into her sad blue eyes. "And if you really want to help, we mustn't waste time. Can you guide me to the queen and her consort?"

Lyka took his hand and led him deeper into the tunnel.

He did not pull it away this time, not yet.

✦

Rowan saw no guard. Through the slim crack he watched the royal couple, a voyeur. The queen and her consort had been locked in a grotto. Masudah stood with his arms crossed, and leaned against the rock wall. Nefer sat beside him on the floor, knees up. One arm rested on her lap and the other's palm supported her chin.

Lyka warmly pressed against Rowan's back, as he'd had to squeeze into a narrow space and failed to persuade her to back away. But that was the least of his concerns. He could barely see anything, let alone the entire room.

Lyka reached past the side of his face and with impeccable aim threw a pebble through the crack.

Rowan grabbed her arm and held it to his side.

Her hand tight against his ribs, she pressed her body against his back.

Masudah looked towards the crack. So did Nefer. They glanced at each other. Neither hurried, but changed their positions, he closer to the crack, while she stood up. He faced the wall and placed his palms on either side of the fissure, and whispered, "Sir Rowan. Take great care. Keep your mind at peace like a windless lake. Then you are silent to them." He glanced behind him, and faced the crack. "Nefer is to leave here soon. I shall accompany her as consort. We are fine. You must find a way out on your own somehow. They will kill you if not."

"But Gregor…"

"Sir Rowan, there is nothing we can do. Not yet. They blame us for the attack. We must, how you say… play along. For now."

✦

Lyka led Rowan to the Surface. He never would have found the exit on his own. Unlike Vugh Deep's cavern entryways camouflaged by encrypted holograms, this one had taken advantage of natural creases in the mountainside that formed a

118

kind of maze. The pair hid among the folds and took stock of the scene beyond under the moon still nearly full.

Rowan realized the dawn of a new day had not yet blushed the horizon since he and Masudah had entered the portal among the fairy chimneys. But he inwardly approved of Lyka's steady stride. "What about you?" he asked. "You'll be in big trouble, but only if they know. It's called aiding and abetting a crime."

"Lyka goes where Sir Red Lion goes."

"No, Lyka. I'm very grateful. You got me out of prison and guided me to my friends. What's more you got me to the Surface. So far so good, but you shouldn't risk your life by helping me any further. Please, go back before they realize what you've done."

"They know. They follow but hesitate. They do not wish to alert the *P'vok'r Yeghbayr*, the Unfinished. They must decide whether to follow us and kill... or to let it be done by the fire from the sky."

Rowan looked out over the moonlit alpine meadow ahead. "Well, I guess we go together. For now." He took another look at the sky, from horizon to horizon. The moon backlit his thin white cloud of exhaled breath.

With Lyka in the lead, they hugged the shadows of the mountain. As the queen's servant, she wore finer but lighter clothing than other Ahan mostly clad in quilted outfits.

She's a big girl, Rowan thought. *She can handle it. I'd probably break into a sweat if we arm-wrestled, nanoids or not.*

"Gratitude, lovely lion," she said, and glanced behind at him.

He admired her striking profile, strong yet feminine, handsome like all the Ahan, and her long white hair shone like silver in the moonlight.

She stopped to tie her black scarf over it while she watched his face.

Rowan could have sworn he had seen her smile. He asked, "Lyka, why haven't the Reps, the Unfinished, surrounded the entire mountain? You aren't under siege."

"Lyka does not know, Sir Red Lion. Lyka guesses they have given up for now. It may be there is only one dragon ship. Perhaps it has been withdrawn to another battle elsewhere."

"I hope you're right. It's been quiet for the past hour. But that Gregor... he's a shady character. What's he up to?"

"He is high shaman, second only to the ceremonial monarch. In truth, the shamanic cults vie for the actual power. But she is good to Lyka. She is kind. Nothing is hidden. Lyka knows her. She is very strong. And wise."

"It's blackmail," said Rowan. "With Masudah as the hostage."

"Lyka's queen will never betray the consort, that is true. She is not born Ahan, yet she is more Ahan than the Ahan."

"How far is it to your home?"

"Lyka has no home, Sir Red Lion. Her place was with the queen. Her home was Lyka's home."

"Then where are we going?"

"Lyka takes Red Lion to her family. Lyka knows nowhere else. It is far, but they will be safe there. He will see."

◆

Travel in the shadows lengthened a journey that may have taken only a single night otherwise. They watched the sky during the day and took turns sleeping where the sun had warmed the ground, and in close proximity. Twice they took the risk to cross open fields to raid abandoned farmhouses. "The farmers, if they knew, would insist," she had assured him. The fourth night fell as they rested in the shadow of an escarpment.

Rowan watched the stars multiply, and asked, "Can you tell if anyone's still following, Lyka?"

"Lyka does not know, but there is nothing in the mind-space of the Ahan, not nearby. Back, far off, there is... noise. She does not understand."

"How close are we to your family now?"

"This cliff, it must be climbed. It is steep, but Red Lion is strong."

The moon behind him now shone silver light on her sturdy curves. He thought it a great pity that she had chosen Menak, a maiden alone.

She bowed her head and pressed her palms to her eyes.

"Lyka, what's wrong?"

She straightened and dropped her arms to her sides, looked up and replied, "Lyka does not *choose* Menak. Yet her heart overflows with the kindness of Sir Red Lion. Never will she forget what he thinks of Lyka. Never." She took his hand. "Come. He and she will be with her family soon... up there."

◆

The skeleton must have been at least seven feet in length, under the dusty quilt. Scuffed tall boots protruded. Two wood-handled knives had been laid across each other over the ribcage, long blades pointed towards the dust-laden pillow on which the elongated skull rested, its unseeing eye sockets huge and forever-stilled

120

jawbone massive. Its remaining long white hair had been carefully arranged, beneath which lay a wreath of the desiccated remnants of what were once flowers. The stone hut in which the bones rested must have been a snug home in years past, set in a fantasy landscape of rock formations that towered in a wide vista of wilderness and over a vast body of water in the distance.

"It is the Inland Sea," Lyka explained. "Once there were big ships."

The barn door had been left open. Among the cobwebs of the attached hut stood a second bed, a small one.

"We cannot light the fire," Lyka said. "The smoke…"

Rowan looked at her and wondered –

Lyka instantly responded: "No, Sir Red Lion. Lyka grieved long, but it is done. These are her father's bones."

"Where's your mother?"

"Lyka's mother is far away. Her bones were carried to Ayl Molorak by Anggh, the vulture god, after Father made the sky burial."

"I see. I'm sorry for your loss, Lyka. But how did your father come to this? Someone must have taken care of him."

"That was Lyka. She carried the bones. She laid the knives. She placed the flowers. She wept the tears."

"Tell me about it, Lyka… if you want to. I'd like to know."

Lyka gazed at him but remained silent for a long time. "He is kind, Sir Red Lion is, so lovely and kind. Lyka…" But she turned away, and stepped outside.

Rowan followed. Together they sat on a mossy ledge with their legs dangled over the edge. The wide view, windblown and deserted, sprawled under the early dawn sky.

"Lyka's father built the sky burial, and he went from the hut to visit it each day with flowers in his hand. Lyka thinks now that was a bad idea. He began to decline further each time. He no longer fed the lovely reindeer. Lyka too grew thin after she ate nearly all the apples and cracked all the nuts with the heavy hatchet. She gave the bad apples to the creatures of the forest. She was so young. To look at her now you would not believe how thin she became. She should be four fingers more tall now, full-grown. But Lyka was not too weak to open the barn door to free the lovely reindeer to graze on the wild grasses. When she turned back to the hut, there was her father face down in the dirt. His heart had broken. The winter… it was very, very long… and cold."

"But how did you survive, Lyka? Did someone come to help?"

"Lyka does not know. Perhaps there were parsnips, turnips, acorns, perhaps onions and garlic. Perhaps grain in the barn. It may be the fairies came. But one day the snow was gone. Then the bones grew clean and white. Lyka talked with the vulture god. She asked that she be allowed to gather the ones that were left and put them back together on the bed. Anggh nodded his head and looked with his red-ringed eyes right into Lyka's own. This meant yes, as soon as the bones were completely white. When the flowers came, she made a wreath and said a prayer."

Rowan could barely speak. "So… how did you get from here to the castle to be in Nefer's service?"

"Sir Red Lion, Lyka thinks he means the queen. She is his friend, yes? He calls her a special name. What does it mean?"

"Nefer means 'beauty… inside and out.' Masudah calls her that. It's a nickname, not her real name, not the name she was given at birth. Her father was a chieftain, a high chieftain. Her parents called her Thema, which means 'queen,' oddly enough. Maybe they knew without knowing."

"The consort is kind, like lovely Lion. His eyes are open whenever he looks upon Queen Havasarakshrrut'yuny. His mind is then at peace. Lyka knows this. It is wonderful… so long as she lives."

The breeze blew cold. Rowan wished he still had his plasma phaser to ignite a firestone. "Lyka, I think we should carefully gather up your father's bones and take them to your mother's sky burial. Anggh might appreciate it. He may grant us protection while we make a hot fire. The ashes of his bones will fly to her."

Lyka threw her arms around Rowan's neck. She buried her face in his chest and sobbed like a little girl.

◆

The air, still and cool, contrasted with the applewood fire hot enough to make the brittle dry bones into powdery ash. The wind gathered and whisked the white ashes to the Ahan afterworld. With one eye on the sky, Rowan had watched the flames turn to coals, then to embers. All the while he kept the other eye on Lyka, who had grown reserved, solemn and silent.

But now she sang. The Ahan had fully functional vocal cords, yet usually reserved them for song only, just as a lyre or a flute is reserved for music. Her strong resonant voice started with syllables, but her melody grew to soar on white wings beneath the ashes high above. Her eyes closed and her arms spread wide, while the wind rose from the chasm below and blew her white hair above her long head. Lyka ended her song and collapsed in a heap, and lifted her fine pale face to gaze at Rowan, her large blue eyes clear deep pools of peace. "Lyka's heart is full, Sir Red Lion," she said. "Thank you, thank you, thank you. Now she knows why she loves him so. But no fear, no worry. Lyka knows her place." She stood and bowed, and moved to Rowan's side and sat beside him on the flat rock that faced the red-gold glow of embers. She entwined her arm with his, clasped his hand, and rested her long head against him. "Father and Mother are together again. Sir Red Lion is lonely. Lyka is lonely."

"You have yet to tell me how you came to be in the queen's service."

"The people in the village did not want Lyka. To them she was a wild thing from the mountain, from those people up there who lived too close to Anggh. What did they expect to happen? But the little girl… how tragic. They collected a few coins of bronze and sent Lyka to the gates of the castle. They did not even have the courtesy to ask that she be taken in. It is said the Ahan are perfected. They were not back then. But the kindness of strangers saved her. Lyka knew nothing but the untamed mountains and the four seasons. Yet she grew to be of service step by step. When Queen Havasarakshrrut'yuny entered the castle gate and climbed the steps to sit on the empty throne, the people hailed their queen. Lyka saw the queen's beauty and her good heart. She saw her wise mind. The queen looked at Lyka and said, 'Come, woman, you shall be my companion and my aide.' And Lyka came. Then the consort came. And Sir Red Lion came." Lyka snuggled closer, and the night fell cold.

Anggh in the form of a giant vulture, spiritual guide and protector god of Aha Domain.

123

XVIII

Wooden Sword

Lʏᴋᴀ ʀᴀʀᴇʟʏ ᴛᴏᴏᴋ her eyes off Rowan thereafter. Under the waning moon in the small hours of the morning they passed the same village that had abandoned her. But in her eyes glowed a persistent smile. "We should not have made the fire, Sir Red Lion," she said. "It was good to sleep a little, but the Unfinished, they may have seen."

"Maybe Anggh protected us. It's thought the Unfinished might not be as strong as they pretend, Lyka. And we're still here, right?"

"Yes, dear lovely Lion, that we are."

"I should try an experiment," said he. "But first, may I ask if you can sense anything in the Ahan mind-space?"

"Lyka all along hears in her mind much noise far away. She does not know the meaning, but hopes the queen and her consort are well. They are in the castle now. But Lyka does not know more."

"We couldn't stay back there no matter how safe it seemed. You do see that now, don't you? Are you afraid of going near the castle?"

"No fear, no worry. Lyka goes with her lovely Lion. The castle is where they must go now if he says it must be so."

Rowan decided not to continue the conversation, well aware of her eyes on him at all times. A few hours passed. They came to an alcove in the mountainside. Black clouds pregnant with rain loomed overhead. "Lyka, can you rest your eyes now, even if you're not sleepy? If you close them and think peaceful thoughts, I'll try my experiment. You can help that way."

"It is as he wishes, lovely Lion. Lyka's eyes, they close." She placed one of her six-fingered hands on Rowan's thigh. "And she thinks of their peace."

Rowan squeezed her hand a little, but placed it back in her lap. "Thank you, Lyka, that will be very helpful. I've not tried anything like this for a long while. It didn't work so well last time. The results were confusing. So no distractions will help the most."

Lyka opened her eyes. "Lyka will be good," she said, and closed her eyes again. Her long hands remained in the lap of her folded legs.

Rowan too sat with legs crossed and his hands on his knees, palms up. Rain pattered beyond the shallow shelter, and the little waterfalls dripped off its edge, faded and stopped. All still and silent – dark and silent. Lyka's radiant body heat grew more palpable, but that too dissipated from his awareness.

"It is the swordsman, not the sword."

Sorely tempted to open his eyes, Rowan did not. The voice in his ears belonged to a man:

"Sawd killed several men with nothing more than a sword of wood meant to teach novices swordplay, no more than a stick."

A vague pale form emerged from the blackness, likely the back of an Ahan head. The voice resembled none he knew:

"Thus is the legend written in *Eld: The Book of Búsala*. It has been a source of power for us since it was etched in ink of octopoda on parchment made from the skin of a sacred ram, by the hand of Búsala himself, the pilot for whom the instrument is named, when the Ahan sailed their great ships on the Inland Sea in ages past. Like the prophet Mtatsum does the heretical sects, his spirit guides us still, as he transcribed the words of the Sky Fathers as they spoke them."

Another form appeared, and morphed into a face – Masudah's, who listened intently to the speaker, nodded acknowledgement and replied:

"In my travels, Azniv, I have seen the busala in use, a navigational device of genius, invented so long ago no one could explain to me its, how you say… provenance. Now I know it came from the Ahan, the first astronomers. Gratitude, Azniv. I am beginning to understand the Ahan way. So you have no comparable technology to the Unfinished nor the League, but are confident in your methods. Perhaps we could compare notes. Khémia too relies on magic. By experimentation I have found that League technology is a useful adjunct, especially as it saves time. And we have so little time now."

Azniv shook his white head, and said:

"Khémian magic has its origins in Aha, so it is no wonder it has saved your brown skins. So far. But you are a fool to dilute it with the materialist machines. They corrupt the soul. Thus Búsala teaches. Thus the Sky Fathers taught Búsala."

Rowan thrilled inwardly to have succeeded in remote-viewing Masudah, and so clearly, and with clairaudience. But what did it mean? Asniv may be one of the council members who had disagreed with Gregor. *If only I could see Azniv's face*. He calmed his mind again and continued to listen – in vain. Perhaps the thrill had severed the connection.

"May Lyka open her eyes, lovely Lion? She is called by nature."

"Of course, Lyka. The rain's stopped. I'll settle my mind a while longer. Then we'll continue our journey."

✦

Rowan had no idea how long Lyka had been gone. He had even forgotten all about her while he attempted another session. But her touch on his cheek grounded him back in his body.

"So soft is dear lovely Lion," she murmured, "like antler velvet or river otter pelt, like the sweet little kitten. So big and strong in body, so soft to touch. Oh, and his great heart…"

Rowan stood up. He placed his hands on Lyka's shoulders and stared into her big glittery blue eyes. "Lyka…"

She pressed a finger to his lips and blinked. "Sir Red Lion, please do not speak." Eyes closed, she withdrew and wrung her hands. "Lyka is like ice in spring sunshine. She is losing her shape. She is happy, she is sad. Be kind to Lyka. She knows not what she does. She is a little girl in a big woman-body." Lyka raised her six-fingered hands to her face and covered her eyes.

Rowan's childhood had been blessed with loving parents for a few years. In only a heartbeat they had vanished forever. He never knew affection again, not until he met Samarit. It never occurred to him to offer it to others. But now an irresistible force made him wrap Lyka in his arms and press his cheek to her long white head. He felt the tension drain from her body.

She dropped her hands from her face and clutched him tight with the desperation of a drowning person. A long moment passed and they parted. Her face had grown wet. "Lyka grieves still," she sobbed. "When will it be over?"

Rowan held her shoulder with one hand and stroked her hair with the other. "I don't know, Lyka. Growing up is hard. It's best begun under the guidance of wise parents until they believe you can thrive on your own. Their confidence in you becomes your self-esteem. Then you're on your way and the whole family is happy to see you go, I mean in the nicest way. They know that whatever storms come, you won't sink. You know, we're alike in a way… orphans. I lost my mother and father when I was very young too. Maybe it's good to be your own parent until you know you're fine alone. Then you can be with someone else or not and still be happy."

126

"He is so wise, lovely Lion is."

"Take your attention off me, Lyka. See what's going on here. What you seek is not outside yourself. What you want is you, not me. I know how hard it is. But don't be afraid. I'm here. I'm your friend."

"No fear, no… but Lyka is, yes… so afraid…"

"Good. It's good to know this. Listen to how you speak to yourself. I was taught this in commando school. Queen Nefer says that the only enemy is within. Don't listen to the enemy. You know there's a part of you, the real you who sees Lyka. She sees everything. But she doesn't judge. Her love is pure. This is whom you seek. She's the one who asked me to be kind to Lyka. Lyka is you, but you are not Lyka."

Lyka clasped her hands around Rowan's wrists, and looked into his face. "There are two Lykas? No…" Her head hung, and she looked away. She dropped her hands, and her face stiffened. "Growing up is hard," she said. "Lyka will be good."

◆

Rowan for a time stepped with a little more spring because Lyka's soft gaze no longer hung on his every move. But now she had grown very quiet, and her weight on his soul told him she sank into an inner pit, another lesson for empaths when they draw close to another. He must not let her drag him down with her. He decided to let go and trust her to work it out for herself. "Lyka, look." From their vantage point in a copse of conifers, Rowan pointed to spires silhouetted in rosy sunrise behind the Fivefold Mount. "It's the castle."

Her hand shaded her eyes as she looked up and across Castle Vale to the crag on the mountainside opposite, foundation of the castle complex.

"It's still whole and undamaged," he added. "I think you're right, Lyka. The dragon ship's gone away to commit mass murder elsewhere. All the same, we shouldn't risk travelling by daylight. While we wait for sunset, I'm going to try my experiment again. I had some success before. The more we know the better, before we get too close. Will you be all right?"

Lyka did not look at him. But she said, "Lyka will be good." She walked off into the woods nearby and sat down under an old elm, where rays of the new day dappled the scene with shafts of pale light and sepia shadows.

Rowan set aside thoughts of Lyka with difficulty, but entered the silent blackness again, that is, until Azniv said:

"You do not speak of this again, consort. You must make no move until I say. Understand?"

The back of Azniv's head looked like a white waterfall as he faced Masudah, whose black moustaches formed a straight line –

"I understand, Azniv, that I am held to ransom. But I do not obey you. I obey the queen. I am consort. Even Gregor says so."

"Pah! Gregor, him I scorn. It matters not. Take care and Havasarakshrrut'yuny will come to no harm. Whatever the outcome, it is all the same to you."

"I do not know how you expect to get away with this. It will end in tears… as you say, Azniv, whatever the outcome."

"Tears are for children. Obey your own interests then. Gregor will kill you when you have served his purpose."

"And you will not, is that it? Why should that be? Gregor and Azniv are akin. But are they still Ahan?"

"You dare to insult. You are a fool! But no matter. Be a quiet fool and your… child bride… will see another day… *but who is there?!…*"

Azniv turned towards Rowan's astral eye. The whites surrounded his blue irises as his large eyes opened wide but unseeing. Azniv and Masudah faded to black.

Rowan recognized Azniv as one of the council members who stood behind Nefer when Gregor announced his seizure of the throne. With eyes opened to the wood where Lyka had sat down beneath the great elm tree, he wanted to ask her about Azniv. But she had gone. He ignored the growing light and searched a wide area in the daylight hours that would have been spent in sleep, but knew he must rest, then attempt to remote-view her. He slept a little. Startled awake – the dregs of a dream remained, in which a great black bird in silence had flown over his head into the foaming storm clouds high above. He sat up, crossed his legs, closed his eyes and let his mind open to the void. A pattern rippled – vertigo – the void went black again until he peered through a feather-edged porthole of a dark cabin at sea – but no, not at sea: he looked straight down on a forested landscape, and drifted over the tips of the deep green conical evergreens. A harp toned softly somewhere. A building came into view, or rather its slate rooftops – and the conical metal tops of its spires –

⁘

A man – yes, Masudah – sat on a window seat with his head in his hands beneath a narrow leaded-glass window. Grey light from beyond cast the prince's shadow on the stone floor. Outside, a mountain forest spread downhill to the vale. The castle had lost a luxurious bedchamber and gained a prison cell.

⁘

Masudah appeared unharmed otherwise, so Rowan set his mind on Lyka. Was she here already? Or had she wandered off, lost in the mountains? He decided the latter less likely. She had grown up in the wilderness, and for a long time all alone.

⁘

Cold gripped Rowan's inner being, a psychic frigidity. The Throne had been encased in impotence. In the empty rooms curled many cats, familiars to the Ahan, asleep in hypnosis, rigid, but clearly not dead. He tried to tune into Nefer's location, but a gentle power co-opted his vision. His disembodied eye turned half-circle –

On the stone floor of a passageway sat a black familiar, the only one with its eyes open. Its tail curled about its dainty feet. The shining golden eyes spoke: "The spell is strong. I am stronger. No fear, no worry." It stood up on all fours, turned and walked a few steps, stopped and turned its black face up and said, "Follow." The little black cat traversed many twists and turns along narrow corridors and walkways, and often peered over its shoulder at him. Up and down spiral staircases in round towers the feline led until it came to a solid door of heavy wooden planks with wrought-iron hinges and rivets, set in a stone jamb with an arched lintel. At the threshold the familiar turned to look into Rowan's eyes. It again sat with its tail curled about its feet, and the golden orbs spoke: "She is within." And it vanished before his transfixed gaze. The co-optation ended.

About to grasp the iron knocker out of courtesy, of course his hand went straight through it and the door. Yet it creaked open on its own. A row of tall leaded-glass windows similar to Masudah's prison chamber cast the same grey light. He drifted into the bedchamber – to one side lay petite Nefer, Queen Havasarakshrrut'yuny, on the huge canopied bed designed for an Ahan monarch. She looked so small and still, like a doll. He moved closer, struck by the brilliant white of the heavy fabrics that draped the bed, like fresh snow in sunshine. In a long gown of white that made her face, head and hands all the more black by contrast, she appeared as if carved of ebony and polished to a soft lustre – and her mouth like a fresh pink rosebud.

"At last. At last you have come, Brother Red Lion."

Once more Rowan's vision rotated, guided in the opposite direction.

There before him on the smooth flagstones sat the little familiar, whose eyes of gold spoke: "I am stronger, yet my strength must grow, gather power, until I can break the spell. You must help."

As if I have a choice.

"But he does… lovely Lion does."

Rowan's attention flew to the window seat – at last, Lyka – translucent, near to invisible. "Are you… are you a ghost, Lyka?"

The apparition's large eyes grew less vague, as did Lyka's handsome face and the long hair on her shoulders, her bosom less evident, the rest of her body even less, but apparently at peace in the grey light, which cast a halo about her white Ahan head.

"Lyka… I've been searching everywhere."

The apparition's pale eyes turned a little blue, and smiled at him, and beamed out: "Her lovely Lion, so beautiful. And he is kind. She will never forget. Never." She turned her fine profile to the view, and faded from sight.

Rowan panicked. He rushed to the window. Beyond, below, lay Castle Vale. In the distance on its far side the wood lit up in the sun, where he had seen Lyka last, beneath the elm. His normally sharp vision had even greater acuity in his present form, and even telescoped.

A tiny figure at this distance, Lyka sat under the branches in sun-dappled autumn leaf, exactly where he had last seen her, knees drawn up, her arms crossed atop; her white hair hung over them as she rested her head. A short reach away sat his own corporeal form, eyes closed, legs crossed, palms open on his knees.

XIX

Spirit *of* Place

The black wings carried the huge scavenger skywards into the spiralling dark of turbid storm clouds. Its talons clutched a bundle of bones.

Rowan's eyes snapped open. He jumped to his feet and dashed across the short distance to the wood where the old elm spread its limbs.

There she sat very still with her head on her arms, and her arms crossed over her knees. Dawn sunbeams gently caressed her hair, made it shine silver-gold, and cast a pale circle about her head.

"I was so worried," he murmured, and crouched to touch her shoulder. "Lyka?" He caught her as she tipped over, and laid her cold body on the ground. On his knees, he took her long hands in his own and pressed them to his face, now wet with tears. The sunrays cast ever longer shadows as their arc traversed the vale, but Lyka and Rowan remained unmoving under the elm, where he lay beside her on the ground, one of her hands still in his own, his eyes transfixed on the blue sky beyond the branches.

✦

The air had grown cold again, now that the light had descended into what the Khémians called the underworld. The trance caused by the limitless expanse of sky had condensed to awareness of the Eorthe plane, the communion of peace at an end.

The moon had risen over the castle. He lifted her body in his arms and carried it away, the burden light. Afterwards he would wonder at it. Perhaps the fairies of Lyka's childhood helped him carry her up to the sharp top of a crag out of sight of anyone but the gods – he did not know. But he suspected Lyka knew. Her presence, her soft blue gaze, touched him, as if she blessed his journey in this life. But he never saw her ghost again.

Rowan arranged stones on a level place to make a bed for Lyka, into which he placed soft leafy branches and moss. He laid her to rest, and smoothed her bright hair, and kissed her cold mouth. The thought of her exposed to the harsh elements made him cover her with autumn leaves. And he garnished them with a bouquet of hardy late-blooming wildflowers. As a final gesture, he envisioned the vulture god, and asked that he show Lyka mercy when he carried her to the Ahan afterworld, Ayl Molorak, and asked that her spirit be reunited with her mother and father in Drakht, heaven. He sat with her in the moonlight for some hours, until the eastern horizon grew lighter. After a final request that Anggh not delay his grim work, Rowan made his way down the crag to the vale to await another night.

＋

The waning moon floated above the castle again. He tried to sit under the elm for another session of remote-viewing. But to concentrate there with the memory so freshly engraved in the surrounds proved too difficult, or rather concentration only on grief was possible in that place. He stood up and drifted through the shadows to a position out of sight of the scene of death but with the castle in view. For a time he lost all interest in the task, immobile in a twilight of empty imaginings. What if he had accepted Lyka's obviously sincere affection? What then? *Did I not take care of her?* The moral enquiry may as well have been a gut punch. *If only Sam were here,* he thought, and ground his teeth. *Why did I leave her to quest after the impossible? I'm wasting the time we have left together. What have I done? Lyka is dead. But she was young and strong. Did I break her heart? How? I should go back to the Longbows…* shocked to clarity by another punch in the gut, before this moment he had never imagined what losing Samarit truly meant – a tragedy more than possible in a world gone mad.

He shook off the dull weight on his being and paced. He must get back to Samarit as soon as possible. But not by abandonment of Nefer and Masudah. His fate had entangled with theirs. He resolved to spy on the castle from afar again, but first he needed to see if he could contact Samarit somehow. *Does distance make a difference?* A hard lesson in letting go followed. Hours went by, fatigue set in. Energy flagged and he fell asleep, his last thought that Lyka watched over him in spirit –

＋

The sky gleamed blue – cumulus clouds towered above the snowy peaks. A black dot grew into the silhouette of a flying bird. It never flapped its broad wings but coasted on the thermals. Closer and closer it rose, until at last it extended its talons and landed right in front of him, and red-rimmed eyes peered at him with intent. But it dived into the canyon, out of sight. Dreamer-Rowan realized he had observed all this from a clifftop. He stepped close to the edge – and in defiance of vertigo peered down to see where the vulture had gone. On a ledge not far below Samarit lay asleep among tufts of golden grass. Far below that the descending silhouette of Anggh winged in a slow spiral, and wove in and out of the misty rainbow of a waterfall that plummeted into the abyss. Samarit rolled from her side, sat up and stretched. She yawned and turned up her beautiful face to look directly at Rowan; her smile, so familiar, and all teeth intact –

◆

The moon still rode high among the stars above the vale. Assured that Anggh had blessed him, perhaps as a reward for his care of Lyka's body, Rowan decided to accept this interpretation as best. It allowed him to continue the journey in faith that Samarit remained well.

The thicket he hid within stood in shade as the sun rose, so he moved along the mountain's base to find warmth. Too many days and nights outdoors must have dulled his wits. Only a short distance had been crossed when he found himself surrounded by tall Ahan.

They carried no weapons, but just like the first night he had met them, they formed a circle.

And this time he knew he had walked into a trap for a second time, but absent of Gregor. None of these Ahan wore feathered cloaks. The only one Rowan recognized bore Azniv's face, who penetrated his mind:

"You are careless with your feelings, felid. Their range is wide and a beacon to us, yet their cause is to be regretted. If you were not a fugitive, the Ahan would take pity on you and conduct a rite. It would have started with the proper sky burial we will conduct for Lyka. She was a traitor, yet one of us, an Ahan. You, on the other hand, will be cremated. Alive." Azniv signalled to the others. As a group they with their captive filed across Castle Vale and up the long staircase to the castle.

◆

The windowless room Rowan found himself in, he guessed, must be in the basement, a cold and damp place with less than no luxuries, the opposite of the room Masudah had been locked in. Only enough dim light seeped beneath the heavy door that he could tell where the walls were without feeling for them, although he only had to lean on one to easily touch his elbow to its opposite. The only thing he could do he did. He slid to the floor and drifted his mind to a transcendent, more inclusive dimension of this world, what Ogna Longbow had called "far-sight." The League military called it remote-viewing; the Khémians called it star-travel; Rowan may as well have called it lucid dreaming, all facets of a single gem. The important thing was to expand awareness of his environment in order to solve a problem, in this case, ultimately, how to get back to Samarit. In the interim there had to be a way out of this dungeon –

"Sir Rowan, what are you doing here?"

"I could ask you the same thing, Masudah. If the situation weren't so dire, I'd think it funny that we meet this way."

"Well, yes, I see what you mean. And I mean that, how you say… literally. I see before me a picture, as in a cinema. It is good, not so?"

"Lyka is dead… I might have killed her, I don't know. I'm in a prison cell. Actually, it's a prison closet. They say they want to burn me alive."

"Not so good then… Sir Rowan, yes, I see it now. Lyka, her heart had chosen you, not so? Ah, this is sad. I sorrow for your loss. You did not kill her. The Ahan obsession with perfection leaves them vulnerable, especially the females. If their affections are thwarted, they become Menak, maidens alone. Add to that the power to die at will… tragic."

"*What?* How can they die at will?"

"Despite the formidable physique, an Ahan is a very sensitive soul. It makes them great artists, and this is why the world knows them not. They delude themselves that they are Eorthe's stewards, as they have hidden themselves to avoid its noise and trouble. The Primordial Architects assigned this power, to choose to die if under duress. The elderly do not linger. They give away their possessions when they have just enough time to disperse their few belongings among those who may need them. Then they may wander off into the mountains and, well, Anggh does the rest, sky burial or no. I sorrow that Lyka has left us… I pray she reaches Aaru, the Field of Reeds. But in Aha Domain I should say Drakht via Ayl Molorak, what some among of the League domains, including the few faithful in Vugh Deep, used to call the Otherworld."

"It doesn't matter what it's called, Masudah. She's gone and that's that. We're still here. We've got a job to do."

"Indeed, spoken like a true warrior." Masudah looked to Rowan, nodded assent and put his hand, which conveniently appeared now too, on Rowan's shoulder. "But you know, Lyka was a fine person, a gentle, kind, good, lovely and humble woman, a true Ahan despite her lack of intellectual sophistication, an unimportant detail completely. These people, these renegade shamans, are no longer Ahan. They are deeply afraid and deeply in denial of that. It makes them arrogant and dishonest. They are not perfected as they believe. Their only desire is to survive, and have sold their souls in a vain attempt to rid themselves of the fear of death. In Khémia we would say they have been seduced by Stormbringer, He of Bones of Iron. As you say, that is that. I should nearly agree, except that I too had once been seduced, dear Nefer also. Now she is a true queen! I say there is hope, so yes, I agree of course, we have a job to do. Let us do it well and They of Bones of Silver shall bless us and shed a light on our path."

"Masudah, in my opinion Nefer has always been a queen. But you should know she's in a coma. They haven't killed her, only incapacitated her. I think she's in this world in the form of her familiar too. I've seen it."

"I do know of the coma. But I am surprised Nefer is not here to greet us in spirit. She often says that her power must gather. If not, it will be dissipated too soon and all may be in vain. She is chained for now, but she will break to freedom. You will see. I did not know about the familiar, yet I am not surprised. Nefer has become much more than the ideal Ahan. Perhaps the familiar was in honour of your felidness, if I may say so, a manifestation just for you. There are so many domesticated felines in Aha, more than in Khémia where in places they are even deified. Instead here they are considered emissaries of nature as aides. This is the cat, it *is* what it teaches. As a familiar, the cat brings a special mystical influence to the work of the shamans who, up until the Apep increased their rampages, worked only to maintain and strengthen the Ahan bond with the Divine.

"These wise men and women," he added, "the true shamans, sacrifice personhood, as they are open hearts to the higher powers. They were once truly humble in their sacred role. Some of them are still, but many have been silenced, some forever. Gregor and his kind have hardened their hearts. They head for disaster. It is a logical consequence, so this is how the scales must balance. Nefer, Queen Havasarakshrrut'yuny, is a balancing weight from outside Aha Domain, of perfect measure to offset the reptilian power in their world, the Apep, those whom the Ahan used to call *P'vok'r Yeghbayr,* difficult to pronounce, like much of the Ahan language. It means 'little brother.' This name has gone out of fashion. Now they are called the Unfinished. It means the gods forgot to make them whole. It also means they deserve to one day, as the saying goes, be finished, as in unworthy of existence. But dear noble Nefer's coming was prophesied before she was but a baby bump in her mother's belly. The prophet was not clear about this, but it seems somehow Stormbringer has co-opted whatever is going on here to weight the scales in favour of evil. Does he want to turn the planet into an orgy of gore, fire and ashes?"

"If you're seriously asking an ignoramus like me," Rowan replied, "it's his idea of a fun time. That's because he's insane. He's Maçina the Artificer by another name... wow, get me. Now I'm buying into all this mythological stuff too. It's hard to keep track of all these different gods and goddesses... why can't everyone just get along?"

"My good friend, you are right. There is no need to label anything if it does not aid understanding. It is enough that we love one another as we love ourselves, not so? But to love ourselves we must first love, how you say... the grand picture. All these images and names, they are tools only. Use them, repair, then set them aside and enjoy, it is to be hoped never that they may be needed again. If you may forgive your friend Masudah for repetition... only when we come to love the whole can we love the part. This is what the Apep never knew and now the Ahan forget."

Rowan heaved a virtual sigh, as he had no physical lungs in the out-of-body state. "I hear you, brother," he said. "You're preaching to the converted. So now what do we do?"

XX

Fire Sacrifice

Humidity had corroded the door's iron hinges. With difficulty it opened, and not without a rusty screech that grated sensitive felid hearing. Rowan's nanoid enhancement remained in effect but in steady decline, thus his pupils did not contract quickly enough to prevent temporarily blindness when the dim light flooded in from the dungeon's passageway beyond, and the reek of sewage with it. Two of the three tall Ahan men outside grabbed his arms, pulled him out, yanked him to a standing position and manacled his wrists in iron. One led the way while the other two followed, and shoved him if he dragged his heels. They ascended a number of winding and slippery stone staircases to emerge in a courtyard that overlooked the vale. The silent denizens of the castle had waited for them, apart from Nefer and Masudah. Several stood with bronze-rimmed steel kite shields that bore the Ahan sigil, Anggh's winged silhouette in black on a red field. At their side a drummer kept a slow and insistent beat. In the distant overcast afternoon view beyond the battlements of the courtyard and the narrow vale below ranged white-capped mountains.

The new lord and still high shaman, Gregor, conductor of an orchestration of murder, stood before the people. At eight feet in height, the dictator stood tallest of the tall Ahan wherever he appeared, as usual draped in a long black cloak of vulture feathers.

Beside him hovered Azniv and the members of the queen's council, at least the ones present in the cavern chamber when he had seized power.

To one side stood a square platform of unmortared dressed granite blocks. On top of that, split cedar logs and kindling had been stacked. The courses above the cedar looked like hardwood logs of some kind, with a heavy stake some ten or eleven feet in height in the centre.

The drummer stopped. The breeze whistled. No one moved except the three guards and Rowan. They stood him between the platform and the other Ahan. The guards climbed up and lifted him onto the logs. They tied him with chains to the stake, including his neck and brow. He faced his murderers squarely.

"Felid," said Gregor, "murder it is most definitely not. This is an execution for a seditious act. You are an alien undesirable, a fomenter of treason. You force us to conduct a disgraceful means of transition to your Otherworld, death by fire at the stake alive. There is only pain in it, and none of Anggh's redemption, who carries in his talons the soul to Ayl Molorak, from where those judged

137

worthy ascend to Drakht." He pointed to his long massively-browed chiselled war-painted face. "Look well, felid, at these tears of blood. We do not shed them in frivolity. But we must, for the sake of pride and honour and to keep our race pure. We are superior, the elder race, thus our right is divine." With an abrupt motion he raised his big black-gloved fist, and his long white hair shivered. "To Anggh the fire sacrifice!" With his other hand he stabbed his metal-tipped wooden staff to the flagstones once, but with ringing force, and the gang of killers telepathically screamed their war cry.

At this Rowan's skull threatened to split at the sutures.

Two men brought torches and set them in metal stands at the forecorners of the platform. They turned, bowed to Gregor, turned again and arranged the kindling beneath the courses of logs at Rowan's feet. They turned again to face the mob, their timing perfect when their throats opened in song, on the beat.

Under different circumstances Rowan might have found it striking and beautiful. When singing as one voice, the Ahan demonstrated their true selves. *How can they sink to such evil?*

The song came to an end prematurely, however, and trailed off out of tune. The torchbearers pointed to the sky. The choir turned their heads as one and stared into the distance –

A giant black vulture rose on the wind from the vale, and grew larger as it drew more near.

Rowan gasped – its wingspan must have been thirty feet or more. More astonishing still, a gaunt figure rode its back, a woman with long white hair –

Behind him out of sight an elderly woman's voice spoke, and moreover vocally: "Gregor, you say there is no redemption without Anggh. I say there is no redemption without a soul for Anggh to redeem."

Rowan tore his gaze from the giant vulture in an attempt to see the speaker. The chain at his neck chafed, but he struggled to catch a glimpse in peripheral vision. He could just make out the same old woman who rode the vulture, now atop the parapet of one of the towers that flanked the courtyard.

"You are a coward, Gregor," she said matter-of-factly. She moved within view, an Ahan woman long in years, slender but hale, elegant, poised and serene. "Resign gracefully now," she said. "You know it is the right thing to do."

Gregor's eyes blazed blue fire that inflamed his mental transmission: "Your discordant song lacks melody, Aynt. It is meant for the felid's ears, not mine. It is *your* soul that is forfeit. You malign me, yet you are a witch of black magic, a heretic, a sorceress. Therefore you are a liar."

The torches in the two Ahan henchmen's hands blew out, and left thin wisps of smoke to curl. At the same moment the chains that bound Rowan to the stake snapped and resounded like the crack of whips, and the manacles clattered to the logs at his feet.

His mind reeled: *I'm the coward… I'm seeing an alternative ending to this nightmare because it's just too terrible… I'm the coward!*

"No, kitty baby." Samarit stood before him, in the black form-fitting warrior guild uniform that suited her so well.

Nefer's little black familiar leaned against the ankle of one of her five-toed combat boots, its golden eyes on Rowan.

Samarit turned to face Gregor and his band of fiends, and her uniform grew a long cloak of black vulture feathers. She nearly doubled in size, thus exceeded Gregor in stature. Her single dark plait came undone to hang white and straight down her back.

The little familiar grew to black-panther scale. A guttural growl escaped its bared fangs.

Gregor stared at the woman open-mouthed. His staff bounced to the ground with a wooden clatter. But he soon rallied, inhaled, clapped his gloved hands together three times, mellow and merry his tone now: "Bravo, Aynt. Your showmanship, extraordinary! Such flair. If entertainment were wanted, you would be the clown of choice. Alas, today we must work." With a flourish that parted his vulture feather cloak to reveal a chain-mail vest, he raised his arm to direct the crowd to overwhelm the old woman. But grim resolve soon transformed to puzzlement. He turned to look behind –

The entire choir had faced away. They pointed to the sky. They pointed to the giant vulture about to swoop down upon the courtyard. It came so fast they scattered and hid wherever they could. Most ran back into the castle, straggled by the bearers who clanged and clattered their metal shields to the pavement. Azniv had been the first to flee. Right behind him Gregor trampled several of his own men as he forced his way through the arched entryway.

Doubt strangled Rowan's mind with an iron grip: *Madness is the price…*

But an old woman in a long cloak, white-haired, blue-eyed, lean for an Ahan, stood before him. "*The*

Aynt, witch *of* Aha Domain.

139

power of waiting is a gift, Sir Rowan," she shouted above the din. "*It has no price.*" Her six-fingered hand gestured to him, and she added: "*Come down from there.*"

He stepped from the pyre to the courtyard, and shouted, "*Who am I to thank for saving my life?*"

"You may address me as Aynt. You will find it a name tainted with innuendo, intrigue, hyperbole and lies. Slander is rife in my long history with the Ahan."

"*But… aren't you Ahan?*"

"I am the sun. I am the moon. I am the sky. I am Anggh. I am none of these things. The people call me Aynt because that is what they see, an angular old woman they deem a black witch, a sorceress. They no longer know Anggh whom they worship. That would take courage. Their religion has been devoured by the monster of fear, a democratic ogre, however, as it welcomes all." She studied his face. "Do not fear me, Sir Rowan. No one need fear me if not unjust."

"*I'm in awe, that's all.*"

The old woman shrugged. "Well, that will have to do for now. Come."

✦

Unlike his superior, Azniv wore only a necklace of vulture feathers, and on his feet red slippers. In the dim chamber he knelt before a fire in a bronze brazier in the form of a pan with symbols engraved within its concavity and set on a kind of altar or low stone table upon which rested an arrangement of bones he peered at, which must have been burnt in the brazier.

Rowan sensed the man's searching, seeking mind.

Azniv fidgeted and repeatedly adjusted his position.

Rowan decided he had better end the viewing session while still incognito. "I'm not sure what I just saw is important," he told Aynt. "I guess his shamanic duty is to try to read the future in the bones, if that's what he was doing." He shivered. The wind blew cold here above the tree line.

The old sorceress, apparently unaffected by the icy breeze, sat beside him on a rocky ledge that overlooked the Inland Sea. "For now," she said, "it is important only that you stabilize and expand your dreaming power. Everyone has this gift, but it remains latent until a teacher can guide the determined student, whose attention span must be great. Gifts such as this tend to atrophy with age as well. You are young but, with my help, dreaming will grow more clear than clear by the time you are a shaggy old felid centuries from now. We shall work together until it is reliable, to the benefit of both our causes."

"I wondered why you pulled me out of that pickle I was in," he croaked. But his voice relaxed to its normal sonorous depth, and he added, "You should know I only want to go home. That's my cause. It just isn't anywhere in particular yet that I can be sure of."

The old woman peered into Rowan's eyes. After a moment, she said, "But it is with a particular someone. Good. It will lend power to the work. The 'where' can take care of itself. Today no one can be certain of their locus, not that there ever was in the history of the world a place that never changed. All is, ever was and ever shall be flux and nothing but."

"That's what I've come to understand… endless change."

"Then let us together influence a change to our mutual benefit. You have told me of the cause you fight for. Now I will tell you of mine." Aynt stood up.

An inspiring figure, to Rowan the archetypal guardian of Aha Domain, he watched her lean erect frame and her white hair blown about in the abrasive wind. She had taken shape as something within the scope of his understanding.

"Do not think you can ever know me, Sir Rowan," she said. "I am not what I appear to be. Nor are you. But that is another lesson for another time." She studied his eyes. "When you are ready… perhaps I am not the one to teach it. Today we have work to do. You are to play an important role in it. But you must be disciplined to do it well. We have made a start already. Now, listen."

In an instant he no longer shivered on that cold height above the expanse of restless water. Now he basked in warmth and comfort, in a small cavity at the base of a massive tree, perhaps an oak, home to some otherworldly being. It reminded him of an illustration of a fairy home in a book when he had first begun to learn to read and write back in Perkona Ola, a measure of how far he had progressed in the intervening years.

"Yes," she said, "it has been a long road, Sir Rowan." Aynt had comfortably settled in a big armchair beside the cheery fireplace. She puffed on a pipe with a long curved ivory stem and burled bowl shaped like an acorn cup. Curls of bluish smoke wafted towards the chimney flue. "Yet it has barely begun. At its end you will find peace. You must find it first within yourself. You must become the peace you seek. Then it is everywhere and everywhen, as it indeed always was, ever is… and ever shall be…" Her eyes closed, her hand dropped –

Rowan leapt from his own chair to catch the pipe before she set herself ablaze. But he soon understood it was not she who slept. He did – and dreamt of the rock beneath his feet, hard as ever, and the blue sky above his head, home to a yellow sun that blessed his skin with warmth as its reflection played on the surface of the great waters below – and the soft solace of a warm breeze –

Her voice came from everywhere at once: "The world is being reborn, Sir Rowan. This means it must die at the same time. Yet there are distinct leaps in the transition. We are about to leap now. Will we land safely or will we break our necks?" Nowhere in sight, her voice now between his ears, she asked, "Do you know why Azniv and shamans like him wear red slippers?"

Rowan assumed it must be a rhetorical question, and waited for the answer.

"If you asked him, Sir Rowan, he would say his ancestors before him wore them in honour of their own ancestors, who walked in the blood of sacrifices."

"Aynt… are you saying shed blood is necessary?"

"No, my young friend. I did not say that. They were necessary to the Ahan rites of old, so they believed. In their primitive age, shedding of blood seemed to work at first. Its power came from the fact that it is so strongly associated with the heart. They did not understand they had only to open their spiritual hearts. But their minds took everything literally, thus believed living hearts of sentient beings when sundered would open a window into spirit to free them from limitation. But the superstition became a habit. Do you know why Azniv and others like him burn the bones and spread them on the sacred table?"

"To read the future in the oracle of the cracks?"

"If you asked him, he would say so. Azniv would add that it is wise to have one's eyes open lest one stumble and fall into a pit. He does not know the future *is* the pit, as is the past."

"But the prophecy… Nefer, I mean Queen Havasarakshrrut'yuny… her claim on the Ahan throne had been predicted."

"Ah, yes. In my form of old, as the prophet Mtatsum, I planted a seed. The seed was good, the ground was good. Thus it came to pass."

"In a past life?"

"No, my young friend. I am unborn, therefore I cannot be reborn."

◆

With a jolt he sat upright, no longer dreaming. He believed he sat all alone on that cold windy ledge that overlooked the grey Inland Sea.

XXI
Anarchy

Aynt had not explained the cause she fought for. How was he to help her? She had spoken of mutual benefit. What was his role?

"Small steps, my young friend."

"Aynt… I thought you'd gone."

"I have never come, therefore I cannot go."

"Is that why you're invisible? I mean no disrespect, but… I might be losing my mind. I can't be sure I'm awake. I can't even be sure I wasn't burnt alive. Maybe I'm hallucinating. Maybe this is the afterlife, the Otherworld."

"Good. You are learning quickly. Question, examine everything. What you call dream and what you call waking are much the same thing. Indeed, sanity whilst in either state, a clear mind committed to truth at all costs, this is what we need. And you are sane, in my opinion, a risk worth taking."

He looked away from the misty sea to his open hands, and replied, "Dream or not, I just want to go home."

Aynt appeared in an instant bodily beside him. The chill air immediately grew warmer and the wind slowed to a soft breeze. The great body of water called the Inland Sea sparkled below in the sunshine. "You will not recognize it unless you are freed by the truth," she replied, "but take care. The truth is not easy to determine. Let me portray truth as the big tent of a circus. You are a small boy who peeps through a hole in the canvas. Inside the ringmaster introduces the entertainers. The forty pretty dancing girls entrance your eyes. Fear not when the most beautiful climb above the crowd to swing from the trapeze and fly through the air without a net or when the lion tamer sticks his head between the beast's fearsome fangs. Be that brave too. On the edge of their seats the entire world sits in thrall. Yet be wary of the clowns. They are tricksters. Do not trust them, but laugh at them if you like. The absurd can entertain and delight. But these jokesters represent the mind in chaos when it forgets its source. The clowns' job is to remind us of that."

"Aynt, isn't this just playing at life like the Primordial Architects did?"

"Life is play, but serious play. The wise are no *dilletanti*, but masters of their art. You speak of the Time Before Time, when the Genitors played their games, then went home. The resultant many species of what you call *sapiens* thereafter scattered, in fear of each other. Why? Because the others differed in some superficial way that disguised the spirit in common. They wandered long as nomads, then settled as tribes and clans in remote parts of the planet, widely separated. Once their immediate needs were seen to, they looked to the limitless night sky and wondered who they were, whence they had come and whence they would go. Something seemed oddly incomplete about their world. To many something about it was all wrong, but a mystery. Yet curiosity is a sentient being's nature, to learn and to grow, to seek completion. The learning mind needs symbols to embody meaning, stepping stones to further growth. These are the gods, who acquire a life of their own."

"But are the gods only acts of imagination?" asked Rowan. "The ones I've met, if that's what they were, seemed quite real."

Aynt lowered her brows, glared at him and said: "*The imagination is not a faculty, it is everything!*" She turned away, shaded her old eyes and studied the horizon. "Listen, my young friend, in times of old, a traveller, say a merchant, upon having made their way to another land, obeyed the gods of that place and worshipped them. The gods were specific to locale. They were not universal, although they resembled each other often."

By way of reply, Rowan added, "They had the humanoid form in common, and the humanoid mind. The gods who developed out of each tribe, clan or region were effective when no one interfered, but when friction arose from increasing populations that competed for the same resources, the god of the tribe that won the battle was adopted."

"Very good, my young friend. As an educated person you likely know the narrative presented in history books better than does this old-country witch. To make a long story less long, the gods of every nation today are shaking in their boots at the prospect of Maçina the Artificer. This does not inspire confidence in the people. Here in the queendom of Aha the shamanistic religion of Anggh is a caricature of its former glory. Like a beautiful still life of a bowl of fruit, it fails to satisfy hunger. The people feel doomed. They are at heart great artists, not great warriors. Violent, manipulative and exploitative dictatorship of the likes of Gregor and Azniv is a symptom of a diseased institution subject to a diseased imagination, a weak compensation that cannot save them."

Rowan sat pensive, but nodded assent. "So what do we do? Is your cause to depose Gregor and unite the Ahan? You have the magic powers. Then what? How can the artists defeat the dragons? Sing them to death?"

The old sorceress nearly doubled over in jollity. Her chuckles, chortles and giggles irrupted for some time. She drew a breath and settled down, yet hilarity burst out again. But she collected herself and wrapped one arm around Rowan's shoulders, and with her free hand pulled the red tuft on his chin. "My young friend," she said, "you do not disappoint. I knew you were special."

◆

"I feel something rising like an ocean swell. It's unstoppable."

"Do not listen to your feelings, Sir Rowan. They cannot be relied upon. They are unstable reactions only. This is the mind's interpretation. It is a poet, an image-maker, a dreamer whose temptation is to wallow in feeling and call it truth. And we are within the vibrational field of an ancient race of artists. Their civilization was once their great work of art. It was once a masterpiece. It has become a cheapened and worthless imitation of itself."

"Could this wave then be a revolution, a will to clarity and sovereignty?"

"Let us say so for now, my young friend. It is time to move on. We need specific details. You have resonated with Azniv's energetic signature before. Tell me, what is his current intention?"

"He's determined," Rowan answered, "set on overcoming any misgivings to commit an act he knows is wrong. So he's convinced himself it's the right thing to do. I feel fear of widespread panic, his own too, and losing control."

"Never mind your feelings, my young friend. Remember that. Now, what is he doing and where? Describe what you see."

"He's talking to a group of other council members… some of the faces seem familiar. I don't know the Ahan language… but these people are plotting to assassinate someone."

Aynt paced back and forth like a tightrope walker on the very brink of the steep sharp blade of rock that comprised their perch.

He gripped its edge, and did not dare to stand up.

She, however, stood with ease, with her hands clasped behind her back, the subject of the composition, so to speak, who looked out over the Inland Sea. The spectacular panorama shone bright on such a fair day. "Time is a construct," she said. "But useful, something like an inch is useful, however imaginary. Now, move ahead along the stream of time. Not too far. Until mastery, your visionary power will tend towards greater fantasy. Only look to the days ahead… just a few."

"All right. It's difficult… not for me, I mean it's tumultuous. I see lots of quick movements, chaos, I feel panic… I mean the people within view are moving in crowds, at first in concert like a flock of birds, but then they scatter… it's tumult. I see Gregor. He stands erect, defiant. But… he's faking it. I can see his knees quiver. They're hidden by that long cloak he always wears. But I see them."

"Civil war." Aynt pivoted to face him. "Now it quickens."

◆

From the peaks to Castle Vale and the Fivefold Mount stretched a distance of some twenty leagues as the vulture flies, two or three days on intrepid foot over mountainous terrain. But the construct of time did not constrain Aynt. The next thing Rowan knew, they stood on the parapet above the courtyard where she had appeared after first beheld astride the giant vulture. Stunned, he stared, unsure if they stood in both locations at once.

"My young friend, please, you waste dreaming power." Her voice sounded at the exact halfway point between his ears: "Contemplation of the inexplicable is fine if there is no external challenge, but that is not what we face now. Still your mind and focus or your next thought will be of your survival. If unrestrained, clinging to it could lead to at least temporary insanity, otherwise known as panic." Aynt peered at him and winked. "Worse, you might wet your pants. This is the danger when the student has mastered to a degree a teaching. Belief in your feelings leads to assumptions. Wild anxious imaginings spring up untamed to dazzle, confound and misdirect. These are the clowns I warned you about. Stick to the facts, not your interpretation of the facts. This is the science of magic and the magic of science."

"I guess," Rowan admitted, "I just want to feel safe. But I can ignore that and soldier on."

"You will tend to feel better as your confidence grows. Confidence comes from knowledge and the successful application of it. Or not. Failure is the best teacher of all, better than me. But no misgivings. To feel secure will be a side effect, neither something you should grasp at nor cling to. Now, enough of that." Aynt pointed one long finger to the sky above Castle Vale. "Watch."

The giant vulture, a mere dot in the sky, grew to a winged silhouette that coasted the thermals, and descended.

Rowan kept an eye on Aynt in peripheral vision. To his relief she remained at his side.

The windows and entryways to the courtyard below filled with Ahan alerted by the guards. They dared not venture any further.

Rowan wondered why the sentinels had not noticed the witch and the felid on the parapet, but he suspected he might be invisible now and hoped it would not come at too dear a cost.

The huge bird circled high above the castle, the people shouted, gesticulated and pointed to the sky, and some even fell from the windows. A few pushed their neighbours out into the courtyard. Fights ensued. The guards did nothing to stop them. The smoulder of tumult ignited once more. Chaos spread like flame in tinder.

Rowan no longer looked down from the parapet, but from within the castle, in fact inside the packed throne room in chaos.

Two factions clashed in a horrendous din. High Shaman Gregor and his supporters on the high ground held the followers of Vice-Shaman Azniv at bay, who struggled up the wide steps and trampled their own wounded or dead, long knives and swords their weapons of choice. Soon the floor grew slick with blood. Gregor's face grew more animated and fierce, as did Azniv's in a fight to the death.

A prolonged battle ended in the last rebel weapons clattered onto the flag-stones. A hollow silence permitted Azniv a haggard voice, and he glared out of the remaining eye in his pale blood-spattered face, and croaked: "You have tied my hands, Gregor, but you cannot chain the people…" He spat blood, and with more force continued: "They now know your soul is forfeit for the fire from the sky that destroyed our mountain portal. Soon the whole of Aha Domain will know it. You curse me, but it is *you* who are doomed, devolved for all eternity. You are no Ahan. You are no leader. You collaborate with the enemy. *You are a coward and a traitor!*" Thus Azniv uttered his last words. At a nod from Gregor, the condemned man's remaining eye grew wide, and his mouth agape spurted red death as he fell to his knees, then on his face into a spreading pool of his own blood, a dagger plunged into his back above the manacles on his wrists.

✦

Rowan's attention immediately went to the queen and her consort –

She lay still, asleep in limbo, her familiar curled at her feet.

Masudah paced his cell in the turret like a caged animal.

"We need do nothing, my young friend," said Aynt. "Have faith."

"But Gregor's in control now. He'll kill them."

"Will he? We shall see. For now he has more than enough on his plate. He may choke on that before he can get that far. If you are worried, then look to see if that is true."

Despite the suggestion, Rowan could hardly prevent the inner visions –

Two steps at a time, a group of armed Ahan climbed the staircase to the queen's chambers.

Another group had already burst in upon Masudah, who stood before them in defiance, not that it prevented them from tying his wrists and forcing him down the narrow spiral staircase into the wider one of the tower base. Down, down and further down they went until they reached the throne room.

◆

Queen Havasarakshrrut'yuny remained comatose upon the white bed in her white gown, the little black cat nowhere in sight now.

The battered silent henchmen lined the sides of the royal bed.

At the footboard stood Gregor, staff in hand. Added to the red war paint, the blood of the mutineers on his long face and the long black vulture feather cloak had congealed. The first few notes of a chant emerged from his mouth, stopped and started again. He closed his eyes and added an insistently deeper tone to his spell, and droned on. But he opened his gaze in silence.

The henchmen shuffled, restless.

The high shaman struck his staff on the floor, not once but three times.

The men stared at Nefer.

She lay still as if carved on the lid of a sarcophagus. From behind them, she said, "Gregor, how are you? It has been a while, much too long."

The men rotated their heads as a group to face the door.

Gregor too spun about, eyes wide and mouth agape.

The men glanced at each other.

The high shaman only stared at the little black cat in the doorway.

Its tail curled about its little feet – and its golden eyes fixed on him.

The henchmen half-circled the cat. They fixated on the little creature as if it were a devil in disguise.

Gregor pushed them aside, but halted.

The little cat rose to stand on all fours and peer up at him.

Gregor clasped a hand to his own throat.

"Has the cat got your tongue?" the feline asked, and sauntered between the men's bloodied boots while all eyes followed. It jumped on the bed, where the queen sat in observation of the visitors, and the little cat curled up in her lap.

She stroked its black fur, and said, "You know, I had such a strange dream. In my crazy dream a rebellion raged, a coup if you can imagine! The castle was in an uproar. But awake now, I see all is well."

The henchmen glanced at each other. And they looked to Gregor.

His glazed eyes stared at the queen. Not only his knees quivered now – every feather of his cloak shook – his large eyes rolled up into his head and he collapsed backwards.

In one fell assail the henchmen pounced upon their leader, who had once towered over even the tallest Ahan, and dispatched what was left of his soul to the nethermost.

XXII

Frequencies

MASUDAH HAD BEEN forced to his knees on the platform before the throne, his wrists still manacled behind his back. A wooden block had been set in position, and his neck inserted into the vee hacked into it. Two long knives had been stuck into the wood and crossed to keep him in place, as evidenced by the blood. Behind him stood a muscular bare-chested Ahan with a makeshift black mask like a blindfold that encircled his long white hair, yet with holes slashed in it so he could sight a precise aim of his battle axe and separate the ex-priest's head from his body with (it was to be hoped) a single blow. The executioner's blue eyes glared, he poised for it, yet did not – or could not – move.

The victors cleared a space of the corpses so they could witness the death of the traitor from Khémia, consort of the deposed queen. Covered in blood, they stood crowded along the breadth of the steps and across the floor below, fidgeted and shuffled, and averted their gaze from their dead friends and neighbours. The restive energy of the mob forced one of them to shout at the executioner: "*What stays your hand, man? Do your duty! Off with his head!*"

The headsman remained frozen in place. Several of the first row of watchers rushed up to push him aside. The most energetic among them grabbed the axe from his hand. But he too stood fixed, arms raised, the axe firmly grasped but unable to strike. After a third man tried to replace him and suffered the same fate, the crowd retreated a few steps, mouths slack.

Another Ahan near the back of the room, spattered in blood like the rest, shouted: "*The Unfinished murdered our friends and family with fire from the sky. This brown foreign devil led them to us, he and his black child-whore. Kill him!*"

No one obeyed. Instead their eyes darted about the room. Each Ahan tried in vain to distance from his or her neighbour.

Although she remained invisible, Aynt's voice spoke in the very midpoint between Rowan's ears. By the expressions on the Ahan faces and the way most covered their own ears with their pale red-stained hands, they must have heard her words in the same way: "Ignoble ones, you have been deceived. You are complicit by self-deception. Your nobility is destroyed. Like your brothers and sisters who lie dead at your feet by your own hands, you could have chosen faith and freedom. You did not. You are cowards. You choose the coward's fate: slavery to guilt. Unlike the P'vok'r Yeghbayr, those you call the Unfinished, you had been blessed with a conscience by the Sky Fathers. This is why you are your own judge and jury. Execution will be visited upon the guilty, not the innocent." Aynt materialized in the flesh at the side of the blood-spattered throne, a tall gaunt figure of great age but unbowed. With a sigh she raised her hand, four long fingers touched to its palm and two pointed upwards.

Poised to strike the killing blow to Masudah's neck, the battle axe in the would-be executioner's hands twisted and severed his own head in its stead. But its work had not finished yet; with unflagging vigour it flew around the room spinning and separating, and sought the necks of the guilty Ahan wherever they tried in vain to flee. Alas for them, any means of exit had slammed in the faces of the heads soon to be detached from their frantic bodies.

The gory scene, too much for even a commando to bear, faded as Rowan looked away.

◆

He found himself as before at the rocky ledge above the Inland Sea, where he sat on a bench of rock with his elbows on his knees, hands clasped. Nothing had changed. The blue dome of the sky remained embellished by a few high cirrus clouds that looked like wisps of unbloodied Ahan hair. The warm sunshine from above and the sparkling water below did nothing to cheer. Their beauty held no comfort. He brooded for a long while, unmoving. The sun had made its unhurried way westwards across the heavens, and descended towards the Khémian underworld, the far side of the planet. Aware that Aynt sat beside him, unsure for how long, he wondered if perhaps she had just become visible. But he did not speak.

In time she said: "The wise grieve neither for the dead nor for the living. But this is a lesson for another time. Our work has begun, that is what is important. Our duty now is to wait."

Rowan glanced at the old woman, called a black witch by the Ahan, and muttered, "Wait… wait for what?"

"But this is your power, Sir Rowan, my young friend. And you ask *me* what we wait for. Waiting knows no what."

"There's always a what."

"Accept any outcome as a gift. This is the next lesson. All you must do is your best to act without hesitation when the truth reveals itself. If your heart is pure, you will know what to do. This is your duty, no more. Let the result take care of itself."

Rowan looked out over the great sea, and sighed. "I'll try."

151

"There is no try," Aynt insisted.

"Let me understand. My reach will exceed my grasp. Is that right?"

"There is only action."

"Then can I ask about magic? I mean, the brief dictatorship has in effect ended. The news will soon spread throughout the Ahan realm. You could have pulled it off without shedding a single drop of blood. I'm sure of it, you're powers are that great…"

Aynt raised a palm, and said, "There are cosmic laws that must be obeyed, otherwise the fool destroys herself. They define the witch's field of action. Moreover, I cannot interfere with the destiny of the Ahan, never mind the world. I can only follow duty to the truth. Whom you speak to now, your friend Aynt who appears in your mind, manifests as needed in whatever form is appropriate to the needs of her people. You saw me first as a guardian spirit of the Ahan. That is not wrong as far as it goes, but it is a very superficial way of knowing. It is not who I am. But this is another lesson for another time. If we survive the coming wave of transformation that threatens to engulf not only our world Eorthe but the entire universe, that will be the time to more effectively explore it."

"Aynt, that sounds like a what called a when, the future. The way you speak, it's predetermined. Can we then know the future with certainty?"

"You ask questions worthy of a child. But you are young, despite your many orbits of the sun. The felids grow slowly, yet their roots go deep. Late in the season they can bloom magnificently."

"In other words, shut up and get on with it."

"There is only action. Act well or not at all. This is true art."

"Gregor broke the law," said Rowan. "He broke himself and all who cast their lot with him. He tried to make himself the law. You said the Ahan were given a conscience. But the reptilians, are they innocent in some way? Despite their path of violence and belief that the rest of us are chattel and vermin? Or game at best? It seems the Sky Fathers left out that key capacity in their case."

"Good. The hatred in your heart is diminishing. Our enemy is no longer so two-dimensional because of your open investigation. Your intellect has grown. Its integrity is more firm, and now it is a worthy tool less prone to misinterpret the evidence. To answer your questions, ignorance of the law *is* lack of conscience. The consequences are identical. It makes no difference if it is the ignorance of ignoring it, of having forgotten it or the ignorance of lack of capacity to comprehend it, as is the case with the morally weak Unfinished."

Rowan replied, "What's hopeful is that you said violation of the law results in self-destruction. The Reps will hang themselves in the end."

"Abandon hope, my young friend. You do not need a crutch. All who love the good, the beautiful and the true must participate by walking the way of the law. It is not only for witches, it is for everyone. The law is all that is. If lazy or stupefied, they too break the law by slack complacency, like leaning on a rotten staff. There is only action; even non-action is action. Thus we must qualify ourselves to be able to wait properly, in calm and alert ability to respond with confidence to what the truth reveals. Only then we act."

◆

"I see Queen Havasarakshrrut'yuny. She's with Prince Consort Masudah. Maybe it's better to say Masudah's with her. She's in her power now. The people are bowed at her feet, except the council standing in front of her in the courtyard, the wide one where the giant vulture appeared. It's a lot smaller group than it used to be… that goes without saying."

"They do not understand Havasarakshrrut'yuny," said Aynt. "Their minds are still under the spell of tradition. They worship the past, the great heritage of the Ahan and its lofty ideals. The prophecy of her coming is sacred, yet the humiliation of having to give their power away rankles the cults of lesser power who cannot use her as a tool. But she has demonstrated power over the late Gregor. He was white, she is black. He was big, she is small. He was banal, she is mysterious and not to be defied, his superior. Anyone could be next if they cross her."

"Gregor's followers called her a whore, a black one, and a child. They called Masudah a brown foreigner and a devil."

"Good. Your statement neither speculates nor makes assumptions. The facts speak for themselves, no? There was division, yet Gregor's followers were no different to the others. Their fear was greater. They had authority to lose."

"If I were them," said Rowan, "I mean the council, I'd have had enough sense to see that Gregor was heading for the ditch, but I'd hang on with both six-fingered hands to whatever authority I still had."

"Good. Your statement shows that you look through the eyes of others. This is helpful. It is not easy to drop one's mask and don that of another in imagination. This ability differs subtly from speculation, yet the distinction is vast."

Whilst he pondered wearing another's mask, Rowan's imagination drifted to Blue, his long-lost elder sibling. At first he had raged against her betrayal. His attitude softened considerably later for a reason he could not fathom. He had speculated that blood is thicker than water, although that old saying did not satisfy. He looked through Blue's eyes now: because her self-worth had been damaged in youth by the depraved abuse and brutal suppression of the Reps, her immaturity and brilliant potential conflicted with the compromise, and created terror that she would never feel content unless she destroyed all attachments so she could start over, free of the Blue identity, another person entirely. She had wanted freedom at any cost – an emotional reaction unguided by wisdom, which became delusion compounded by long denial –

"You mind is wandering, my young friend. Leave the past in the past. It will come to the fore when it needs to be examined for assimilation when you have prepared a ritual space to contain it safely in order to transform it. This is true alchemy. Right now we must focus on the task at hand."

Surprised to be no longer surprised at Aynt's knowledge of his innermost thoughts, he replied, "Yes, Aynt. Would you like me to continue to observe the royal court?"

✦

Aynt and Rowan had toggled back to the parapet above the courtyard. The instantaneous transition again electrified to the point of partial paralysis. Like the Ahan, despite her underfed elderly appearance, he considered her a terrifying entity awesome beyond imagining, a witch-goddess. No wonder so many Ahan feared her power. The infinite unknown appeared as free fall. The parapet disappeared from view, as did Castle Vale and the world. All rotated rapidly and dissolved into a near vacuum but for *vertigo* –

"Hang on, my young friend! Do not lose your mind!"

Aynt's strong arms lifted him up and out of the vortex that threatened to suck him into oblivion like a whirlpool. The world reappeared, including Castle Vale and the parapet.

"I warned you before about the circus clowns," she said. "Now you have forgotten the lion tamer. It does no good to explain that you are safe. You would never believe it. You are still very much attached to the belief that you are a nobody with a lot to learn. This makes you shaky. It is correct on one level, apparently, but in truth we are not different." Aynt pointed to the sky. "Watch."

Still unsteady, Rowan looked up –

Beyond the thin clouds high above hovered a triangular silhouette, like a tiny arrowhead.

His body wanted to dive for cover. But there was none, unless he jumped forty feet to the courtyard and hid inside the castle, assuming the doors and

154

windows had been accidentally left unlocked. He knew even that would do no good if what he saw in the sky was what it appeared to be. *"Aynt!"* he cried, *"Is it a hologram?!"*

"Everything is a hologram."

His eyes refused look away from it. *"In my world there are holograms and then there are fire-breathing dragon ships!"*

"Your statement shows you know that your own and others' perceptions differ. Very good. I suggest yours may be a bit on the melodramatic side. But then you are young."

"We can't just stand here, we have to do something!"

"You are not wrong, my young friend, just disordered. Your power is to…" Aynt paused and gestured to him to speak.

"Wait… so?!"

"We need not do anything but just stand here."

Rows of red lights at the lacklustre pointed craft's edges flared, and the incredible white light flashed –

◆

"There's no such thing as nothing… right, Aynt?"

"Good. You understand. But then an eight-year-old could grasp the logic with ease."

"There can't be nothing, no-thing." Rowan scratched his head. "Otherwise non-existence exists. Even if it did, I'd have to be there to witness nothing. I would exist."

"No-thing is the child of a barren woman."

"But are we dead then?"

"Why do you ask?"

"Because we're in… whatever it is… a swirly cloud. The last thing I remember is the dragon ship, then a bright light."

"We are just beneath the top of the shield, the frequency dome, where the fire from the sky meets the shield of the Ahan, at the exact moment of impact."

"Has time stopped? Never mind, it's a construct, like an inch."

"You are correct on both counts."

"Nefer, the queen I mean, mentioned the shield," said Rowan. "She said it was still functioning when they went underground. I heard the Reps hammering on it when I was down there. I'd assumed it didn't work above ground…"

"This is the difficulty with assumptions."

"Right. You got me. Why didn't it work when the lodges were destroyed? Azniv blamed Gregor. Gregor blamed the queen and Masudah. And me."

"Gregor tried an old trick," Aynt answered. "It worked for a while. He was a powerful sorcerer and secretly disabled the shield. After the lodges had been destroyed, behind Havasarakshrrut'yuny's back he convinced most of the council the Ahan should be under his protection, with their assistance. He promised to reward them well and take special care of their families. The queen had not the personal power, he argued. She was a foreigner. Just look at her, he said, she was so small and so black. Yes, there was the prophecy, but they could afford no risks now. And the Unfinished were inferior and therefore no match to the strength he knew how to draw from the sacred traditions of the Ahan, from their ancient race and their land itself, despite their enemy's superior firepower."

Rowan frowned. "That's despicable. He intentionally permitted the enemy to kill his own people. He took advantage of their terror. He gained their permission to shove Nefer aside and take over, take Masudah hostage and keep the prophecy intact."

"My young friend, this is why I was called into manifestation, but the shield is the Ahans' achievement, a manifestation of their collective soul, their archetype if you like, but more abstract than this old witch. It is simple, yet a work of great beauty. I love to see it in effect. But we must move on." Aynt touched his forearm and said, "Look up."

The shield grew more radiant above them as the cycle of time rolled into gear again. The bright white flash had lasted a mere instant, thus the shield had become invisible again. The dragon ship turned in a slow arc, then like an arrow loosed, sped towards the west until it vanished.

Vertigo soon threatened to overwhelm as gravity took over, but Rowan hung on to Aynt with a tight grip. From the back of the giant vulture high above Eorthe, he observed a landscape of mountainous terrain green with forests through holes in a ragged layer of clouds below the creature's wings. In the distance a large body of water gleamed. The sun reflected on its surface in a soft sheen. The flyers descended in a tight spiral until they drew close enough to reveal the Ahan castle quite intact: the spires, the parapet, and the courtyard where the people had assembled. They pointed up at the big bird, scattered and hid. The huge vulture set its feet upon the flagstones, and folded its black wings.

XXIII
Restoration

THE COURTYARD'S MAIN porch bordered with a limestone peristyle bore a gabled copper roof beneath which one of the two tall doors of old oak opened enough for an armoured guard to stick his helmeted head out, and the rest of him followed, only to be edged aside by Queen Havasarakshrrut'yuny in typical Ahan attire, apart from a vulture-sigil pendant. "Gratitude, watchman," she said to him, "that will do." She strolled through the front columns and into the open space. "*Brother Red Lion,*" she called out, "*are you all right? However did you get up here?*"

"Queen Nefer." He bowed his head, and answered, "Of course I came with…" He turned about to look to Aynt, but she had gone. The giant vulture too had disappeared. Rowan stood with his back to the queen and peered at the tiny black speck on the horizon that might be a large winged creature.

Nefer had in the meantime walked to stand beside him. "Well, however you got here," she said, "I am glad. Masudah will be glad also."

He turned aside to look at Nefer, the queen. Her two slim black hands offered a grasp of his own, which he took.

Her fresh dark face beamed up at him. "You look a little battle weary," she said. "Come with me."

Together they walked hand in hand through the columns. A burly guard now stood at each of the double doors and held them open. They entered the hall to be greeted by Masudah. His narrow moustaches a blackbird in flight, his warm brown eyes shone, but speechless, he grasped Rowan's forearms.

◆

The throne room underwent renovation. The platform and the main floor had been dressed with new flagstones, but the throne itself had been removed to be refinished in a special workshop. Stonemasons, carpenters and labourers restored and cleaned the remainder under the direction of a designer who pointed to the equivalent of blueprints, surrounded by a few of his staff.

"This remains officially the throne room," said Masudah, his moustaches on the downstroke. He closed his eyes briefly, but continued: "Now also it is a choir chamber and will remain so until the newly quarried marble replaces any lingering negative vibrations and restores the space to its natural resonance with justice." In a moment he sighed and brightened. "Plans are for the amphitheatre to be expanded for a larger choir, now that we know how to make use of the geology of the Fivefold Mount upon and into which this old castle is built. It will act as a resonator and an amplifier. I have redesigned it as an instrument of stone, based on Khémian architecture's sacred geometry. That will modulate the vibrations. We must create a frequency Dome of global dimensions, but modest at first, enough for the castle environs, then all Aha Domain. As it grows, its centre will descend ever deeper towards the core of the planet. So doing, it will of course expand across the planet as well, reinforced wherever needed by additional amphitheatres, then it is to be hoped a network of restored pyramids across the globe to anchor and refine the effect. Everywhere but Khémia they had fallen into obscurity and decay long ago following the Great Mireflood. First I must build more refined scale models and make experiments. But even the early test case is very effective. It is really a question of fine-tuning the aesthetics, itself a major factor. This is what I am learning from the Ahan."

"This is inspiring news," said Rowan. "So the choir is cleansing the room as a kind of ritual space? Because of what happened here…"

A shadow crossed the prince's face, but he confirmed, "Precisely, Sir Rowan. Khémia has long used sonic means for healing and more, thus I have been able to contribute something, but it really has been dear Nefer who has composed, I should nearly say engineered, the hymns for this work. The Land of the Song-Eyes has no written language, only songs of knowledge, for the sole purpose of acting as a living archive for the ancient wisdom of the Antediluvians. Wakan understanding of music is therefore great. She has an extraordinary ability, perhaps inherited from a previous existence as an Ahan or a Khémian or both. Perhaps we met in a past life and agreed to continue our work where and when it would be most needed."

"It's a lovely notion, Masudah."

"I sense your doubt in the theory, my friend. It is good. One should not believe anything blindly, nor comply with peer pressure."

"It's clear to me, Masudah, that Nefer has saved Aha Domain. I saw the frequency Dome. I was there when the dragon ship attacked. It was right above this castle when the fire from the sky rained down. The Dome stopped it like a shield. The Reps went away disappointed, back up north and west."

"It must have been amazing… but of course, this is why we are able to discuss it now! Ah, Sir Rowan, my Nefer is a true miracle. We are blessed beyond measure. And to think only a short time ago, it seems, I was reviled as an outcast and a refugee, despised even by myself. She has taken the Ahan's natural unconscious shield and awakened it, so to say, as the Khémians have long since done."

Masudah took Rowan to a smaller private wing reserved for the royal family. Their view overlooked the part of the vale where Rowan had last been with Lyka, including the crag on the mountain where he had laid her to rest. The sight of it now in warm sunshine made his heart leaden.

"Your rooms are here, Sir Rowan. You are welcome at any time for as long as you wish. Your true home is in the west with your Samarit and the Longbows, but your second home is with us, always."

"Thank you, Masudah. If you don't mind, I'd rather stay in another part of the castle temporarily, if I may. Anywhere is fine, an empty closet, whatever."

"Understood, Sir Rowan. We must honour the fallen in our own way, in our own time. Lyka was a victim of the old order as well. Nefer as queen needs time to restore Aha to the Ahan, not that we may have much of it, time I mean."

◆

Rowan retired to not a closet but alternative chambers, a suite of well-appointed rooms that even came with a personal assistant, a young Ahan woman who bore no small resemblance to Lyka. In fact she must have been the other servant girl in Nefer's dining room at her mountain lodge when he and Masudah first arrived. Sírun's pale skin glowed with subtle translucence like flawless alabaster. She stood tall, blue-eyed, with long white hair worn woven into a single plait that hung nearly to the small of her back, and exposed her shapely ander ears, not pointed like Samarit's, but her hairstyle reminded him of the Longbows so far away; a typical Ahan woman, but taller and more slender than Lyka her looka-like, who had been of the voluptuous type that complemented the more heavyset men. Rowan wondered if beauty were something the Primordial Architects had selected for genetically in her people.

"Sírun, I don't need your service really, but maybe you could tell me the story of your life. It will help me to know your culture better. Please, if you don't mind, take a seat and we'll talk."

Sírun *of Sahmanayin Bay.*

Sírun nodded assent in the way servants do, and took a seat he held for her in one of the two armchairs that faced the tall glass doors that opened onto a vibrant green garden.

"Which part of the country," he asked and sat down, "are you from?"

"Master, I am from a fishing village on the eastern coast of the Inland Sea. It was very small, near where the old town of Arratadzerrnut'yun used to be, on the Bay of Sahmanayin."

"Please, don't call me master. It's a title that recalls bad memories. You can call me Rowan. I've only seen the Inland Sea from a distance. What happened there?"

Sírun bowed her head in deference, but replied, "Excuse me, I am to address you as Sir Rowan as an alternative with your permission, as instructed by Queen Havasarakshrrut'yuny herself. But yes, my village, in fact the town and nearly the entire bay area was swarmed by refugees who had escaped the destruction of their homelands in the west, those who could travel by water and allowed by the Unfinished to land on our shore. These were the Horn'd People, who had never heard of us. They are there still, but infest the cliff caves above the beaches, as they burnt our houses to the ground. They are a small, primitive rodent-like race, who usually walk on all four limbs. They feared our stature and white skin. We had no defences but fishing knives, axes, pitch forks and diggers, pruning shears, nets and oars. They are small but very quick, fight well in swarms and have sharp teeth and claws."

"And, I venture to guess," he said, "horns. Maybe eventually Aha Domain can reclaim the Bay of Sahmanayin."

"It could be done, Sir Rowan, and may one day, when the world is safe. Then we shall make sure they are repatriated to their homeland in the west. But for now we leave the Horn'd People alone, as they have nowhere else to go. The fish keep them content. They will not come anywhere near Castle Vale. It is too far for their little legs over the steep mountain passes. The rivers are too wild for their canoes, and there are waterfalls."

◆

The next morning Rowan had been invited by Nefer and Masudah to listen to the choir at work to test the throne room. Renovation work had been postponed for the duration of the session. The choir consisted of a hundred singers, women and men in equal numbers. No instruments accompanied. Nor was there a conductor, although one of them may have served that purpose telepathically, as their timing was perfect when their song began.

Whenever Rowan had heard the Ahan sing, his soul moved in ways he could not help but surrender to. Unlike before, this song in a sense destroyed objectivity. Only after it ended did he understand he had been listening in rapture. A power from beyond absorbed the singers, and he too had been swept along in the current and fused with it. A transcendent force that might be described as wholly good alone existed in that moment, a good with no opposite, the most faint of evil thoughts impossible within the range of its vibrations. How could there be, absent even of thoughts of the greatest good?

✦

Later the opportunity to speak at leisure to both Nefer and Masudah at the same time arose as they took their evening meal on a private balcony that overlooked Castle Vale. The sunset imparted a rich glow to the peaceful scene. The three friends watched the colours of the sky mutate.

Rowan asked, "What can you tell me of the witch called Aynt?"

The queen and her consort glanced at each other and spoke in unison, but the prince conceded to the queen, who answered, "Aynt is a black witch, they say. No one knows how old she is, but she has been a part of the folklore so long there are ancient fairy tales translated from Old Ahan with her as the main character. These stories are said to be from before the Sky Fathers last visited, two million years ago. For the most part, they are not flattering. But in one… perhaps Masudah knows more, but in one she was once a queen. Like all royalty, she had a flaw to maintain the Ahan balance. It is said her particular flaw in that lifetime was a tendency to secretly rejoice at the ill fortune of others."

Masudah added, "In other versions of the story that I have heard and read, she has a different flaw. In some it is the inability to empathize with those of lesser intelligence. In a word, snobbery. In others it is simply her bad table manners or lack of personal hygiene, sometimes poor grammar. These tales are obviously intended for children's ears. I tend to think that Aynt is too mysterious for anything but the most subtle intellect and is likely not what we think of as a person, that is, not like us, but not like a goddess either."

"So what is she? A demigoddess? Did she have anything to do with the current configuration of the Dome?" Rowan, unused to drinking wine, asked more than one question at a time of a monarch, just not done. Fortunately, Queen Havasarakshrrut'yuny remained Nefer.

"We do not know, do we, Masudah? We have never met her manifestation."

The prince frowned. "But I have heard her voice… in the throne room…"

Nefer quickly added, "As for the Dome, Brother Red Lion, I struggle with how it came to be. Your question intrigues me. Until now I did not know how to even think of the miracle. In an instant I awoke from my coma completely. I remember strange dreams, some. Also I remember visiting Masudah in the turret. He remembers me as if I were there. I only remember trying to make him feel better, but invisible and powerless."

"This is amazing to me, Nefer," Masudah said. "You were so sure of yourself. You assured me repeatedly that your time to act would come. Until then I should be patient and brave. But then… you tell the rest, Nefer."

"Well, now that you mention it, I may have met Aynt while not in my body, so to say, while in the coma under Gregor's spell. But here is the strange thing… until now I would have expected that she be an old hag, like the pictures in the storybooks. But I believe now she can take any form. I believe she came to me in the form of a little black cat."

"The cat remains," said Masudah. "But Aynt has gone."

"I've met her," said Rowan. "I've met Aynt."

"*Really?* Please, tell us, Brother Red Lion. Tell us what happened."

"I think Masudah's right. She's not like us, but not a goddess either. She called me her friend. And she was my friend, although at times I thought I was going to lose my mind when she shifted time or whatever you want to call it. But she promised to help me get home."

"As it is said, time is a construct," said Masudah. "In Khémia this construct is not considered only a subjective fantasy as is the case for many, but a work of true imaginative vision in the hands of a master. Perhaps Aynt is such a master. Please, tell us of Aynt."

Rowan recounted how he met the witch and their subsequent adventures together. "I'm not quite sure why she chose me," he added. "I don't remember asking for teachings. Maybe I just happened to be in the wrong place at the right time, on the pyre. She had profound, mysterious and paradoxical things to give to someone more qualified than me, that's for sure. I'm not even Ahan. Anyhow, I found her pretty terrifying, but the fear was my own mind's projection. At least I learnt that much. I got used to her a little. I even cracked a sarcastic joke that might have made her see me as of some use, so maybe I helped a bit. At least she thought it was hilarious and made me feel that I'd contributed. I believe, as I sensed at the beginning, that Aynt is a guardian spirit of the Ahan, whether they like it or not. She was proud the Dome was all their doing. But she's not going to hold their hands while they retool. She only corrects their course a little when they need it."

"Indeed," said Nefer. "I remember laughing when I suddenly knew how to raise the Dome as a shield against the Unfinished. It seemed to me already there in a way, but weaker than it could be. But how this came to me I do not know. I even wondered if perhaps the little cat had something to do with it. It had a great sense of humour, in its catlike way. And it could speak mind to mind, which I dismissed as an illusory lingering effect of the coma. Yet I did not appreciate who it might be until now. Gratitude, Brother Red Lion."

"You're very welcome. You know, I first saw her riding the giant vulture towards me. The last time I saw her she rode the giant vulture away from me. I want to see her again more than anything. I could even put up with that monstrous bird. At the same time I never want to see her again if it means another lesson."

XXIV
Rites *and* Whispers

THE CASTLE FELL again into an uproar. A visiting delegation, who wished to petition that their home county Karzún be guaranteed protection under the Dome, insisted on daily performance of rituals in their lodgings within the castle city complex. The Karzúno had not felt they needed permission; the fact that their particular interpretation of Anggh religion required blood sacrifices, according to the tradition they believed vital, should not be a problem, they said, as it was the Ahan way the Sky Fathers had established in the beginning.

The royal argument stated in no uncertain terms that the presence of blood outside a body interfered with the choir's work. Introduction of polluting vibrations into the castle environs due to the occult potency of it, the danger of a portal into the afterlife dimensions torn open through resonance, must not be permitted.

The Karzúnos' sole intention had been and remained appeasement of their god Anggh.

But the resultant interference patterns not only weakened the natural barrier between worlds, it slowed renovation of the throne room and the expansion of the amphitheatre. Reason demanded, said the queen's advocate, that concentration on those projects be the priority so that all of Aha Domain could benefit as soon as possible. Until then it was best to remain underground in most counties until the Dome had expanded, as was only fair to all.

Rowan took care to not let himself be seen in the attempt to observe the traditional Ahan blood rituals. He knew how to do that without resort to magic. Overcome by intense curiosity, rather than try to remote-view the rites, he wanted to breathe the same air as the practitioners, for one thing to find out if their incense might be psychoactive and in what way. Of course neither the queen nor her consort showed themselves. Since neither they nor he had been born Ahan, it may have stirred latent resentment, and moreover drawn attention to the use of blood as a sacrament. The prophecy of Queen Havasarakshrrut'yuny's coming to rule from beyond Ahan's borders was respected everywhere per the tradition, but her small size, black skin and foreign birth were nevertheless subjects of gossip. Her rumoured magical powers were exaggerated by some, doubted by others. Although all proclaimed her beautiful, to those who looked no further than the surface of things she remained all the same the opposite of the Ahan ideal.

Rowan discovered the Karzúno called the blood ritual Banishing P'vok'r Yeghbayr. They paraded an effigy of a reptilian into the large common room of their lodgings, and imbued it with all the evil in the land. They beat, tore, crushed and smeared it with the blood of a large snake. In their sect, the shaman's slippers never avoided the blood spilled on the floor. The shamans burnt the effigy on the altar to Anggh. A second ritual involved ritual dismemberment of the snake's corpse. It, along with an image on a scroll of a reptilian being crushed by a vulture's claws, the shamans also reduced to ash. Much chanting and an impassioned song ended the rite. The song of prayer to Anggh had been stirring, as always. It filled Rowan with feeling, as if the blood on the altar incited his body to move, but caused a gnawing dissatisfaction without a goal. He wanted to jump out of his skin. The inchoate energy only needed direction, a leader who would show the way to whatever unquestionable action necessity dictated. Rowan understood outcomes are best left to the universe, but regardless, at this moment he wanted nothing more than to give power of outcome away to a leader. The future leader would know what to do to put a merciful end to the demanding feeling –

"This is the difficulty with assumptions."

Rowan jumped and bumped his head on the balcony's balustrade behind which he lurked. His mane stood on end. Aynt had spoken into his left ear. She had not taken care to whisper.

The worshippers below emerged from their pious revery and as a group turned their heads towards the back of the room. The crowd of pale Karzúno faces looked up directly at him. And they filed up the stairways and surrounded his position in less than a thirty seconds.

"The foreigner, the felid, spies on us," the tallest man said. "The queen and her consort have no respect for the true tradition. How could they? They are foreigners too. They do not respect the Ahan way, so they send their spy. They do not trust us."

Another Karzúno, a woman, agreed: "So why should we trust them? We are Ahan, not they. We must leave the bunkers. It is too much to ask of us to stay in those dark damp places. It is sheer arrogance. Where else are we safe? Here, under the Dome. We should claim Castle Vale as our campsite."

A third Karzúno added: "Why stop there? The castle complex is large and can house many. Our elderly and lame need care under a proper roof."

While the delegates debated their options, Rowan slipped away. *Well, that was easy*, he thought. *These people are farmers and merchants, not warriors.*

✦

"Now I've done it, Masudah." Rowan sat down before the prince consort's desk, and added, "Curiosity killed the cat, to use an unfortunate expression. I've made your job, and Nefer's, all that much more difficult."

"Indeed," replied the prince, and the wings of his moustache pointed downwards. "But for Aynt it would be far less likely, however. It suggests it is ultimately to our benefit, this exposure of fear in our midst. We cannot tolerate it, not now. We must make every moment count to restore the Ahan power to its maximum. According to my calculations, what everyone wants is within reach. But they must be patient a little more. One moon at least. Then all Aha will have temporary shielding. We will then be ready to begin to test the amphitheatre's range, and with in addition the help of the Karzún region's most skilled artisans and singers."

"I take it they were thinking it over before I poked my nose in."

"You are correct, my friend."

"In my own defence," said Rowan, "and Anggh knows I need one, as you say, if not for Aynt the delegation would have been none the wiser."

"Perhaps it is best to neither be doubtful nor gullible when dealing with such a being as Aynt. She is not like us. In this age she displays the powers of an immortal goddess."

"I thought they had only the one, Anggh the vulture god."

"Officially it is monotheism. Aynt it seems had been rejected as a candidate for deity status long ages gone. It is said she abandoned the people to become a star in the heavens, a black one. Khémians too believe it is possible for a mortal to enter the realm of the gods and remain. This is in fact the ruler's only goal, whether king or queen, who sacrifices his or her Eorthely life for the sake of the people, thus vanishes from our prosaic existence up to the stars to become a star, a god… this is the most literal, how you say… exoteric understanding. For the esotericist, the nature of light is the key. 'Star' means high, brilliant, pure, a power beyond reach, eternal. Exoteric or esoteric, by these means the nation is blessed by the highest power. The rulers accumulate in numbers over the millennia, hence purify power through enlightenment, and are literally the exoteric measure of it by quantity, the esoteric by quality."

"Aynt's got star quality, definitely."

"But she is something else, this Aynt. If you are correct, Sir Rowan, she is a manifestation of the Ahan race, only a more defined one, its collective soul, its archetype, expressed in form, emaciated, however. She is formidable as a guardian, with little tolerance for ignorance of the law. She only interferes when absolutely necessary. Otherwise the people never learn."

"Masudah, I think we may be right about Aynt. Intervention was necessary. This somehow really will be ultimately to our benefit."

"Despite what I said, Sir Rowan, we must have faith… in ourselves. I say let us clarify our vision and deal with this before it demands more attention than it deserves."

"I'm impressed, Masudah. As an ex-priest, you're now more free than ever to be creative. What do you suggest we do?"

◆

"We mean no disrespect, *Khosnak* Pulvis," said Masudah to the delegation leader, spokesperson for the Karzúno. "Our friend and colleague Sir Rowan Berry Longbow acted on his own, we assure you." He looked to Rowan, who nodded confirmation. "We beg you to consider," he continued. "If you can remain patient through the cycle of only one more moon, we will be in a much better position to support one another."

"It is with humble intentions that we come here, consort," Pulvis replied, a middle-aged woman of the voluptuous variety with a very serious demeanour. "But you must understand that we would not petition if it were not extremely important. We have no faith in your clever machine. We know nothing of these modern ways, so unspiritual, nothing like the tradition. You foreigners force us to use our singing voices for speech! Faint praise is paid to Anggh. The way you people speak of His Most Holiness, He is a figment of our imagination. But He is as real as you or me. He attends every sky burial faithfully. All He asks of us is to conform to His will by sacrifice so that He can perform His sacred work, to bear our souls to the paradise of Drakht. We must obey. We must pay our way to heaven. I sorrow for the personal inconvenience to you, but we insist."

"Of course," said the prince in a pleasantly modulated tone, "we understand your situation and empathize. Try to understand that it is your hearts you must open to Anggh, but not by literally spilling blood. This is nothing to do with spirituality, which is by definition beyond the, how you say… corporeal, the gross body. But this is no time to debate theology. We must be practical. Yes, we have repelled the Unfinished, temporarily, and by the way according to tradition, but with songs newly designed for the purpose. Now we must expand our ability and reinforce it while we have the opportunity. This is what Khémia has to contribute, new knowledge to enhance Ahan tradition. We must work together while the window is still open. But, Khosnak Pulvis, it *will* close."

The impassive *khosnak* studied Masudah's brown face. She stood only three inches taller, but her pale eyes stared down as if from the moon. "Now I am glad this has happened, this intrusion," she said, and glanced at Rowan. "It reveals the bankruptcy of the leadership. You, consort, speak for Khémia, but we have it on reliable authority that you are in exile, an outcast, deported on charges of inappropriate and immoral behaviour while on a diplomatic mission. I speak of your child bride. Our tradition reviles lechery, prophecy or not. You do not speak for us, not you, a failed priest of a foreign religion. I have decided. We will speak to the people through the council, of which I am Karzún's representative."

◆

"*Oh! How could you!*" Queen Havasarakshrrut'yuny's face took on the red tint of rage. Because of her very dark skin, it showed most fiercely through the glare of black fiery eyes and clenched little fists. "You should have consulted me before saying anything," she said, "or even acknowledging the delegation. You had *no* authority unless I granted it. Now I cannot prevent a confrontation when I had hoped to assuage them less formally. Now I cannot avoid the council's ire, who will be required to debate an issue relegated to the primitive past. The Karzúno understand this. You, Sir Rowan, I had expected better of than indulgence of curiosity in such perilous times. And of *you*, Masudah, the royal consort, once a respected diplomat, I would have expected at least common sense!"

Rowan and Masudah stood before Nefer in the barrel-vaulted office of the royal chambers, eyes averted and hands clasped behind their backs. She glared at them from atop her huge ornate Ahan desk, feet set apart and fists on her hips when she was not pacing back and forth. She need not have stood so high; Rowan expected Masudah felt as low as he already did, likely lower.

"*Now get out of my sight,*" she shouted, "so that I can think of how to save the situation. *If possible!* It is only because you blame Aynt, Sir Rowan, that I even consider not banning you from the castle. If Aynt has intervened, it is for good reason. But, I insist, we do not need Aynt, Anggh or anyone to save us. She need not have interfered. We can save ourselves. That is the true Ahan way, if they but see it that way, *no thanks to you two!*"

Outside now, as they exited the office antechamber, Rowan exhaled and asked Masudah, "Did I really blame Aynt?"

"I do not remember that you did, Sir Rowan. But you had to inform Nefer… you had to inform Her Royal Highness of the facts. You were only presenting all the information."

"I wish I didn't need to defend myself at all. I made a mistake, but must accept the cost. If the queen throws me out… I deserve it."

"No, my friend, do not think this way. I am shocked by how hot-tempered my Nefer can be as well, but this is her fiery nature. She is young, still very much a wild thing. Perhaps I too have much to learn, despite the grey hairs of late. Perhaps I feel I must act the daring lad to deserve my royal young bride. Ah, life is for learning. But we must adapt like true warriors, how you say… take it on the chin, not so?"

◆

"Sírun, have you any news of Queen Havasarakshrrut'yuny's meeting with the visiting delegation from Karzún?" His young attendant had just surprised him with mid-morning tea, an unaccustomed luxury.

She spoke vocally, in Common Tongue: "Yes, Sir Rowan. She has already met with the Karzúno khosnak and the council and more meetings are planned. Whether they will be permitted to safely camp in the vale is undecided as far as I know. It is rumoured the council is divided and there is now a legal debate."

"Please, join me for tea. Tell me more."

Sírun remained standing, nearly at attention. "Apologies, Sir Rowan, but I must decline. If my superiors knew of it my reputation would suffer."

"I thought your superior was the queen."

"Yes, at the queen's request I am your personal attendant, it is true." Sírun shifted her feet and cleared her throat. "But off duty… I mean it would make things difficult for me when away from my post."

"Really? How so?"

"Well… I am of low status, a refugee from an impoverished region who must prove herself to retain residency in the castle. Whom I speak of as my superiors are castle-born and have the most influence. And there is always gossip. One in particular presses me for details. In fact he would like nothing better than I take tea with you. I only wish to do my work, not act as a spy. Nor have I aptitude as a courtesan. They tell me I can learn, but I am not like that. It is not wise for us to converse casually, in my opinion, sir. I only report your mood as vaguely as I can so as not to lose my position. I only wish to be neutral, not compliant. I do not mean with respect to your orders, sir, of course."

"I see. Of course I don't want to create trouble for you, Sírun. Thank you. You may go."

"Gratitude, Sir Rowan, but… to be clear, I need this work. And if I may say, if you let me go, the queen may not be offended, but it would be a great setback, as I have no home to return to should I fail to succeed here."

"No worries, Sírun, I don't feel I need a servant, but please keep your job. And I respect your wishes. Gossip can be extremely destructive. And I appreciate your honesty. It will be strictly business between us… and please bring tea twice daily from now on."

Whilst brooding on what the news meant and who among the aristocrats might be Sírun's social harasser, a knock came at Rowan's study door. She had let Masudah in –

"Sir Rowan, I have news you must hear immediately."

"Come in, Masudah. I'm all ears."

"Have you already heard anything, my friend?"

"What I hear from Sírun isn't encouraging, but I don't want to involve her any further. It might become a problem."

"Yes, it appears so. Anyone who is close to the queen is now suspect. Some are subject to persuasion to take sides. It seems the civil war is not yet put to rest. But perhaps it is, how you say… a storm in a teacup. One hopes."

"But what's this about a legal debate?"

"Yes," replied Masudah, "the prophecy is the case. It is questioned by Pulvis and her party. She has not declared it, but I speculate that she intends to legally slow Nefer to a standstill to make her look incompetent. This is very dangerous, in my opinion, but I am but a lowly consort."

"Now, Masudah, Nefer calls you a prince at times, at least when she's in a good mood, which is always. Well, except for that one time. To use your words, do not think this way. I too am determined not to speak self-defeating words anymore… as I was taught as a commando."

"Ah, yes, you are right, Sir Rowan. We cannot afford it. Here is how I understand the situation: for a long time the land of the Ahan was a unity, hardly avoidable in a telepathic species. They had no explicit laws until recently. By 'recently' I mean the past three centuries. Their natural inclination was to accord with natural law, so none were needed. As I understand it, the Apep, what they call now the Unfinished, are a manifestation of a negative influence that has slowly infiltrated the Ahan world by, how you say… osmosis, that is, psychic osmosis. Thus they have a rudimentary legal system that is enforced by a military class, established when other races became dimly aware of the mythical Ahan and envied them by making them the subject of superstition, either as superior beings or in possession of treasure that could be exploited. The system grew into a monarchy, the king or queen a ceremonial figure, a symbol, however, with little real power, but meant to separate state from religious authority. To ensure that it remained balanced, the tradition of the Oracle was instated. A caste system developed, at first a natural one based on the gifts and talents of individuals, especially defenders. Later, castes became inherited as the pernicious influence spread. The Ahan leadership thought it too trivial to investigate, and things deteriorated unchecked. Their ideals hardened into the fundamentalist inter-pretations of the religion of Anggh. They nearly became fossilized in some sects. Of course a fossil is not the original, only an imprint, the original form replaced with, in this case, unquestioned and, how you say… sacrosanct materials. As an ex-priest, this interests me and is not a problem. Any religion I know of contains seeds of wisdom, otherwise it is of no use and will not survive the travails of life. Yet it is strange how the mind can take the symbols literally, such as blood, thus we do not explore their deeper meanings. If we do, we find common ground."

"I have to remind myself that it's all down to Aynt," said Rowan. "This is her doing really."

"Alas, my knowledge of such beings is limited. I can think of no Khémian myth to offer that may shed light on her mystery. This recent act of hers seems very much trickster-like."

"I remind you," said Rowan, "that you advised that we should make no assumptions when it comes to Aynt… in case Stormbringer is on your mind."

"Ah, who was that Masudah? He sounds like a wise man." The prince shook his head. "But here is something else I have been thinking about: the Ahan are telepathic and usually only use the voice for song. Their belief is that music in that form has the most power on the Eorthe plane, more than telepathy… the coherent vibrations have physical effects and literally restructure the world if performed correctly. To them it is a superior physics. Language, although closer to the intellect, especially spoken telepathically, is secondary and supportive of song for this, how you say… coherency. But recently I have heard voices whisper in Old Ahan. Yes, vocally. At first I thought my ears deceived me. But no."

"What does it mean, Masudah?"

"I think it is a form of black magic. I cannot tell whether these are spells, but if so I fear they may be a devolved form of song, the sorcery of manipulation."

Rowan considered. "Maybe Gregor and Azniv weren't the only shamans to be terrified into such practices."

"It may be that I as consort am their target. Perhaps I am meant to hear the spells audibly for some reason, perhaps to instil fear. I cannot tell who among

171

the Ahan are the whisperers. You must likewise take care, Sir Rowan. I have told of this to Nefer, and she agrees."

"Will do, Masudah. Any tips? Obviously your songs work to repel anything negative, what I'm calling the sorcery of giving the universe a shot."

The prince chuckled. "Indeed. I would have thought so too, Sir Rowan. Now I am not so sure. When in the field of the choir, I believe we are safe from all harm. Yet this may be naive. Yes, our new songs are extremely effective against the fire from the sky, the Apep's most powerful weapon. At least until they adapt. And yet the simplistic doubt of a fundamentalist sect has brought our work to a halt. Some Ahan faction may be taking advantage of this to work more subtle effects. All I can suggest is your obsidian pendant to armour the body-mind. Alas, the gods and goddesses of Khémia may not have jurisdiction in Aha."

"But aren't they universal principles, potentials that acquire specific cultural forms wherever necessary?" asked Rowan. "It seems to me these godlike beings are identical, but it might be more complicated than that… paradoxical. In fact I don't think appealing to Anggh could do us much good, since we're not from around here. But I may have one advantage, Masudah. I'm going to try to contact Aynt. I'm not sure how that's done, but since this mayhem is a result of her influence, maybe I can appeal for help as a friend."

"I wish you good fortune with that, Sir Rowan. You are a brave man to invite such power, but let me notify Nefer beforehand. We do not wish her wrath to descend upon our heads a second time. That was a painful lesson. And one hopes contact does not require being nearly burnt at the stake this time."

XXV
Invocation

WITH THE QUEEN'S approval, Rowan had sole access to the largest courtyard, but only late at night when vacant. He looked out over the dark vale from the parapet where he had stood with Aynt before. Moonlight illumined the scene at times when the cold murmur of the breeze parted the clouds. He tried to think of nothing but the old sorceress, yet his eye nevertheless wandered repeatedly to the high place where rested Lyka's skeleton. The peak above the crag like a knife tore at the clouds just there. And regret pierced like a persistent blade from within at each heartbeat –

"Awaken, open your eyes, my young friend. I am here."

Rowan flinched and shivered – he had fallen asleep standing up. His gaze darted, but sensed no one, except there – in the shadows – the moon briefly passed over a rift in the clouds and revealed his own form sound asleep hunched in the doorway. The cloud returned, and he stared at the after-image of the familiar stranger –

"The body-mind-sense complex is your equipment here on Eorthe," she said. "It is a fine specimen. You do well not to abuse it with weeping overmuch for what can never again be."

"Aynt…"

"It is I."

"Am I weeping? I must have eyes, but tears… there are none. I can see, but it's all clouds and shadows."

"You gaze into a mirror, my young friend, through tears, projections of mind. Wait, watch and you will discover much behind the sad mask you wear. You will discover the unknown, yourself."

"But… I am myself."

"Precisely."

Rowan decided that he had better prepare himself, whatever he was, for another lesson. He had asked for something, but did not remember what. Yet here came the answer: a pit of crushing despair. The memory of Lyka grew overwhelming, fused with vague memories of his mother and father, Blue, and Samarit. "If this is a mask, how do I remove it?"

"It is removed."

"It doesn't *feel* removed."

"Should it?"

"I just want to feel... less heavy."

"Do not resist. What you seek is hidden by your seeking. Let go."

Free fall. The wind rushed in a gale from below, he plummeted into the dim void, grasped at nothing and tumbled head over heels in the grip of non-stop gravity. Down and down and endlessly down he fell – he must give way to the inevitable – but it did not come. Defeated, he released his stranglehold on life a little, resigned to his fate should it come now or later. *This is the end* – a reddish glow below like lava brightened in ever larger flashes – sharp spikes and spires of rock transformed in spasms and agonies of sparks into magma, a roiling, boiling sea of molten death rose to meet him at an unbelievable speed that dragged on *forever* – he only wanted it to end, and surrendered utterly –

✦

With a start he awoke – but with a memory of looking at himself sitting in this very doorway that opened onto the parapet. Up above, the moon appeared to race across the sky, an illusion caused by the clouds torn by the wind, which triggered an avalanche of other memories of this night. He jumped to his feet, teeth clenched, and his mind cried out: "Aynt!"

"No need to shout, my young friend."

Rowan spun about – alone on the parapet. No one in the courtyard – but Aynt's voice – at the exact point between his ears. "I'm sorry, Aynt," he replied. "Obviously I'm not the sorcerer's apprentice type. You know, these teachings or whatever they are... there's no word for them."

"I *am* disappointed," she said. "How about 'interesting'?"

"Well, if I were a poet I'd think of something... but now I remember why I asked you to come, in my inept way..."

"Skill is not the issue, I assure you. Do you think I appear at the summons of any mortal? You are my friend. I am here for you."

"Believe me, I'm grateful, even though I had to nearly die a thousand deaths in that caldera just now... that was worse than the big bird."

"How do you know you did not? Look up."

Through the holes in the cloud cover, the silhouette of the giant vulture raced across a backdrop of stars – but no, it hovered in position, another illusion caused by the wind in the clouds. "Oh no... are we going for another ride?"

"My young friend, I thought you would never ask."

✦

174

"I see Nefer. She's with Masudah." Rowan's inner eye closed, his outer eyes opened, and he looked out over the Inland Sea from his seat on the familiar rocky ledge. On such a bright day, pleasure in the majestic vista of sun, open water and sky should have been restorative and very welcome. But not today.

"Very good," said Aynt.

Rowan remained silent. His eyes refused to close. His heart smoked.

"Look again, my young friend, fear not. I have said nothing is what it seems. That is never more true than at this moment."

"It was all for nothing," he groaned. "We're doomed."

"A projection of mind, Sir Rowan. This is a gift."

"How can what I just saw be a gift? Was Lyka a gift? Was Blue a gift? But you don't know them."

"I know you," said Aynt.

Rowan stood up and walked the few steps to the edge of their viewpoint. The warmed air rising up the cliff face gently caressed his face and tugged at his mane. Vertigo filled his body when he looked down the couple of thousand feet of sheer drop, the only obstacle to letting his "equipment" fall to its death. He leaned into the breeze and looked down. There would be a fiery explosion of fear, then the pain would end –

"*No, kitty baby. Don't leave me. Come home.*"

Rowan stepped back from the edge and spun around at the same time – no one there, not even Aynt. But something had changed. He sat down on the ledge and stared at his feet.

"This is good advice," said Aynt from beside him. Her strong warm arm wrapped his shoulders. "Go to where the heart is."

With Samarit's voice still fresh in his mind, he closed his eyes to focus. But she had vanished.

Only Nefer's and Masudah's remains – instead of their heads bowed in surrender to the flames, lashed to the stake back to back, their skeletons now hung loosely chained to it, and dropped bone by bone into the fire. Sparks leapt into the night.

Behind their kite shields the Ahan guards held to repel the heat, the fanatics' pale eyes stared out of the gloom at what they had done. Hope had fled, but passion stayed, reckless and futile. The winged sigil of Anggh in black on a blood-red field glittered as the fire's reflections writhed in the steel shields.

"Your power is to wait," Aynt said.

He nodded assent. "I'm going away now. I did my best."

"That is all," Aynt agreed, "anyone can ever do."

"You said you would help me get home. I won't hold you to it. I haven't held up my end of the bargain."

"There is no right and wrong for a free being," she replied. "There is only knowledge or ignorance of cosmic law." Aynt tugged on the red tuft on his chin with her free hand. "It is my function to guide the Ahan. My young friend, have I failed?"

Rowan did not know how to answer. If such a powerful being could fail, only the prospect remained of a similar fate for Samarit and the Longbows: immolation at the hands of the reptilians.

Aynt stepped to his side. Her shadow touched his feet. "Come," she said. "On the last day of the world plant a tree."

◆

From the back of the giant vulture, Rowan dared to look through the voids raked from the cloud cover below by the cold wind that filled the night. The queendom of Aha beneath remained dark. Aynt did not pilot. Nor did he. Alone he rode in trust that the big bird knew the way. The clouds enveloped them completely, altitude impossible to judge, but they might be on a long slide down a spiral. They broke through the canopy of dense mist at last – the big vulture could have touched the castle spires with its wing tips. The giant creature hovered mid-air instead, flapped its huge pinions above the main courtyard and scattered the people below. They had encircled a makeshift witch pyre, having thrown a torch onto the kindling. In the growing fire's light abandoned kite shields reflected orange and yellow flames in their metal –

More than anything Rowan wanted to leap from the big bird's back, but at a height of more than fifty feet, he could only agonize over the danger gaining on Nefer and Masudah even without the vulture's fanning of the flames.

Nefer looked into his eyes, her mouth open pink but speechless.

Masudah could only twist his neck to try to see, as he had been lashed with chains to the stake behind her.

The vulture dropped in altitude.

Rowan dived. He rolled to a stop before the flames, leapt across and tore at the relentless chains. With no time to waste, he forced his arms between the bodies of his friends and the stake and lifted with all his brawn. All three fell across the logs and partially out of the growing fire. Rowan pushed the weight of the stake and the two bodies attached upwards and away to relative safety. He too rolled several times, enough to snuff the licks of flame on his smoky body.

176

The pain seared hot as he stumbled to one of the reflecting pools that bordered the courtyard, where he snuffed the hissing smoke from his charred form, and lay on his back in the ripples of shallow black water.

The giant vulture hovered, and its huge wings wafted draughts of cold air over the scene. Its red-rimmed gaze fell on him, but it turned its huge head to the side, and prepared to ascend.

Aynt astride its back, her long white hair blown in the wind, gazed down at him too, typically Ahan without expression, but she winked and saluted.

A powerful downstroke splashed water in his face, and Rowan watched the giant vulture's wings take her higher and higher until they passed through a hole in the clouds that closed after them.

He rolled to his side to rise from the water to his friends' aid – too late.

Sírun snapped the chains with a bolt cutter. Aided by a first-aid kit, she attended to the royals' cuts and bruises from their amazing rescue, and burns inflicted by the hot steel chains.

Doors opened, as did shutters on windows, which permitted Ahan eyes to see and Ahan minds to clear. *"Anggh!"* The entire castle shouted: *"Anggh has spoken! Anggh has spoken! Long live Queen Havasarakshrrut'yuny! Long live Prince Masudah!"*

          ✦

"We do not mind that you have no hair, Brother Red Lion. It is beautiful. It means we are alive. I means there is hope for the Ahan. It means there is hope for the world."

"And thanks to my suggestions," added Masudah, "which for some reason are not only listened to politely now but implemented, the burns will heal soon. Those commando boots saved your feet. They are but a little scuffed and singed. The royal cobbler is studying how they are made while she repairs them to as-new condition as well as is possible without nanoid recharge."

"Please thank the cobbler for me." Inch by inch Rowan sat up in his bed in the castle infirmary so as to study his face in a hand mirror. "It could have been so much worse," he said. The loss of his chin tuft, elegant whiskers and eyebrows was not the worst; with the remains of his red mane shaved, his blackened felid ears stuck out for all the world to see, but he said, "You look pretty good yourselves, considering… Your Highnesses… do I really have to call you that? It's a bit sibilant."

Nefer's white bandages stood out stark against her lustrous black skin. "It is we who should call you that," she said, "as you came from on high to save us." Her pink lips smiled and revealed perfect white teeth. "You may call us whatever you wish. Do you agree, my prince?"

Masudah's intact moustaches spread their wings. "I still cannot get used to this title 'prince.' But if one am I, it is a singular blessing to be consort to Her Majesty. But yes, Sir Rowan, my name is yours to give."

"Well then, I might as well call you Prince Masudah too, and Queen Nefer. I probably don't need to ask how you came so close to meeting Anggh in person. But if there's one thing Aynt taught me, it's not to make assumptions."

The royals glanced at each other. Nefer spoke first, her countenance solemn: "It was Anggh who brought our saviour to us. I met his eyes as he hung above the pyre. His voice was in my mind. He asked if I should live or die. My answer was to ask if Aha Domain should live or die. The flames grew higher. But Anggh nodded, as if to say Aha should fulfil its destiny. Then his voice spoke once more. He said it should meet its fate on the path it took to avoid it."

Prince Masudah added, "Then behold, there flew Sir Rowan down from the skies. I imagined I had already crossed over into the underworld, soon to have my heart weighed in the scales. It was too amazing to be real. Ah, it is no wonder I am an ex-priest. There at the threshold of doom my faith was weak. It was not until my hard head hit the flagstones upon being yanked from the flames that I awoke to find myself in this world, alive."

Rowan chuckled. "Well, I wouldn't call it flying exactly. It was more like a barely controlled fall. There was no time to try to coax the big bird any lower. Come to think of it, maybe it's mortal after all. It might have not wanted to lose any feathers to the flames."

"You remember, Brother Red Lion, that my prince had told you of the argument with the council, especially of the cult leader, Pulvis the Karzúno khosnak. I was ready to agree to many of her demands, and without reference to the prophecy, only because it was humane. They would camp in the vale, despite the envy of other counties, which I would leave to her to convince that it was just. The infirmary would be at their disposal. Look around you. Most of the patients cared for here are from Karzún. More are coming. When you are well enough to look, you will see their tents and their campfires, their children above ground and yet safe, safe for now, we sincerely hope. We still have much work to do. And we must make up for lost time."

"Pulvis, I am sorry to say, will be exiled," said the prince. "The ex-khosnak was permitted by the tribunal to return to Karzún, but stripped of her rank."

"But she got them what they wanted, didn't she?"

"She did, but they now fear the risk she exposed them to, a tear in the veil between Eorthe and the afterlife. They believe she is a black witch in secret. I tell you, superstition is alive and well in Karzún! But she is proud. Also afraid, I think, of what her tribe would do to her. Some would shun her the rest of her days, and thereby split their unity into two factions, as others are grateful to her. Perhaps she believes it is better to be a martyr to her faith, to give her own blood to Anggh to strengthen the cult. She has demanded instead to be taken over the passes to the Inland Sea. The company of guards, some from Karzún, will watch as she descends the pass to the Bay of Sahmanayin."

Rowan frowned. "But Sírun told me her territory had been invaded by a species called the Horn'd People. They sound mighty nasty the way she tells it."

"It is true, they are most unpleasant, Sir Rowan," agreed the prince, "little better than animals. Unlike beasts, however, they are just intelligent enough to be extremely dangerous. At least animals do not kill for pleasure and exploit their environment's resources until they are depleted, after which the weak among the Horn'd simply die off. If times are hard, cannibalism is not unheard of. This is their way. Apparently this is another of the Genitors' practical jokes. But we live and let live for the time being."

"Ah," said the queen, with a sunny smile, "here is Sírun now."

The young servant bowed to each of the royals, and to Rowan.

"Sírun, my dear," said Nefer, "it is good to follow protocol when my subjects are present, but from now on I hope you will call us your friends."

The young woman's voice caught in her throat. Her large blue eyes even grew moist, most unusual for an Ahan, that is, to display emotion at all, at least as far as Rowan had noted. She looked down, with her palms pressed together, and murmured, "Gratitude, Your Highness. Gratitude, Prince Masudah. Gratitude, Sir Rowan. I only did my duty."

"When the entire castle did not!" Nefer pointed out. "But that is behind us now. We must only look ahead."

XXVI

Cure *and* Care

Under Masudah's direction, the healer Udarek in charge of Rowan's case experimented with a large and rare crystal fully a yard in length, very pure, until now housed in a museum. A dowsing expedition centuries earlier had found it in a mine not far from where Lyka's bones lay. Azniv had not followed through on his promise to give her a traditional sky burial. The council had agreed with the queen that she should be left just as Rowan had placed her.

Heavy with some exotic mineral, the crystal wand the old Ahan doctor wielded with authority, once Masudah convinced him it indeed could work wonders. After years of minor complaints, apparently the result of treating the ill without protecting his auric field properly, the healer said he felt reborn in its proximity. The traditional medicine of the land he also used to good effect: white gold elixir, along with a compound of special herbs to allow the skin to heal more quickly without scarring.

Rowan often ran his hand over his bare burnt skull. The prickles on his palm reminded him every time of his early youth in the orphanage. Back then, however, he at least had a fringe of mane around the exposed tattoo on his crown. He stroked his pate and evaluated his progress since those early days. When Sírun, who sat at his bedside for several hours each day, asked about the tattoo, he told her his story. As he spoke, he knew the little Syx person to be intact, although he believed he of course no longer identified with the boy. Free to investigate the lad's character, he discovered great love for his young and vulnerable self. And it interested him that he regarded Syx both as a parent would their child and the boy who became father to the man. But the injustice of the murder of his parents and the corruption of his sister Blue interfered with the contemplation, now that he had opened up a little to Sírun.

"Little Syx must have been a very beautiful child," she replied.

"I have no idea. There was no such thing as a mirror in the orphanage. No one else had green eyes, and the Heptas never mentioned it, so I didn't know even that much. In any case, we were convinced we were hideous and must not admire one another in any way. That was a sin. If any boy showed kindness, affection or sympathy, they were never seen again. Anggh only knows what happened to some of them. I only know others were beheaded even for minor infractions. When I think about it now... but it hardly bears thinking about."

"I sorrow for little Syx," said Sírun. "Would that I were his guardian. I would love him and care for him, and he would grow happy and strong, like Sir Rowan."

"You're very kind, Sírun." He gazed at her and took in her beauty, a trait she shared with most Ahan. They resembled one another more than other *sapiens* species, all of whom varied in appearance, except the reptilians. He saw Lyka in Sírun's face, yet a completely different person, with a unique vibration that defined her presence, which made the identical-twin resemblance quite secondary. "We can't be happy all the time," he said. "Right now I'm sad. When I look at you I see someone I cared for very much. She died. Sometimes we're weak too. Like me right now, an invalid."

"You see another? This makes *me* sad. I am me. I wish you to see Sírun. She sees you. She knows you. To her you are strong, and very, very brave. You came from the sky on the back of Anggh to save our queen and our prince! I never dreamt I would witness such an act. It will become a legend retold for thousands of years. I want to make you happy. What can I do?"

"You do so much already, thank you. Your visits are very welcome. But don't you have other things to do? I know it's your job, but I don't insist that you hang around. They take good care of me here."

"I have no other duties, and no one else to care for. My father and mother and brothers did their best to fend off the Horn'd. But I ran away... a coward."

"You? No. *No way*. You're the only one of all the Ahan who didn't sell out. You stood by ready to take care of Nefer, I mean Queen Havasarakshrrut'yuny, and Prince Masudah, right to the end. I couldn't help them at that point. I wanted to, but I was worse off than I thought. No, that was truly heroic, Sírun, to defy your so-called superior and the rest, to be a true and loyal friend. *You're* the wonder in this tale."

Sírun's eyes grew even softer. "It is you who are very kind, Sir Rowan. But the people... they do not think so. Before I was nobody. Now I am somebody. Yet they know I never said I agreed with them, silent because I feared ejection from my place here. Some envied my position. Some believed I was the queen's pet. Some said I was your lover. They called me worse names behind my back. Some wished me to be your pleasure girl so that I could divine your mind." Sírun sighed. "Sometimes I wish to go home to the simple life I once knew. It is hopeless and stupid." She looked down at her lap.

"Sírun, give me your hand... now, look at me. It's *not* hopeless. We have a power that we can grow. It's not stupid to want your life back. And you *will* get it back. It may not be in the exact form you prefer, that's all. A great sage once said that we can't step in the same river twice. I say the river flows on forever."

Sírun threw herself on Rowan's chest and wept, the second time he had seen an Ahan cry. Strong memories surfaced of Samarit too, who had also once soaked his vest with her tears.

•

"Nefer, I need your advice," said Rowan. "I may be in the worst trouble I've ever been in, believe it or not."

"You are a wise man, Brother Red Lion. I believe I know what is of concern, but it is good to ask. No one can be wise in all things."

"Thank you for that, but in my opinion, I've got a lot to learn. Even the best intentions can lead to the worst results."

"Your words are truth. I am happy to, so to say, leap to conclusions and bless you with wise counsel. But perhaps it is best for you first to speak."

Rowan studied Nefer, as beautiful as Sírun but in an opposite way: petite, black and a queen. Only their clothing was of similar Ahan style, apart from Nefer's royal vulture pendant. He decided to focus on the silver Anggh sigil, reminded of wise Aynt, but on second thought, it might be best not to be seen staring at the queen's chest. His gaze rose from the pendant to Nefer's dark eyes. "Well," he replied, "this is probably a dumb question… but could Sírun end up like Lyka?"

Nefer answered, "Every Ahan has the power to end their days if an inner psychic mechanism is triggered. It must be an extreme circumstance to enable the will to withdraw the life force from within. This is a gift, but it seems one of the Genitors' more dubious ones, perhaps an experiment as yet uncorrected. According to the ancient wisdom kept for millennia by the Waka, my clan of origin when I was called Thema, I would interpret it as a mistake. But who am I to judge? A Wakan is not qualified for this, and I am only a person in this world like any other man or woman. A queen, yes, but a public servant. It strikes me that Lyka and Sírun were quite different… only similar in that they were both orphaned in youth and came from humble backgrounds. Their looks differed but little, yet it was easy to tell them apart. I chose them as two of my closest helpers because of their obvious good character. They were wholesome, and without, you know… guile. I knew I could trust them. It remains the most important qualification.

"Lyka had a very difficult childhood, as you know. She was very fortunate to have been pawned off on the castle household. But I for one feel fortunate that I knew her. Yet she was bound to confront her lost loves eventually, and Anggh.

I did not see this in time, nor did Masudah. Sírun too lost her family. But she suffers from survivor's guilt. 'Why me?' This is how she thinks. 'Am I worthy?' She asks this and thus must prove herself. She feels she must be most virtuous to be accepted. This is her doubt. But I see your problem, Brother Red Lion. These women are fated to fall in love with what they have lost, to deeply desire to begin again and make it all better. It is gone, but now they see their hope before them, in a new form, but so kind, thus familiar. Add to that a handsome and heroic figure of a man… and they are lost."

Rowan would have raised his eyebrows if he had any. He rubbed his brow ridges instead. "Well, I don't know about the handsome part, crispy creature that I am… and I'm a reluctant hero, believe me. That's another thing Aynt taught me. Nefer, I'm glad I asked. Back in Perkona Ola you could've been a rich and famous celebrity psychologist or a self-help superstar. What should I do?"

Nefer chuckled. "Never flatter a queen unless she is vain. I think this is a funny idea. But as to what should be your action… this is difficult. I think one's attitude is most important. If it is correct, right action will spring from it naturally. I believe you have studied martial arts, not so?"

"Yes. I was trained in many disciplines to qualify as a League commando. Let me guess what you're going to say. In a dangerous situation, the last thing I should be wondering is what to do, distracted by my feelings. Right? I should be a data-gathering robot with every channel wide open and powered up to respond instantly to whatever the rule sets and master algorithm specifies."

"Sir Rowan! Is this how commandos of the League think? It seems to me much like the Unfinished would do. But it is something of a, you know… metaphor. I would say your attitude should be of the highest. Highest what? Awareness… of Sírun, of her life. She is not Lyka. Forget Lyka. No, I mean forget projection of one woman onto another one… this is a big mistake. Never forget Lyka. I will not."

"I could never forget Lyka. But I think I understand. The highest, most comprehensive awareness would include me, wouldn't it? So my attitude should be confidence that I understand whatever benefits everyone, I mean both Sírun and me, ultimately everyone."

"I told you, Brother Red Lion is a wise man."

"But I *don't* understand, not really. That's why I'm asking."

"You are an intuitive empath. Your challenge in life is to know where you end and others begin. This is not easy, as in truth there are no actual boundaries in oneness. This you understand instinctively. Yet in this world people are creatures of the mind, thus there appear to be strong divisions, unbridgeable distances. You did the right thing by drawing a boundary for Lyka. She did not *choose* to cross it, as she could not help herself. She knew not where her own limits were. But an empath's greatest challenge is to say no to carrying another's emotional weight for them. By nature you feel their pain, especially if you yourself hurt another… so you want to please them instead. But you *must* say no at times, always ready to walk away if necessary. You must do this for health, for the vulnerable inner child who was denied the opportunity to discover his boundaries. It may have been easier to appease Lyka's desire for wholeness, but it would have become insatiable; you would have become very unhappy not to be able to please her, and it would not have served the highest good. Her respect would have diminished and become bitter. We are here to grow up, to bear our own weight."

◆

Sírun looked exceptionally calm and composed at her next visit. She sat in the visitor's chair and gazed at Rowan, apparently content to let her eyes wander over his burnt and lightly stubbled features without comment.

Rowan wondered if he might be overly cautious. Maybe she was not a problem to be solved. Whatever the situation required would be the action he should choose. He must have faith in his instincts. Above all, his speech must be pure and from the heart. He would be wise to think before he spoke. "How are you, Sírun? You seem at peace."

"I am at peace, Sir Rowan." The young woman opened her eyes a little wider. "You have made me so."

"Oh… well, I don't know that I really had that much to do with it. Maybe you temporarily overlooked the truth. I only reminded you of it, that's all, you know, like a big brother."

Sírun looked into his eyes and held his gaze. "You are kind, not like my brothers. They teased me. They said I was ugly. They chased me away from their games. They said I was only a girl."

"That wasn't very nice of them. But they were only children, with a lot to learn. Maybe, if you let me, I can make up for that… a little."

Sírun peered at him. "You wish to be my brother, Sir Rowan? But… I do not understand. We are not children. We are grown. This is not a problem for me. Is it for you?"

"I… I see no problem." Rowan rubbed his palm over his head. "My friend Lyka, may I tell you about her?"

"You may, Sir Rowan. Lyka was my friend as well, my only friend. Until came you and the queen and the prince."

"Then you know how she died."

"Sir Rowan, do you wish to tell of how you feel? Do not be afraid of me. I love you very much. I cannot help it. No fear, no worry. My brothers made me learn inner strength."

"Listen… I don't want you to be Menak. *Promise* me you won't go down that road. Sírun, this is very important to me. You must not waste your life. You're a beautiful being and an exceptional woman. The world needs you. You can't fulfil your destiny as a hermit."

Sírun leaned over and took his hand. She gazed into his eyes and caressed his shaven head with her other hand. "My beautiful Sir Rowan. Such lovely green eyes. I will not be Menak." And she kissed him on the forehead.

·

Sleep did not come that night. The burnt flesh got the blame, got forgiven, then blamed again. By the time the dawn chorus of the forest of birds that surrounded the castle announced a new day, Rowan decided he must be as firm with Sírun as with any reptilian he might meet on the road. He must put a stop to her infatuation, but he could not simply use a plasma phaser in slice mode to lop off its head. Action was needed but skill was absent. But he could contemplate stoic principles. That might help. No matter what pleasures may be enjoyed, to a stoic, virtue is the only worthwhile quest, based on reason, not passion, and wisdom as the root of virtue. From it spring the cardinal virtues: insight, bravery, self-control and justice – a narrow, hard path, steep and often in twilight –

·

The now familiar silhouette before the tall window behind the visitor's chair evidenced that he had dozed off at last. "Hello…" he said. "Is it morning? How long have you been sitting there?"

"For some time, Sir Rowan. I watch over you while you sleep. You look so beautiful and full of peace. And I have time to knit. See?" She held up an incomplete woollen stocking, undyed but for the dark green reindeer motif at the collar. "Mouflon wool, for when your feet are healed."

"Right… Sírun, give me a moment to wake up. Then we must talk."

185

"We will talk, Sir Rowan. I have something to say to you. But please rest. I have nowhere else to be."

"You do? I mean… well, it's just that it seems to me you've become infatuated with me… there, I've said it. Do you know what that means?"

"I do. It means intense passion, not meant to last."

"And why do you think that is? Why doesn't it last?"

Sírun peered at him, and paused a moment. "Because the infatuated one does not know the object of their desire? Their desire is all they know, as they lack self-knowledge. But I know you, Sir Rowan. Nothing is hidden."

Rowan frowned and rubbed his eyes with his palms.

"Do you wish to sleep some more, Sir Rowan? It may be well if I first speak what I have to say."

"Well, sleep isn't easy. Please, feel free to tell me what it is then."

"I know you. It is very clear to me that your heart is elsewhere. When I reflect it within, it is warm and deep… but far away. There is someone there with you. There is little room for me."

"That's… true. I mean I do make room for you, Sírun, how could I not? But yes, there's someone. Are you hurt?"

"I am sad." She looked at the yarn caught in the crossfire of knitting needles in her lap. "But I promised to you I will not be Menak. Because you are my friend, and the queen is my friend, the prince also, I am proud to be a person of some importance at the castle. It is our friendship that makes it so, not the prestige. But there are Ahan men who look at me now with light in their eyes. Nothing is hidden, but since I know you, I know what is good and right. This is your gift to me, Sir Rowan, the one that was needed."

XXVII

Limina

"I⊤ WILL GROW, the hair, to its former glory. The scars, they will disappear. But you must not be too vigorous just yet. Come back to see me if you experience any difficulties." The old Ahan doctor, Udarek, returned to his duties after he had walked Rowan to the infirmary door.

Sírun took his arm, he barefoot and with a stout stave for support. "This is good news, no, Sir Rowan? Your beauty returns with increase, and you will soon be just as before, big and strong."

"Never flatter a commando unless he's vain. You're too kind, Sírun. I'm feeling a bit wobbly now and then. Your assistance is appreciated."

"But if it were not my duty I would be happy to do it still."

◆

They had made their way along the halls, galleries and staircases back to his rooms. Once through his doorway he discovered folded on a table a new outfit: a linen tunic and quilted woollen jacket and trousers. No typical Ahan footwear, however. But his League commando boots had been restored to good as new, although without means of recharge of their nanoids to full power; he estimated them at close to half that.

"You will leave us soon," Sírun said.

"What? There's so much to do and little time to do it in."

"It is said time is a 'construct,' Sir Rowan. I have come to know this word since I am at the castle. It means it is in the mind only, subjective. And what will be will be. This is how my mother spoke. Yet it is not merely Anggh's will and cannot be undone. If my mother were alive, I would say yes, and we must do our best, then wait to see what will be."

"You're kind and you're wise too, Sírun. I would add that whatever will be is to be accepted as a gift, however it turns out. Aynt taught me that. I have to remember it because I only want to go home, and it's so far away. Maybe that's what you sense. But I can't go home until I can bring something back that can save my people. Otherwise there *is* no home."

"Prince Consort Masudah says your home is with us… but you will go. I will miss Sir Rowan." She covered her face with her hands. "Oh… excuse me," she muttered, "I must go as well."

Before he knew it, the door closed behind her with a soft click of the latch. Rowan plodded across the room to the study. He threw himself into an armchair by the window, not without a wince.

◆

"Is it the hero's wounds or is it another that makes you brood, Sir Rowan?" Masudah had recovered well from his ordeal, his own only visible wound a small scar on one cheekbone, but he always wore a scarf around his neck now.

"People say I'm a hero, whatever that is. I only did what needed to be done… with a big boot in the rear from a witch and a lift from a giant vulture… and just in time too. I don't feel too battered now, just stiff. My hands hurt a bit. Mostly I'm wondering how to contact Sam. I've seen or heard her in hallucinations, but that was only Stormbringer's tricks or Aynt's influence. I've tried so many times by remote-viewing… why is it so vague and difficult?"

"There could be several reasons, Sir Rowan. Perhaps the fear of drawing attention to the Longbow clan, should the Unfinished intercept somehow. If distance is believed to be a factor, it will be a factor. Yet even the speed of light means nothing in the dimensions that make it possible. And of course… one hesitates to mention it, as it is least likely… you perhaps do not really want to contact Samarit Longbow."

Rowan's eyebrows would have raised, and moreover bristled, had they grown back yet. "That's ridiculous. Why on Eorthe would I not want to contact Sam?"

"Well, perhaps you do not want to know she may be in pain, but you are helpless. You may feel you should have stayed. Has Samarit contacted you?"

Rowan leaned on his staff, stunned. He looked away from Masudah to stare at the mist-enwrapped evergreen trees outside his windows. "Maybe she doesn't know how. Does she?"

"I think not. The Longbow clan, as far as one knows, had been assimilated by the League civilization to a large degree. They still preferred their traditional territories on or near the Surface, but many of their old ways had long been abandoned early on."

"They used to call it 'far-sight.' But she'd been officially trained at the military academy, probably better than I was. Was remote-viewing an elective course?"

"I do not know, Sir Rowan. I am a Khémian… *was* a Khémian. I believe if one enquired of an official at the time, it would have been be denied that they employed such suspiciously unscientific practices. Would she not have told you?"

"You're right. She would have told me." His shoulders slumped. "Am I starting to forget? How is that possible? Do you ever get tired of this constant arrival at a threshold and never crossing it?"

Masudah paused, but answered: "Perhaps I may be of service. I was successful before, when it was necessary to find where was Samarit held captive by Kirzaka, in that Apep stronghold, the… how you say…"

"Mudredd Vale. I'll never forget that vile name. Masudah, you've got to try. Please. It's been too long. I must know at least *something* of how the Longbows are doing!"

"How you say… easy does it, my friend. Of course I will help. But I must consult the queen beforehand. Anything that may affect our efforts already underway must be authorized."

✦

In the days that followed, Rowan paced, with the support of his stave, in front of the study's tall windows that overlooked his garden. Masudah had gained royal permission to experiment with the remote-viewing technique of which he had once been a master, but said he needed to requalify for it. This meant he had to train like a world-class athlete for a special event; otherwise, the results may be unreliable. His duties as overseer of the architecture of the amphitheatre were in the meantime not to suffer lack of attention or logical consequences would manifest when eventually the Unfinished returned to finish what they had started. Their secret agent Gregor had been liquidated, but they were not known to accept defeat, rather to fight to the death.

To distract himself from anxiety, Rowan tried to absorb his mind in study, a method that had worked before at times. Since the Ahan claimed to be the first astronomers, astronomy was the topic he chose. When on the fourth day Masudah visited Rowan's rooms, every surface had been littered with books and charts and artists' renderings. Both men remained standing.

"Sir Rowan, here is my report. I have done three sessions. I have been very cautious, as I believe I must provide to you the truth, just as I had done the first time when remotely viewing Samarit Longbow."

"For Anggh's sake, Masudah, what did you see?"

"Brace yourself. It is not good, Sir Rowan, I sorrow to say. But there is hope. I saw the Longbow clan in hiding, then on the move, then in hiding. It was as if the dragon ship played with them like a large predator, not hungry, and only tortures its prey. Perhaps it is a method of energy marination."

"How bad is it? Have they been decimated?"

"Yes, that is the word. I estimate approximately one in ten Wishbone Warren survivors is dead or injured from small-scale plasma fire from the Unfinished craft. That is my guess, based on their number when you last saw them. For defence, the Longbows have only rocket launchers, but the range of those weapons is of course short, if they even function now. Thus far no Unfinished have made ground-based attacks, nor need they do. They but land to feed on corpses died of fear, but do not ripen them as they prefer. It is only to strike terror into their victims, who are forced to watch."

"And Sam? What about Sam?"

"My friend, please do not be alarmed unnecessarily. Chieftain Samarit was one of the injured. I saw her in the vanguard, guiding the people, then a fine beam of white light shot straight down from the sky. In an instant the ground at her feet exploded. Splinters of rock have penetrated her armour, as it was only of leather. I believe that this attack was intended to injure, not kill. The dragon ship is perfectly capable of pinpointing to within a fraction of an inch its target, even analyzing the trajectory and compensating for the planet's speed of rotation, surface motion, wind velocity and electromagnetic field variations. The only hindrance to its accuracy is natural radiation of the surface composition due to uranium content. But it can widen its beam in a scatter pattern. Of course the Unfinisheds' space station can destroy many cubic miles of Surface if it desires."

"For Anggh's sake, man, how bad are the injuries?!"

"Peace, Sir Rowan, she is resting in care of other Longbows in a small cave. There is not room for everyone, but she is sheltered. I did not see Samarit awake, but I do not believe she is in a coma."

"Is she healing then? Or in danger?"

"I believe she is stable."

Rowan threw aside his stave, limped to the wardrobe and flung open the doors. "Sorry for yelling," he said, and grabbed his refurbished League commando boots, rushed to the edge of the bed and struggled to pull them on.

"Sir Rowan, you are not used to footwear. If you insist, I will assist. Here, allow me… there, now you push… good. But I beg you, Sir Rowan, do not rush off just yet. As you know, it is a very long way to find them. Moreover they are not now where you left them. You will travel faster if you heal a few more weeks."

"I appreciate your concern, Masudah, I really do. But by the sounds of it they may not have a few more days, let alone weeks. They may not outlast such torture. Just tell me where the natural portals are and I'll be fine." Rowan continued to struggle as Masudah helped him with the other boot. "*Ow…*"

"A true warrior, how you say… eats pain for breakfast."

"Well said. I've been getting soft lately."

"We here do not think it a dishonour! The legend of the hero Sir Rowan Berry Longbow descending from the heavens on the wings of Anggh himself to rescue Queen Havasarakshrrut'yuny and Prince Consort Masudah will live on forever in Aha Domain. The people had come to believe the black witch Aynt was only imagination, a fairy-story fantasy, never mind that Anggh could manifest as a giant vulture."

"If I hadn't been there, Masudah, I wouldn't believe it either. Look, I'm of no more use here. I've served my purpose. I can't just hang around now that I know Sam is… is disabled, temporarily." Rowan stood up. "Good. The boots are… acceptable. I'll get used to them. Now, how about those portals, where are they? Is there a map?"

"Ah, I sorrow to report there are no portals near. The only one, at the mountaintop lodges, is destroyed. The Ahan do have maps, which mark accurately other locations, although they do not use them anyhow, and they are just beyond their borders. For the direction you wish to travel, the nearest one is far along the Inland Sea and northwest. The Ahan border is the mountain range that is along that shore, but you must follow the water's edge and head west until you reach a strand that joins it to Fish Lake, a large body of water. Along that strand is a peninsula. You may traverse that region and head north or you can circle around the lake. That is where you will find a portal that will take you roughly one quarter of the distance, assuming you can make it functional. This will not be easy, as I will explain. You may have heard of the fishing town of Arratadzerrnut'yun. It used to be on the Bay of Sahmanayin along the eastern shore."

"A village near that town is where Sírun comes from," said Rowan. "Can I skirt by it? It's infested with the Horn'd. Or the cliff caves are."

"Alas, that is difficult, if one remembers correctly. But we should consult the maps if you insist on risking your limbs, if not your life. The location of the nearest portal is many leagues northwest of Sahmanayin, across uninhabited wastelands and unexplored territories, at least by the Ahan. Travel by water from Sahmanayin westwards would be ideal, but alas, the Unfinished make that impossible now."

✦

"Nefer, thank you for your concern. But I'm sure you understand. If I could be of further service here, I'd stay."

"No, Brother Red Lion, you would still go. But yes, I do understand. If we cannot persuade you to heal completely first, may Anggh bless your journey."

"Thank you, a lift on that big bird is probably the last thing I want, but it would speed things up. If Anggh shows up in that form to offer a ride, so be it. But it's up to Aynt, and Aha is her concern, not some wandering felid far from home. And may your Dome increase in power and eventually save everyone. Everyone except the Unfinished, that is. By the way, where's Sírun got to? I've not seen her since my release from the infirmary."

The queen's dark eyes opened wider. "I do hope she is not neglecting her duties." She looked to Masudah.

The prince shrugged his shoulders, and said, "I have not seen her either, Sir Rowan. But please, my friend, let me try once more to ask you to reconsider. What will you take home to the Longbows? You have come so far for so little, and yet if you stay you will learn much that will help them, just as it will help everyone. I know you will go, but I must ask."

"You're right… maybe I should've stayed with them, I don't know. I thought I was doing the right thing. But what's done is done. I have to go to Sam. I can't *not* go."

"My prince," said Nefer, "Brother Red Lion has saved us, thus saved the queendom so we can save the world. For this he has come. Now he must go. Perhaps Sírun… perhaps she is only unwilling to say farewell. This is the Menak way. It is one of the many reforms I have yet to make. But it will have to wait until Aha Domain is safe."

"But she promised…" Rowan frowned. "She *promised* me she would not do that. What's got into her? I don't get it."

"A woman's heart is not something to 'get,' Brother Red Lion. And let the Ahan be the Ahan. It is their way, at least until I can convince them otherwise on this issue or they convince me. But their beliefs are entrenched. What is more, I must understand them before I attempt any changes. And please remember, Sírun is not Lyka."

Lyka's name still evoked a pang.

✦

A great blessing: his plasma phaser and hand-held scanner remained intact. He breathed a great sigh of relief when they both powered up to nearly full strength when tested after placed in autumn sunlight for a few hours. He told Masudah it would have been reassuring to give these two pieces of League equipment thorough maintenance, but if there were any facilities for that left, they were certainly nowhere near this domain. For some reason the thought of Aynt came to mind. Superstition came easy, yet the possibility of her influence could not be discounted until he crossed Aha Domain's border.

"It is indeed a pity," agreed Masudah, "that there are no means to analyze the condition of your equipment, but you know, the Ahan believe that the technological science you value, as do I also to a degree now, is among a choice of many ways of interpretation of the cosmos. They think the League tools of measurement, mathematics, for example, are creations of the mind, however agreed upon by consensus, but neither absolute nor necessary. We basically agree on the theorem of incompleteness, the theory of relativity and the uncertainty principle, according to the official canon. It is necessary now to point out that they have somehow unknowingly lost the sacred yoke, and it is a struggle every day for me to argue my position. Yet I have much to share, and it is to be hoped there is enough time to prove my amphitheatre will not only enhance the Dome, but save all the world if ours is expanded and more pyramids are restored and new ones built to maintain its strength where the geology is conducive. But the Ahan must teach the world to sing also. That is their obligation, whether they wish to remain secluded or not."

After the heartfelt parting from his friends, Sírun not among them, the descent from the castle presented the first challenge. In a show of bravado he had handed his stave to Masudah to demonstrate fitness for the journey. Rather than the delivery elevator or even the ramp for wagons to the delivery gates, he even managed to move briskly all the way down the thousands of steps to the vale floor, as he knew people observed from the walls above. The offer of a squad of soldiers had been declined; best to travel alone so as not to attract attention from any watchers from the sky, despite the Dome, transparent after all.

He crossed to the vale's head, skirted the Karzúnos' encampment, and must now pass the wood where he had last spoken to Lyka, the last place he had seen her alive. Leaves no longer troubled the old elm's dead branches. He tried not to look at it, and kept his eye on the horizon. He drew near the narrow gap where he would enter the next valley, and something made his ears swivel – but it turned out to be only the rustle of autumn leaves on the ground. No wind crossed his path – perhaps a draught had passed through the wood. He told himself he had only been triggered by his revulsion at the concept of Menak. Soon it would be behind, then far behind. Soon he could rest when out of sight of the castle around the next bend. The pain of tread upon the relatively even ground of the vale floor did not ease as expected, in fact increased. He soldiered on.

But not for long. He must drop the weight of the rucksack for a while, within it the herbal medicines prescribed by Udarek, the old doctor. The painkilling edibles may help –

Awakened several hours later by a squirrel impatient with his presence, he lay beneath a tree dismayed to realize he had dozed off. Precious time had been wasted. He decided he must overcome any discomfort henceforward without medicine like a commando, not a gentleman of leisure. He clenched his teeth, faced the path ahead and step by step hurried towards Samarit and the Long-bows far, far away.

XXVIII
The Walking Stick

THE ELEVATION increased. So did discomfort. Progress he made, some, but too slow. Rowan only used the oral medicine when the day came to an end and the sky showed a few stars between the clouds. Tonight it grew completely overcast. Should it rain, he would be dry enough under the overhang of rock with a ledge at his feet that sloped enough to drain. As a precaution he studied the dim forest surrounds. But before he knew it, he fell deeply slumberous in a dimensionless state with only one object: bliss. He knew not how extremely pleasant it was until the nightmare began –

♦

The crowded cave: unlit except for three dim crystals; pervasive pain, oppressive and dull. It grew sharp if movement were attempted at all. In a word, unbearable. Airless and fetid, as shelter this dank hole had been a last resort. *Even if this is a lucid dream, I can't do anything. I may be only borrowing what Masudah told me he saw, and torturing myself into the bargain…*

♦

With a grunt he snapped back into his body. Every time this happened he could not tell if the vacant form, like an abandoned house absent of its landlord, but who had just returned and slammed the door behind him – perhaps he had just imagined himself back within the limits of his skin out of habit. He did not know. Maybe his body was "in" him, the non-local self, by nature free to experience any locus, not just the habitual body-mind-sense complex. He had neither Masudah nor Aynt to confirm it. As an empath, he *may* have felt what Samarit endured. Or he may have projected his own agony – whichever.

The noisy birds too impatient to wait for the grey light of predawn chirped and chattered, one here, one there, then many.

Meanwhile he pondered the powerlessness shown in the dream. What could he do when the vision of that cave became as unquestionable as the damp and cool forest glade he sat in now? Fortunately, he did not entertain gloom for long, thanks to commando training. These negative evaluations were useful only briefly and only to expose their self-defeating potential. If hidden, they could be dangerous, so self-knowledge was the key to victory. *My power is to wait.* What needed to be known would be known when it was needed and not before. All he need do now was attain calm and confidence, poised to act. *What will be will be* – be that as it may, the thought of Sírun's mother provoked another demon. Two demons before sunrise proved one too many, so he stood up through the pain and tried to stretch. The world spun for a moment, too soon a void –

◆

At first he thought somehow he had not left the castle yet. Less darkness made morning a possibility. Birds sang, called to their mates, who called back. His head hurt. Vision blurred. But he rested on something soft and warm. Wild roses – "What are *you* doing here?"

"My duty, Sir Rowan. No, do not sit up."

Her face upside down, she bent over his. Her long white plait brushed his cheek. A leather pouch of something cold sat on his forehead. Where she had found ice he did not know. But he did as instructed, relieved that she lived, a feeling that would have been more welcome if it had not clashed with another one. He could not describe it, however, so it remained confused, incoherent. He only knew it was not anger. "You must go back," he said. "I release you from your duty. I'm going to a place that's very dangerous. It's a long, long way from here. Anything that slows me down will have to be jettisoned… sorry."

"Do not fuss so. Drink this."

He closed his eyes and swallowed the bitter tea. Argument consumed too much energy. Soon the clouds thinned. The pale sun slanted through the mist and the world birthed a new day.

◆

"Well, I'm orders of magnitude better than a few hours ago." He stood without a wobble. The stiffness had decreased. "Look, I've got to get a move on. Now, like I said…"

She held forth his rucksack so that he could strap it on.

"Oh… thanks. Now…"

She handed him a newly cut walking stick, smooth to the touch and with the bark partially removed, which created an irregular and pleasing pattern of alternating blonde wood and brown rind at each end, in his grip just the right length and very strong but light in weight.

"This is nice," he said, and looked at her.

She stood with one hand on a hip, the perfect symmetry of her beautiful Ahan face cool and collected, and her braided plait with not a hair out of place. A light sparkled in her blue eyes, but restrained. She looked like she had just walked into the queen's office, ready, willing and able to begin a new day of service.

It really is remarkable, he thought, *how she's always so well turned out... even in the wilderness.*

"Sir Rowan," she said, and held his gaze, "if you wish to not waste time, please do not let your mind wander so. Come, the path is here." She turned and led the way along the ledge and out into the forest.

Not knowing how to object, since without her assistance he may have been delayed indefinitely or worse, he nonetheless followed her. "Sírun," he said, "you promised me you would not be Menak."

"I have not broken my promise to you, Sir Rowan."

"But Nefer, the queen... she gave me the impression that you had."

"She is more Ahan than the Ahan, but not born Ahan, pardon me for saying so. She is the best thing that has happened to us for centuries, but she is not Ahan. Not yet. She does not know our ways. She thinks of them as something to be repaired. She is right, but she as yet does not understand."

"Neither do I," he said. "But where have you been for the past, what... week?"

"Sir Rowan, one of the first things you said to me was my services were not necessary. Remember? By this I was hurt. All the same, I wished to serve. I had come a long way as a young girl, on this very path we walk, and grew to serve the queen. She chose me... and Lyka. It was a great honour to be trusted so. But you did not value her gift."

Rowan gasped, inwardly. "I apologize for that," he said. "I'm kind of a dunce at times, which is no excuse. It just seemed a bit luxurious and unnecessary. I'm used to being on my own and taking care of myself."

"But since I was not valued, and you did not want me, I took time to enquire into what was Menak really. I even went to the shaman. She made me sit very still for days. Then she examined my heart. I would not break my promise. I only wished to put Menak to rest."

"I see. Again, I was very concerned, as you might imagine. But it's not because I didn't want you. I mean..."

"She said I was not Menak. She said I was not suitable. She said my heart is for a great man. She said he is young, but he will grow to be like the Ahan of old."

Rowan did not know what to say. *My power is to wait.*

"Queen Havasarakshrrut'yuny *gave* me to you. I was to serve *you*, no one else. I think perhaps she believed I might heal the wound of Lyka gone. Instead I made it hurt all the more, no?"

"I really can't complain now that I know you're not Menak. But yes, it was worrisome for a while. To me a promise is a promise."

"You do not trust me? But I am your *friend*." She halted and turned to face him. "To me a friend is a friend." A golden sunbeam shone down from behind her and surrounded her bright hair in a kind of halo he had seen before.

He watched the crown of light, and said with care, "No more assumptions, I promise. Please forgive me. I'm a slow learner."

Sírun turned around and continued to walk, and always matched his pace without checking over her shoulder.

The sunlight pierced his eyes when she moved out of its path.

"Trust is not to be blind," she said. "It is to know the one you trust, to know their shadow and their light. You need not believe in their words, nor judge, only watch what they do, expecting nothing. It is then that you may trust."

◆

"It has been a long journey for you, Sir Rowan. We are near the summit now. Soon it will be downhill. Then we must be extremely wary."

"A long journey… and I've barely started. Sírun, I'm grateful for your help, how you got me going again with that tea you made…"

"The forest is home to medicines, Sir Rowan, if you know how to look. The bark of a tree and some choice fungus are to thank."

"Interesting. Anyhow, your firestone cuisine was wonderful. I'm in much better shape than when I left the castle. The medicine, the walking stick, finding the path without a map, everything…"

"No, Sir Rowan, do not say it. I will not go back to the castle." She turned away to carry onwards.

Rowan touched her arm.

She stopped.

And he said, "Look at me." He guided her to turn around, and placed his hands on her shoulders. "I want you to live, Sírun, and live well. Find your way to that young man who'll one day be like a noble Ahan of old." He looked into her limpid blue orbs and smiled with his eyes. "I'll be fine. You have no idea how dangerous this trip is. Even if it weren't for the unknowns, the knowns are daunting enough. I could not bear it if you were hurt in any way."

Sírun peered back. "I am given to you, Sir Rowan. In Aha, taking back what you have given is theft. But if you return a gift, you have offered the greatest insult. It can only be done with purpose to offend, the mark of a vile person. It is to show you wish your friend death, and your soul has lost its way. We have not had this conversation. I will tell no one of it."

"Only for now, Sírun. Until the beach is near. Right? Now, why did you say we had to be wary once we pass the summit? I can guess, but what do you think we'll encounter?"

"Of course we will confront the Horn'd People. Any impression that they are perhaps less dangerous because they are small creatures should be cast aside as foolish. The Horn'd are more like one creature with many bodies, like an ant hill or a bee hive. They have a queen. She is big… bigger than you… and very, very fat. She does not fish, hunt or raid. She makes the babies. I have seen her, when I was a young girl. The Horn'd creatures work together as one body. But each has its rank and its duty. One would not think so to look at them, as they are so ugly and dirty, and how they love to wallow in offal. In this they find beauty. It is their way."

"But they don't climb mountain passes?"

"No, they are lazy when they have enough to eat. The Inland Sea is full of fish. The forest is home to much game. The Horn'd People will be spread along the beach of the bay, mostly near the ghost town. They swarm in the caves of the cliffs. But they will have sentinels."

"It's said they have canoes or canoe scows, is that correct?"

"They will have many of both, big enough for the two of us because they fish in crews with nets the ones with three-fingered hands make from vines. There may be old Ahan fishing boats, none still waterproof. Their paddles they hide, but they are small for the little clawed hands of the two-legged; some have only one finger bone, others many. But proper Ahan paddles are not a problem for me."

"I see… well then, this end of the bay is supposed to be rimmed with these mountains all the way along it. There's nothing on my map, but do you know of a way to avoid the beach and travel north further inland?"

"No, Sir Rowan. There is no way unless we have much of a moon to walk up and down, up and down, zig and zag, if we want to go north and northwest. The beach is best and shortest. But we should stay on the water only until we are beyond range of the Horn'd. The danger of the Unfinished seeing us grows the longer we paddle. The route after by land has at least some shelter. Come."

The descent from the summit proved steep, which made Rowan reckon it less likely the Horn'd would be met on the path, yet he redoubled caution. By the end of the day he guessed they must be near the level of the beach. He smelled water. Another clue: an increasing number of skeletons hung from trees, Ahan skeletons, obviously, judged by their size and elongated skulls. Most were bare but some still wore rags of quilted wool hanging in shreds, as if they had been skinned, eaten and clothed again. Some lay as scattered bones on the ground. The scene looked all the more striking because the setting sun shone a golden spotlight on death filtered through the bare black branches of the dim deciduous forest in contrast with the living green of the cedars in the mix. As they stood and

Rowan *and* Sírun part company.

surveyed the grim scene, waves on the shore lapped in faint rhythm from below.

Sírun took his hand and gripped his forearm with her other, and gazed wide-eyed upon the evidence of genocide.

"You must go back now, Sírun. This is the end of the road for you. I'll go on alone. All I need from you now is where to find a paddle or an oar."

"You would never find it on your own, Sir Rowan."

"Just tell me. I'll be the one to decide that."

"No. You will die…" She nodded at the bones. "Like this."

He turned away from the skeletons and took both her hands. "I'm going to ask you nicely one more time. The next time I won't be so polite. Where can I find a paddle once I get down to the beach?"

Sírun glared up at him in silent defiance. She shook her head twice in quick succession.

Rowan released her hands. He handed her the walking stick.

Her eyes opened wider yet. She accepted the stick she had made – but whacked him hard on the shoulder with it.

The sting stung sharp, sharper than expected. His normally excellent reflexes had failed him. She was quick and strong, not one to be crossed. Hate burned in her eyes. He felt sure it was hate, worse than the sting.

The walking stick lay where she had dropped it. She turned away and with haste hiked back up the trail.

His eyes followed her retreat –

◆

In less than half an hour he glimpsed the beach dead ahead, a sandy stretch fairly wide. From his vantage point in a thicket, he spied on the remains of a village, likely Sírun's birthplace. Rowan steeled himself, not only against the Horn'd he may be forced to face, but against the guilt that threatened to suffuse everything. But he could not let it hinder his progress. He had to draw a boundary, for her own good as Nefer had advised. Yet he could not stop himself from looking back up the trail, in the direction from which they had come. But Sírun had gone.

◆

Night fell. No one had said whether the Horn'd were nocturnal creatures. And Rowan had not thought to ask. He gambled that cover of darkness trumped the bright light of day, and limped across the sand to the ruins of the Ahan village.

Only one structure still stood, somewhat. And possibly contained the needed paddle. Plenty of canoes beached in the distance, but no fires burned on the sandy boundary of land and water. He extended attention in a widened sphere: no Horn'd presence, all appeared calm. The breakers on the beach languidly whispered tranquility, no doubt a blatant lie.

In silence he moved towards the salt-air-weathered unpainted wooden hut, and found himself before its half-open door. He listened. Nothing. He pushed it open further to the creak of dry old wood, and made out a dim still figure in the shadows, too large to be Horn'd. Nor could it be their queen – she would be well protected in a cave. And the stench of death here – his vision adjusted – Pulvis. This, rather than return to her people, had been her choice. Why? Why had she not climbed a wilderness crag somewhere, willed herself to death and taken her chances that Anggh would show mercy and take her soul to Drakht, the Ahan paradise? It could only be martyrdom. Rowan spoke to Anggh in silence, and implored that she merited his care. Her skeleton had not been stripped of its flesh like the Ahan who hung in the trees. Instead she had been stripped and skewered on a sharp pole like a sow on a spit and mounted upright in the middle of the room. A frayed short length of rope circled her neck, her full figure now shrunken and wrinkled and saggy. Her white hair that remained stood out straight in a pattern of tufts, the rest torn out. She might take longer to rot in here than outside, a final warning to anyone foolish enough to come down from the summit. The gag reflex defeated inspection. He turned away.

If there were an oar or a paddle in there, he would have to search. He even wondered what it would be like to swim instead. The distance could be twenty miles at least. Neither knowing the currents nor any conditions of the possibly deceptively calm waters, he knew it had to be a paddle or nothing. He drew a deep breath, and into the hut he went. Through all the decay and rubbish that surrounded the corpse – he searched in vain – and he searched the rafters. Nothing. Outside, nothing like a paddle either, nor anything of value.

He cleared his lungs several times in succession, checked the direction of the wind, and decided he may as well stick to the shadows under the cliffs and take a look at the Horn'd fishing canoes. Maybe something would turn up. After a mile or so of this, with no moonrise yet, starlight showed the craft to be made of hollowed out logs, scratched out with little claws, not pretty, but sturdy enough and of acceptable size. The Horn'ds' tiny paddles were of course not in evidence, just as Sírun had said. Rowan looked around for anything, a board, a barrel stave, any substitute.

The moon emerged from behind a cloud above the cliffs and lit up the beach.

XXIX

Impression Ringrise

UNSEEN AND UNHEARD until then came the oncoming swarm. The things literally poured from the cliff caves in an unstoppable flow, a heaving Horn'd horde, swarthy, skittering – silent, at first. As they drew more near, a shrill, shrieking cacophony tore at his ears. He would have to swim for it. He extracted the portable scanner from his other gear, which would have to be abandoned, and strapped it firmly to his belt next to the plasma phaser holster. He pressed a couple of buttons in succession on his five-toed boots, swim-mode enabled, and dived into the surf. When he had swum far enough to look back, of course the filthy creatures were boarding their canoes in crews of twenty or so per vessel, and sported paddles aplenty now.

With no thought of capture to diminish concentration, under the waters of the Inland Sea he plunged, deep below the surface to make his way northwards. But was it north? The moon uncooperatively hid behind the clouds, but that may be a blessing in disguise. The current lower down flowed strong and steady. He hoped it favoured his intended direction, however murky in places. But unused to such exertion – he needed air. He poked his nose out of the water, which brought relief – and excited heightened shrieking – he had been spotted. *They must be able to see in the dark…* and with great acuity at this distance. He started to dive, but something caught his collar and pulled hard, and drew his head above water.

"*Quick! Get in! They come!*"

Rowan crawled into the canoe, and was handed a paddle, new and of very smooth blonde wood, the dark bark partially shaved to create an irregular but pleasing pattern at each end of the shaft – had he time to appreciate it. The two fugitives out-paddled their pursuers. When he looked behind, moonlight revealed that the swarm of Horn'd had retired from the chase and were heading back. Yet he poured all strength left into breaking dark waves off the bow, which left a long wake at the stern until well out of range of pursuit. But his skin had become a sausage casing afire. "How far north do they extend, the caves?"

"The caves are behind us now," Sírun answered. "The elevation of the hills will decrease, but the beach will narrow and become rocky. We should get off the water as soon as possible."

They jumped in and waded, but once on land, and had scuttled the canoe, Rowan said, "I had to leave my gear. All my prescription medication was in there.

But I have the scanner. And the phaser. We should find a safe place to get dry. A firestone… I'll ignite one."

"You will not need your pills," she replied. "I can find what you need in the forest in the morning. Come. This way." She had spotted a cleft in the sandstone cliff, not quite a cave, but with enough headroom for both of them to stand up, large enough to include her gear, and floored with clean dry sand.

Rowan rolled a small boulder into the middle, kissed his phaser and powered it up. The row of indicators in its barrel lit up in a jewel-like row and blinked off one by one – and the last glowed a dim green. He quickly stripped off his wet clothes and wrung everything out. But he glanced up and met Sírun's eyes, and only then thought perhaps his manners were lacking.

"No fear, no worry," she said. "It is my duty to serve you, not for you to serve me." She too quickly peeled off her outfit to wring it out.

Rowan turned around in the narrow space and stared at the rocky wall. "They're beautiful… I mean the paddles, they're beautiful… were."

"A new walking stick I will make come the morning."

"I'm trying to say… thank you and I'm sorry at the same time. Thanks. And I *am* sorry. But I don't expect forgiveness."

"I forgive for *me*. I do not wish to be angry. It is very painful for an Ahan to be angry. It destroyed Gregor. And it killed Azniv, and so many others."

"Well, I don't deserve it. But I don't want you to feel pain because of me. Somehow by trying to do the right thing I do the wrong…" He sensed her eyes on him. Now his face flushed hot, and he hastened to clasp his hands behind to cover his backside.

"The burn wounds," she said, "they should be treated when the sun wakes, when I can distinguish the healing herbs from the poisons. For that I need strong light. No fear, no worry. You are very beautiful."

"It's not that. It's just… you know… propriety."

"But I am your friend."

"Right, that you are. I promise I'll try to be a better friend to you."

"Please do not make promises you cannot keep. There is no try. There is do or not do."

"Of course. Aynt told me that too. I should know better."

"Speak no more of this, Sir Rowan. Resentment is released. It is washed off in the Inland Sea. No fear, no worry. I am strong. Nothing is hidden… you are young, but you will grow."

✦

He awoke at Sírun's gentle touch on his cheek. The firestone still glowed a faint dull orange, and the sky through the cleft, as much as he could see, looked blue and clear.

"Please, do not stir," she said. "I will apply the ointment I have made. I will not hurt you."

He rolled over, and said, "I don't know what I did to deserve you, Sírun. I'm the problem, not you. Obviously you can take care of yourself."

"By serving you I serve myself, Sir Rowan. We are one."

"That's a little over my head, but I won't argue. In the meantime the big weight on my mind is that I left my map behind."

"Do you mean this map?" Sírun showed him a brown leather tube the size of a spyglass, capped at each end with brass. "I make a joke. This map I copied at a castle library."

He twisted to study Sírun's mysteriously unreadable face, and wondered if she were an angel in disguise – only he did not believe in angels.

+

When they had readied to go, he was presented with a new walking stick finished in the same way as the paddles. It looked and felt even better than the first one.

"Do not speak, Sir Rowan. Just take it. Do *not* give it back."

Even with no trail Sírun found the most direct path to take them ever further along the shoreline northwards beneath the rough terrain that loomed above. In time their route turned northwest, along crooked tracks animals had made through an unpeopled land that must have been inhabited in the ancient past, the evidence in the form of dolmens, chambers of stone created by two or more megaliths topped by flat slabs of rock tens of tons in weight – who made them, how and why – a mystery. With a dearth of caverns to hide in, were they shelters from meteorite showers perhaps more common long ago?

After more than five days, the trek, mostly along the coast, led to a long-abandoned ghost town near a narrow sandy isthmus. According to Sírun's map it connected to the far side of a very large coastal lagoon, itself joined to a salt-water lake or lesser sea much further north, the large body of water Masudah had said could be skirted around its eastern shore. A shorter, more risky route west across the isthmus remained an alternative. Once they had traversed that stretch of ground, they would be within range of the natural portal that would send them roughly one quarter of the distance to the region where he hoped to find Samarit and the Longbows.

"Let's rest here for the afternoon, Sírun. We can cross tonight. It will be safer then, as safe as we can allow ourselves to hope."

"Here in the shade it is good," she said. "I will find food. We will enjoy, then sleep. I shall return soon. Please rest."

◆

As always, Sírun returned with bounty: wild roots, herbs, tubers, greens and berries, even some nuts to add to her supply of dried fish.

"If only we had some wine," he said. "This meal is near perfect."

"I find only peasant wine, red. Will that be acceptable?"

Rowan laughed from the heart for the first time in many moons. After all had been relished to the full, a short sleep of deep peace came, as if all were right with the world. And a dream –

◆

He and Sírun silently contemplated the end of day, when the white sun descended into a cauldron of gold, magenta and purple. Sacrilegious it may be to stir, but stir they must.

"Sir Rowan, look up."

Indolent, in a state of great contentment, Rowan smiled at her and gazed at the heavens – and clenched his jaws tight. The big bird. The huge vulture. "Oh no. Does this mean what I think it means?"

Silence.

Alarmed, he searched the darkness.

Sírun had gone, vanished.

◆

With a sharp spasm he sat up, wide awake. The sun dipped into the underworld as the Khémians called it. But something felt wrong. He looked up, but beheld only the dark sky. However unsettling, somehow he knew she truly had gone.

"This is beyond the boundary of my dominion."

The voice had sounded at the midpoint between his ears. Rowan sat very still. "I don't know what to think," he replied. "But I guess I should be grateful all the same."

"It is your world. You may think as you wish."

206

The last of the molten sun slipped beneath the rim of Eorthe.

"Will I ever see Sírun again? If there is an actual Sírun."

"Is there not? I have sent her home. She is safe."

"Thank you for that… but she never said goodbye."

"She would not."

Rowan sighed. "Well, it's just kind of… open-ended."

"Should it be closed off? My dear young friend, this you can work out for yourself."

"Maybe I got attached. I'm too sentimental."

"Is detached better? To withhold attention is best? What about non-attachment instead? Think, my young friend."

"Right. My power is to wait. Thinking is a skill I'm still working on. Any other advice?"

"If you mean regarding your journey, I have none. This is past the limit of my authority, here before the lagoon. Beyond is a strange land to me. If you mean regarding your life, you must be your own adviser."

"I just want to go home."

"My young friend, may your eyes give light to the day."

✦

The stars glistered above, and reflected below in the still waters of the lagoon, which made the isthmus of sand look like a bridge across the heavens.

He crossed without incident. *It's better to be independent,* he thought. But it felt like a setback. Sírun had been a good friend. *I grew soft. I grew weak. She was like… a mother.* Hers was a mother's love. Another demon rose up to choke his heart. *The only enemy is within.* But it could only be a devil if he were unaware of it. In a way, it only wanted attention, like a child. *Maybe it's Syx who needs it.*

The new walking stick — a great aid, like a fifth limb. Every step reminded him of its maker and every footfall reminded him he had taken one step closer to Samarit. Yet with each the urgency increased. Fortunately, the peninsula remained fairly flat and forested. He followed the western shore of the lesser sea, under the trees whenever possible. Topside here had been emptied of its natives like the rest of the world, except Khémia, Land of the Song-Eyes and part of Aha Domain — perhaps Eorthe's polar regions, but too difficult an environment for any species, never mind the cool-blooded reptilians.

Nothing remained of the wooden houses of large villages said to be native architecture before the people went underground in centuries past. From what

Rowan had seen in the Hall of Memory in Perkona Ola, the culture that once thrived in this wild country had been gifted in the arts. Everything these tribal peoples made had been decorated in stylized, abstract and timeless motifs. In fact they influenced the most sophisticated fashions in the League when daredevil archaeologists had brought back earthenware, tools, jewellery, textiles and so on, which spawned an industry of consultants, artisans, designers and manufacturers to clothe the people and furnish the houses of the in-crowd in style. Among the artifacts there had been very few weapons, however. And they deliberately burnt their settlements to the ground every few years for reasons unknown. Rowan suspected a similarity to how some artists in Perkona Ola had destroyed their own work, to emphasize the ephemeral nature of things and to begin again, perhaps true to the Beginner archetype, consciously or not. Moreover, there would then be no temptation to make a commodity of it.

◆

According to the map Sírun had copied in a castle library, he stood near the point at which the route departed from the shoreline and proceeded to the north, inland, no more than two days from the natural portal, if nothing delayed.

A little further on, he had decided to leave the beach, but spied signs of people at the woods' edge – an abandoned campsite. No one had made use of it in some time. Dead leaves had blown in and scattered about, undisturbed for possibly many months. The tents had partially collapsed. Whatever had been edible and hung ten feet high on the trunk of a tree had long since been scavenged by a creature tall enough to reach it. The beast had left long and deep scratches as it took the opportunity to sharpen its claws. Uneaten as yet by wild goats or too many insects, a notebook lay open in the dry grass. Rowan picked it up and dusted it off, intrigued by the sketches and handwriting in Common Tongue. The last note before the blank pages read: "Not one of my colleagues has returned. It has been six days now. What am I to do? Perhaps it is best just to stay put. Difficult."

He leafed back to the front of the book – which appeared to belong to an intrepid daredevil field researcher, a biologist. Obviously, wherever he or she hailed from, curiosity was not a sin. To follow one's scientific passion topside was a defiant expression of freedom, but nearly suicidal if only because of the reptilians, let alone any hostile cryptozoic flora or fauna. The sketches and drawings especially fascinated, glimpses of an unknown creature whose habitat lay just offshore. Its whole figure was never shown, only whatever revealed itself above the waterline: humanoid, greyish smooth mottled skin, wide-set bulging eyes and a very wide mouth – no visible neck, only a triple roll of fat like a collar, and hand-like clawed webbed digits at the ends of thick limbs. And as befits an amphibian creature like this frogman, no hair, although long thin strands of something like it hung from its receding chin. The handwritten notes speculated the cryptid might be another of the Primordial Architects' experiments, an undiscovered species rather than an anomaly. Rowan looked up from the book to the placid waters under the eastern sky and wondered. But he carefully placed the book back among the tufts of blonde grass where he had found it. The spirit of place had apparently manifested a guardian of the deep best not disturbed again.

◆

The animal tracks continued along the waterways for some distance. He followed the map and the compass in the scanner, left the wetland behind and headed across flat grasslands due north. After a day of uneventful but nevertheless anxious exposure to the sky, Rowan came to the halfway point, where he made a slight digression to the northeast now that he had passed the narrow swamplands north of the lesser sea.

In only one more day he would reach the natural portal, described on the map as Gate of the Shining Ones. Masudah had said it would take him roughly a quarter of the distance to the region where Samarit likely still holed up in the cramped cave. The prince consort had only made one comment that indicated its unusual nature. He had said that a password, the name of the doorkeeper, must be pronounced exactly, and he had made Rowan repeat it many times until satisfied that the pronunciation was correct. At the time it seemed a bit like Khémian mystic superstition, as if a deity presided over special portals they called gates, doors, or sometimes pylons, much like obelisks but in pairs. The gate itself the prince considered a goddess, in this case Mistress of the Knell, a detail only important if the difficult pronunciation of the god's name proved incorrect, ominously translated as Dancer in Blood. That night Rowan had a dream –

◆

Again, in the dim cave with the Longbows – but Samarit not among them.

Rowan panicked, searched everywhere and beseeched the people. None could hear him. None.

✦

The nightmare took some hours to shake off. To preserve sanity, he decided hidden anxiety had purged, like mental vomit. He must have faith that Samarit remained alive and that he would see her again, and the ever-stretching time until then would be over.

Dawn came slowly, in a hundred shades of red through the mist on the steppe. Finally, after the day had worn on under leaden skies, on a large knoll in the fading light, the monument loomed out of the dusk – Stone Tomb, huge slabs of sandstone apparently heaped at random, yet with intention to create many grottoes rich in petroglyphs and proto-cuneiform that spoke of the deeds of old gods, another colossal megalithic feat of the ancients. If he had been in better condition, he would have run the last few miles. But his heart nearly burst regardless. He powered up the scanner to locate its exact position. Before he got too near, Rowan practised the password in silence. Superstition or not, he could afford no delay. He drew closer, close enough for proper orientation. He suppressed fatigue, set up the scanner and faced the still invisible portal. Courage gathered, and he spoke the true name of Dancer in Blood, the gatekeeper.

Like all the portals before, the gate revealed itself first as a rippled series of distortions in the visual field, as if on a clear surface into which a stone had been thrown. Unlike the portals before, except the one into Aha Domain, the passage proved neither smooth nor chaotic, but an instantaneous transition from the wind-swept steppe in twilight to an observation deck under a vast transparent dome that overlooked a barren and jagged terrain – in the distance a slightly convex plain pocked with meteor craters and patches of white, like snow or ice. Beyond the glassy overhead canopy, a fantastic display of stars free of an atmospheric veil dazzled mind and eye. But most amazing of all, what the Ahan astronomers called the planet Zhamanak dominated the skyline, as if the place where he stood were not situated in the same orbital plane of its luminous rings and other many satellites, but a rogue moon with an unbelievable view. *No… this is worse than the big bird. Now what have I done?!*

View *of the* ringed gas giant Zhamanak *from* Penetra Dor,

one *of its* many moons *and* moonlets.

The adventure continues…

Please leave a review!

Please consider leaving a review at Amazon.com or whichever site you purchased this book. Prospective buyers place more trust in the opinions of honest reviewers like you. George R.R. Martin, author of the epic fantasy series A Song of Ice and Fire, of which *A Game of Thrones* is book one, says that a range of reviews is helpful to the author, so I invite you to share your thoughts in a review after reading this book. Furthermore, I subscribe to reader-response theory, which recognizes the reader's role in creating the meaning and experience of a literary work. The theory argues that literature is a performance art such that each reader creates their unique text-related interpretation. That means you are a partner. Your opinion matters.

Thank you and keep in touch! You can do that on the contact page at my website. Also, consider signing up for my newsletter there to be informed when the next trilogy in the series will be published, along with excerpts and possibly illustrations from published and forthcoming books.

RupertSmithson.com

Book Three:

Mistress *of the* Knell

IF YOU ENJOYED *Bones of Silver, Bones of Iron,* you will want to continue the adventure in The Stars Hereafter Chronicles with book three, *Mistress of the Knell.* Here is an excerpt from chapter 15, "Analogue to Digital":

◆

AGLET, UNTRUE TO his word, but true to his nature, was now unwilling to give Rowan a choice. He would be forced to join in the scheme to refine the variables of existence to a more manageable form, that is, patterns of information within the operating system. From there Penetra Dor and its technological infrastructure could be interfaced with and controlled from within the array of servers positioned in the most stable geography beneath the moon's surface, its ancient ice caves. "Here we go, Longbow, my friend. Eh? You won't feel a thing, except relief that you're free at last when the process is finished."

Rowan had been rendered helpless by a paralyzing injection. Androids had strapped him to a large metal table that looked like it belonged in a veterinarian surgeon's operating room. It could be raised from floor level to twice his height, causing wonder at its purpose when Penetra Dor had been a thriving holiday destination. Apparently it had been adapted for Aglet's purpose now, to scan and extract the existential data – as he called it – from the body in order to collect it for storage in a kind of holding zone from which it would be distributed to backup servers and for deployment at the core of the operating system. At its heart was where the "real" world – as Aglet called it – would be experienced in any form desired, as long as it conformed to his will.

"Thank you for volunteering to go first, Longbow. I'm sure it will be a flawless transition, but you never know. If all goes well, I'll be right behind you."

Only Rowan's eyes remained mobile. He rolled them in Aglet's direction and glared – to protest, in vain – and curse, in futility.

"Don't look at me like that, feline. I don't like it. You should be grateful. I'm giving you freedom. Isn't that what everyone wants? Why do we do all the crazy things we do otherwise? I'm your friend. Remember that on the other side." Aglet attempted to force a smile. "If you survive." He rolled his wheelchair to the control desk and checked the monitors. "Let's just tweak this first…" A long strained silence ensued. "Eh? What the…?"

213

From Rowan's position on his back he could not see Aglet, but he could hear the confusion in his voice. Panic arose. Is this how it ends? *Sam!*

RupertSmithson.com

www.ingramcontent.com/pod-product-compliance
Lightning Source LLC
Chambersburg PA
CBHW070817120626
46556CB00002B/547